RAVE REVIEWS FOR
EVELYN ROGERS!

THE GROTTO

"*The Grotto* is gothic romance at its brooding atmospheric best."

—*Midwest Book Reviews*

DEVIL IN THE DARK

"Woven with suspense and an evocative flair for the darkly dramatic, this is a perfect midwinter read."

—*Romantic Times*

WICKED
*HOLT Medallion Finalist for Paranormal Romance!

"Evelyn Rogers brings this charming story of a man too wicked to be good and a woman too good to be good to life."

—*Romantic Times*

THE LONER (SECRET FIRES)

"An enjoyable story and a must for those who have been following the McBride saga!"

—*Romantic Times*

SECOND OPINION

"This plot sizzles with originality. Poignant tenderness skillfully peppered with passionate sensuality assures readers of fabulous entertainment."

—*Rendezvous*

GOLDEN MAN

"A sexy sensual story you won't ever forget. When it comes to finding a perfect hero, this book has it all. Fantastic! Five Bells!"

—*Bell, Book and Candle*

IRRESISTIBLE

"You are too familiar, Captain Saintjohn."

"Then match me. Call me Nicholas. I'd like to hear you say my name. Just once, if you can manage no more. Since nothing can pass between us."

She took a deep breath. "Nicholas. There. Are you satisfied?"

"Satisfaction is not what I seek."

"Again you speak in negatives. What is it you do want?"

"Oh, I want satisfaction, damn me to hell. I said it wasn't what I seek."

I am not a passionate man.

Could he possibly believe his own words? If she began to unbutton her gown, she knew he would not stop her. In an instant they would both be lying in a tangle of discarded clothing and all the past hurt and the firm resolutions would be as naught the moment he pressed his hands and lips to her bare flesh.

THE Ghost OF Carnal Cove

EVELYN ROGERS

LEISURE BOOKS NEW YORK CITY

A LEISURE BOOK®

December 2002

Published by

Dorchester Publishing Co., Inc.
276 Fifth Avenue
New York, NY 10001

ISBN 0-8439-5115-X

Visit us on the web at www.dorchesterpub.com.

In memory of Patricia McCrory,
a caring woman and a good friend
who made our shared visit to the
Isle of Wight a joy.

THE
Ghost
OF
Carnal
Cove

Chapter One

A wind-borne cry, high-pitched and mournful, greeted Makenna Lindsay the first time she walked onto the sands of Carnal Cove.

A chill shivered through her. Was it the keen of a child? The moan of a lost soul? Fanciful ideas both, but they would not go away, though no one was in sight on the crescent stretch of beach.

Nerves raw, she halted halfway to the water. Night was almost upon her. She shouldn't even be here, considering all the work that awaited her. A pounding heart told her to run back to the path into the dunes, the narrow trail that twisted upward to the sanctuary of her cottage. But that would be a cowardly act, and she was not a coward.

Or so she kept telling herself. Leaving London had not been cowardly. It had been smart.

The damp wind tore at her cloak and stung her cheeks. With the setting sun at her back and the moon hidden by clouds, the inlet was cast in shadows. As she looked around her, all she could pick out was the curved section of shell-strewn sand that formed the isolated beach, less than two hundred yards in width, the grassy dunes rising into rocky cliff, a dark sky empty of birds.

And the water, of course, endless, rolling, the final boundary of this small, secluded part of the world.

A massive structure sat atop the cliff that rose from the far end of the beach, a dark, rectangular dwelling whose unlit windows and solid walls made it appear more an extension of the rock than someone's home.

You'll be moving near Windward House, the ferryboat captain had told her only hours before, when he learned of her destination. *'Tis a dark and gloomy place, I'm told. There's few who wander near.* He had not offered further information; uninterested, she had not asked for more.

She turned from the cliff and, despite herself, listened for another cry, but heard only the incessant drone of the wind, the pounding waves, the flapping of her cloak.

"Hello," she called out. "Is anyone there?"

Caught by the wind, her words whirled around

2

her and died without echo, leaving her all the more alone.

Sighing, she moved slowly across the beach, drawn onward by the pull of the ocean, by the pounding of the waves on the shore. Across the strait that separated the island from the unseen English coast, the water pulsed in white-tipped peaks banded by dark pits of shadow. A rickety pier stretched from the shore some thirty yards into the water, the lone evidence that man had ever walked these sands.

Her artist's heart quickened. She needed her paints to capture the play of curving light and dark against the gray right angles of the pier.

Later. Most certainly later. But not now, not her first day in this alien setting that was to become her home.

She moved close to the water's edge, mesmerized by the movement of the waves as they crashed onto the shore, reaching the tips of her shoes, dampening the hem of her clothes. With each thrust of the ocean, a thousand tiny pockets of air foamed against the dark, wet sand. She watched them die, only to be reborn in the next wave.

A strange sensation settled on her, as if she had come to a place she knew well. But that was impossible. She had been raised in London, had known only the cluttered boundaries of the Thames, not this endless expanse of ocean, not this pounding, not this wind. She had scarcely heard of the Isle of Wight, except that it was off the southern coast of Hampshire and was the site of Osborne House, the Queen's summer home.

But then she'd had to leave the city, not knowing or caring where she went, and in packing up her home had come across the deed that brought her here. A fated finding? She did not believe in fate. Men and women brought about their own destiny. One man, one woman in particular. She had been as much at fault in her despair as he.

She shook off the thought. Far more important matters faced her now.

Darkness was falling fast. She ought to make her way to the cottage in the remaining light. But she could not. Drawing the stinging salt air deep into her lungs, she loosened the hood of her cloak and let the wind catch her hair, tossing it about as it did her skirts. She reveled in the prickle of salt spray against her cheeks. Always sedate, always reserved, she felt a wildness smolder in her, a thrill of anticipation and foreboding that set her heart pounding in her throat.

"Looking for sailors? I doubt you'll find them here."

With a cry, she whirled, her heavy-soled shoes marking a circle in the damp sand. A man tall and dark as a thundercloud loomed not ten feet away, his feet set apart and firmly planted on the shore, as if no storm could move him from his place. He wore no cloak, and the wind off the water molded his dark shirt and trousers to his muscular body, whipping his long, black hair as wildly as it tore

4

at hers. Though his face was shadowed in the dying light, she could feel his scowl scorching the once-cold air.

The shock of his appearance stunned her into momentary speechlessness.

"What are you doing here?" she said at last, barely able to raise her voice above the roar of water and wind.

He had no trouble being heard. "Apparently disappointing you."

Disappointing wasn't quite the word she would have chosen. *Terrifying* came closer to the truth. The cry had been bad enough. The presence of a stranger—a man—standing so close was more than she could bear. All the smoldering wildness of the past moment shriveled to a trembling that even she saw as pathetic. She wanted nothing to do with men, and here was one—as manly a specimen as she had ever seen—standing a few feet away in the secluded cove she had thought to be hers alone.

Suddenly she realized what he had said to her. The heat of his words forged the trembling into anger.

Water sucked the sand from beneath her feet. She had to move closer to him to steady herself, daring him with the lift of her chin to read anything personal into the few steps.

"You think I'm looking for sailors?"

She would have laughed had the accusation not been so outrageous. She would rather a slimy monster from the deep crawl out of the foam onto the sand, a fact she proceeded to tell him.

He was not impressed.

"Do you not know the appearance you make?" he asked. "The billowing cloak parting to disclose a woman's body, the hair like silver blowing wantonly about a face upturned to the last remains of the day?"

He made her sound enticing. It was a description as ludicrous as his accusation. And as ridiculous as the fury she could feel in him because she dared to walk about the beach.

Catching her hair in her hands, she held it tightly in place.

"Are you so foolish as to think I believe the legends that give the cove its name?"

"The possibility exists. Stories of trysts between the village girls and sailors have existed for decades. Some believe them." His voice softened into insinuation. "Others wish they were true."

"This is absurd. Who are you? One of the sailors lurking about for a village girl? Look elsewhere. I am neither from the village nor am I a girl."

Neither spoke for a moment, each letting the roar of nature whirl around them. The power of the elements coursed in her blood. More disturbing, she sensed strong feeling roiling in him, a tumult beyond anger, though she could not define it further, any more than she could understand its source.

"Who are you?" He ran a hand through his hair,

doing nothing to tame it. "No, no, I do not care. You have wandered to a place you do not belong. Go away."

He spoke with sharp authority, as if sharpness could bend her to his will. She was not accustomed to such speech. The few men and women close to her had been soft-spoken, though she had learned that softness had little to do with kindness. A knife slipped softly into a human heart.

He did not know he gave his order to a woman beyond intimidation, in any form. Her momentary fear had been because he took her by surprise.

"I was not told anyone owned this cove," she said.

"I do so by right if not by deed."

She looked beyond him to the stretch of beach, past the pier and up to the dark house atop the cliff at the cove's northern edge. She should have asked the ferryboat captain more about the place, but there had been other stories on his mind, tales told with lascivious pleasure of the legendary copulations that had taken place in the island cove. He'd actually used that word, seeking, she supposed, to raise a blush to her cheeks as he explained why the inlet once known as Craven Cove had taken on a second name.

He had also mentioned rumors about the cottage, hinting of a mystery that kept the villagers away. But he had said nothing specific, and she had given his words the same scant attention she gave Windward House.

But that had been before the stranger's arrival. Its menacing presence seemed all-important now.

"You live there." It was not a question. He did not respond.

She gestured toward the dunes. "I've moved into Elysium."

It was a foolishly grand name for the cottage set into the grass-covered hills on the cove's southern boundary. Between Elysium and Windward House lay a high, curving heath of more grass, more rocks, more desolation.

Again, no response, though she knew he listened with the concentration of a hawk. With the last traces of day at his back, she would have liked the hidden moon to cast a silvery light onto his face. All she knew was the height and breadth of him, and the dark aura that seemed to come from his soul.

Too, she knew his strength of will, and the inexplicable hostility with which he viewed her intrusion into his world. As if she could do him harm. She, who wanted only peace and seclusion and a change to heal her broken heart.

Over the past month, she had found a will she never before possessed and, too, a combativeness that had once been as foreign to her as flying through the air.

She gave him a taste of both.

"I'll need a deed to keep me from returning to Carnal Cove," she said.

She meant it as an ultimatum. She wanted to be

the first to leave, to walk from him as best she could across the shore, back straight, head held high. But the wind took on a ferocious power, as if it would hold her in place beyond any will, any hostile wish.

Striding against its force, he closed the distance between them, his boots hitting solidly against the heavy sand, the full sleeves of his shirt whipping in a sharp cadence, its open-throated front like black paint against his broad chest. She had to tilt her head to look up at him, and release her hair to wildness so that she could curl her hands into fists.

As if anything she could do would stop him from whatever course he chose.

The moon decided at that moment to grant her wish. Easing from behind a cloud, it bathed his features in light. Thick brows over eyes as dark as his hair, strong nose and mouth, too rugged to be handsome, and sharp lines to his cheeks that cast shadows over the lower half of his face. His skin was weathered, and fine lines etched the corners of his eyes. Eyes that studied her with more intensity than she could endure.

And with more than condemnation. He stared at her as if puzzled, uncertain, as if he saw in her something he had not expected to see. The look did not last. He pulled back from her, though he did not physically move, and the dark eyes hardened to stone.

9

"Damn you for coming here, whoever you are. Leave. I will not tell you again."

Any defiance she could summon died in her throat, and a trembling weakened her knees. His was a force she had not known existed. If not for the wind she would have collapsed at his feet.

He turned abruptly and walked from her, his long strides taking him across the beach with a sturdy, rolling gait.

She stared after him, a receding thundercloud, removing his stormy determination from her presence, leaving a sense of confusion tearing at her mind. All she had done was move into a cottage that by law belonged to her and take her first walk on the beach. In the doing somehow she had breached a protective boundary that was as inviolable as it was invisible.

But she had boundaries of her own. No matter how forceful he was, she could not tolerate a man injecting himself into her objectives. That he was used to having his way was as clear as the fact that she was driven to having hers.

The conflict between them held no promise for the peace she sought. Somehow she must convince him she posed no threat to his own peace, his solitude. The last thing on earth she wanted was to find herself in his presence again.

If she could, she would call upon her ancestry and place a Celtic curse upon his head to keep him from her. If she believed in curses, which she did not. She placed no faith in the powers of the supernatural.

Makenna was a practical person, levelheaded, and until recently given to little show of emotion. Somehow, using her very ordinary skills, she would let him know what a truly mild creature she was, mild yet stubborn. She would not bother him if he would not bother her. How that arrangement was to be worked out, she had no idea.

Gradually, as she put her mind to the problem, the wind began to ease and the moon to silver the cove with a steady light. She should have been relieved, by both the stillness and the illumination. Instead, her skin prickled with a sudden chill she could neither explain nor ignore, much like her reaction to the cry. She pulled her cloak tight around her, but the cold would not go away.

Movement along the water's edge caught her eye, a pale shift of light that undulated in a rhythm matching her beating heart. A moment passed before she realized the light was more substantial than that cast by the moon. Someone else was with her, someone dressed in white, someone who might have witnessed her encounter with the man.

"Who's there?" she called out, but heard only the moan of the now-dying wind.

Was that a gesture she saw? A raised hand beckoning her closer? She was not sure, yet she felt compelled to skirt the encroaching tide and make her way toward the vision.

She hurried past the slanted steps that led onto the pier, but no matter how much distance she covered, she could draw no closer to the woman. How she knew it was a woman, she had no idea. Perhaps it was the paleness in contrast with the darkness of the man.

The fickle moon chose that moment to hide once again behind a cloud, leaving her in darkness. When it returned, the vision was gone. She stood for a while waiting for another glimpse of whoever—or whatever—the beckoning figure had been. She waited in vain. Finally she had to admit she was alone.

It was a condition much wished for, one with which she should be content. But contentment escaped her. Her world—what she had hoped would be her isolated world—had been invaded in its infancy, by dark and by light, by an all-too-real man and a wispy vision that must have come from the recesses of her troubled mind.

As if she had bade it do so, the moon, aided by a sprinkling of stars, held steady to light her path past the pier and away from the ocean, winding upward through the rolling dunes and vegetation to her destination, to Elysium, her cottage nestled near the top of the hill.

Safely inside, she bolted the doors and turned up the lamps, brightening each of the three rooms. She had scarcely glanced at them, so strong had been the pull of the water the moment she first walked through the kitchen door. As she looked around her now, the feeling that had struck her on the beach, that she had come to a place she already knew, returned.

The feeling was curiously settling, removing the turmoil of the past hour. It was as if the cottage had been waiting for her a long, long while, though that made little sense. Still, the thought and the feeling comforted her.

All was not perfect, however. In the bedroom she stared in dismay at the trunks and boxes that had accompanied her from London. A few items had been shipped ahead, linens mostly and the lamps. Before her lay the rest of the possessions she had chosen to keep, all but one, which was to be delivered the following day.

Though she was far from poor—her inheritance would provide a livelihood for the rest of her days—she planned to live simply; she would not need much.

The train ride from London, the sailing on the ferry, the slow lorry ride from the village dock had all left her exhausted. Grateful for the already made bed, too tired even to eat, she barely had energy to find her nightgown and fall on the welcoming mattress.

But she was not too tired to think of the man on the beach, remember his words, his commands, the dark power he used to threaten her, if only by implication.

It was not the threat that lingered longest in her mind. Mingled with an image of the elusive, beckoning light was the uncertainty in his eyes before he had issued his final command that she depart. Such doubt did not go with the rest of him.

Makenna liked order and precision. Nothing on her first journey to the cove had been orderly, nothing even made sense. Troubled, she closed her eyes, fearing that despite her exhaustion she would find rest as elusive as the light. It was her last troubled thought before she slipped into the velvet release of sleep.

A broad, dark hand dragged her deep into the brine. Her eyes, mouth, lungs filled with stinging water. Desperately she fought the steely fingers but could not pull free.

Without warning, a force that seemed to come from the center of the earth thrust her upwards, breaking the hold of the hand. Light as air, she burst through the surface of the water, shattering it like glass, and awoke with a start.

Sitting up, she hugged the bedcovers to her and waited for her heart and head to calm. Gradually sanity settled on her. She had been dreaming, that was all. But dreaming where? The panic returned, until she remembered her new room, her new bed, her new home.

Slowly she became aware of a distant banging. The noise must have awakened her. She waited a moment, but the commotion gave no sign of abating. Reluctantly she pulled herself from the warm bed, eased into her wrapper, and padded barefoot through the darkness, cautiously picking her way around the boxes into the parlor.

Right away she found the source of the cacophony. A shutter had pulled loose from a front window and was pounding against the stone house in the wind.

Striking a lamp, she returned to the bedroom, removed the rope that had bound one of the boxes and hurried back to the front of the cottage. When she opened the door, an unseen force held her in place, an invisible barrier that kept her from entering the narrow portico.

This was ridiculous, she told herself. What was happening to her? Fear of the unknown, of change, that was all. The shutter slammed against the stone, as if warning her to remain inside. The situation was more than ridiculous. It was insane. If she did not secure the shutter, she would get no more sleep on this windy night.

Holding the lamp and rope close to protect them from the wind, she forced herself through the door. It was like walking through a wall of ice, the fanciful effect, she told herself, of a harsh awakening from a terrible dream. She would read no more into the sensation than that.

Outside, the air was surprisingly warm, though the wind tore at her thin nightclothes. Setting the lamp beneath the window, she bound the offending shutter closed. For a moment the air grew still and all was quiet. In the eerie silence she realized how quickly she had gotten used to the sound of the wind.

Then she heard it, the sound of sobbing as if a child were in agony. It was nothing like the high wail she had heard when she first walked onto the cove. That sound had been coldly unnerving. This one tore at her heart.

Lamp in hand, she stepped away from the portico and onto the narrow path that led down to the sea, stopping at the edge of the hill and listening to the crying. The wind returned, this time more gently, closer to a breeze, whirling the sound around her until she could not locate the direction from which it came.

The moon was down, and in the narrow, diffused circle of light cast by the lamp she could do nothing more than sense the ebb and flow of the water. But she could make out the outline of Windward House looming high on the cliff to the north, and the light coming from a top-floor window.

Someone else was awake. Her stomach tightened. Could it be the stranger from the beach? Did he look out on her pitiful lamp as she looked up at his window? If she concentrated hard enough, would she sense his thoughts?

She could well imagine them.

You have wandered to a place you do not belong. Go away.

Another thought struck. Could the sobbing come from that lighted room? Could someone, perhaps a child, be lost in such despair that his misery tore from him in sobs that carried across the dark, forbidding cove to her small cottage?

She could not rule it out as impossible. Neither could she allow the notion to affect her, certainly not to the degree it was doing on this strange, black night. She turned from the light, from the water, and found consolation in the sight of her own open door. When she hurried back inside, she felt no wall of ice, no restraint. No longer could she hear the sobbing of a child. For the moment at least, Elysium gave her the comfort that she sought.

She must have imagined everything but the banging of the shutter. Her real enemy was not forbidding strangers or crying children or mysterious lights.

Her enemy was a dark imagination, nourished by raw emotions, exhaustion, upheaval in her once-orderly life. After she got used to the cottage, the water, the wind, and after she got the rest she so desperately needed, her days would settle down into routine.

She could accept nothing less.

Chapter Two

A pounding at the back door awakened Makenna to bright sunshine. Head reeling, she leapt from the bed. After her midnight wrestling with the shutter, she had thought she would not sleep. But she had, like the dead, without dreams, without unsettling sounds.

What time was it? Unfortunately, her clock lay buried somewhere in the containers surrounding her bed. But the hour was late. The light blinded her, and she stumbled about the room, bumping against boxes and an iron-hard trunk as she hurriedly tugged on the clothes tossed aside last night.

Whatever else she did today, unpacking was high on the list.

"I'm coming," she shouted as she ran her fingers

through a tangled mass of hair. With one shoe on, the other dangling in her hand, she hastened to the kitchen and threw open the door.

Only then did she wonder who might be on the other side. The man on the beach seemed a chilling but remote possibility. He was far more suited to dying light than to the birth of day.

A middle-aged couple greeted her with deferential nods, each in the plain, sturdy clothes of working people, and she let out a sigh of relief. The man, tall and bony, bore a ruddy complexion and coarse features, and sprigs of brown hair stuck out from beneath a well-worn bowler. As for the woman, short and softly rounded, gray wisps of hair rested around a pleasantly smiling face.

They were a contrast in size and color, yet went together like a pair of gloves.

"Didn't mean to waken you, miss," the woman said. "The letter said we was to report bright and early on this Monday morning. Not so early, is it, but it's fair bright enough."

"Now, now, no need to overwhelm our lady," the man said with a nudge, doffing his hat and twisting it in his hand.

They both looked so normal Makenna wanted to hug them, a totally unacceptable reaction for one who sought strength in solitude. Unacceptable or not, she was glad to see them, almost giddy in fact, after all that had been happening since she arrived.

"You're Mr. and Mrs. Jarman, are you not?" she

said, extending a hand, forgetting the shoe. Embarrassed, she jerked her hand away. This confusion was not the impression she meant to convey to the couple an agency had hired to serve as cook and handyman.

"Would you be wanting me to buff the shoe a bit?" Mrs. Jarman said. "You'll find I'm a hard worker and can do most anything."

At such sweet words, Makenna could do little more than stare. Yesterday's train had been dirty with cinders, her fellow passengers surly, the ferry captain too ready to impart lascivious legends, and the lorry driver who'd brought her from the village to Elysium was full of dark hints about the cottage, for good measure adding tales of storms that had struck the Isle of Wight.

And, of course, there was the stranger of last night. And the crying. And the light. She brushed them all from her mind. Mr. and Mrs. Jarman seemed so ordinary, so cheerful, she could believe that her decision to come here had been a good one.

The Jarmans followed her into the kitchen, wiping their feet first on an outside mat.

"Pardon my asking, Miss Lindsay," the woman asked, "but were you all right here during the night?"

"Why wouldn't I have been?"

"No reason," she said, avoiding Makenna's eye. "But there must be. Are you referring to stories about the place? If you've heard them, please tell me."

"There's nothing to tell. It's a feeling folks have." She caught a look from her husband. "I'm foolish to be mentioning it at all."

Clearing her throat, she continued with a more benign assault. "I did what I could Saturday, yesterday being Sunday, you understand. The vicar's a kindly soul, but he does like the Sabbath to be remembered. I did a little straightening, getting the bed ready for you, working at the stove, but there's more to be done, as you can see."

She took off her cloak and bonnet, hanging them on a hook by the back door. Already she wore a sturdy apron. It looked as much a part of her as her hair and eyes. She smoothed the wisps of gray from her face and rolled up her sleeves.

"You take care of your needs and I'll be getting you a bite to eat. Nothing like a good hot breakfast to start the day."

Makenna rarely ate breakfast, but there was no stopping the determinedly cheerful woman from her duty. An unexpected lightheadedness overtook her, and she turned away. It was the kind of feeling she would have expected if she were with child. But she wasn't. She had made certain before she sold her London home.

The fact that she was thinking of children was another sign of her troubled mind. She had never been around them. And she had never harbored maternal feelings. Hers had been a world of adults.

It must be the sobbing from last night. The *imagined* sobbing. She had to stop remembering it. Despite the pathos of it, the sound had seemed separate from Elysium and therefore separate from her.

"Are you feeling a bit tweaky?" Mrs. Jarman said. "You sit right here at the table. A cup of tea will put color back in those cheeks. I found some old china in the cabinet, chipped and stained, but it'll do right well enough. Tea don't mind the cup it's in, my late mother used to say. O' course she was talking about vanity, but the saying fits here, too."

"I'm fine," Makenna managed.

She lied. She was not used to such cheer. Nor was she used to bright sunlight streaming through curtained windows. London had been drawn draperies and heavy upholstery. The servants had been solemn, efficient workers who knew their place. As a child, she had learned soon enough they were not her companions. Hired nannies and governesses had served in that capacity as best they could.

And there was her mother, of course, a woman who seldom smiled, but whose love had been constant and unconditional. How Makenna missed her now. Since Jenna Lindsay's death two years ago, her only child had done little right.

Hurrying from the kitchen and through the parlor, she closed herself inside her bedroom. After a moment to enjoy the quiet, she took a close look around. Here, as elsewhere, the furnishings were simple: an iron bedstead and high, quilt-covered mattress, bedside table, wardrobe and chair, and covering the worn stone floor a simple rug that might have been woven by one of the village women of years past.

And of course there were the boxes, and the trunk. She opened the latter and stared in dismay at the heavy clothing of London. She was out of mourning now, but the lightest-colored gown she could come up with was a pale gray. On this late spring day, it seemed far too somber. But it would have to do. After all, tea don't mind the cup it's in. Neither should she.

A jug of water sat on the bedside table, left no doubt by her new housekeeper on Saturday. Pouring the water into a basin, she bathed and donned the gown, then set to work with brush and comb to tame her hair.

The brushing was not easy. Her flaxen hair, so pale it looked close to white, was long and thick.

. . . hair like silver blowing wantonly about a face upturned to the last remains of the day.

The stranger's words came back to dim the brightness of the morning. He had a poetic bent, when he chose. But he had also accused her of looking for sailors, an accusation thrown out more to anger her than to touch on truth.

23

He had judged her well. She had indeed been angry.

Why she was giving him so much thought, she did not know. Smoothing the covers of her bed, she returned to the kitchen and to the incessant good cheer of Mrs. Jarman. The husband was already at work repairing the cottage's front shutters. And without a word from her. Between the hammerings, she could hear the hum of what sounded like a sea shanty.

"Did your husband go to sea?" she asked.

"He did, a long time ago. Fancies himself an old salt, he does. He was still a sailor when we met, but he gave up the life."

Could Mrs. Jarman have been one of the village girls who gave Carnal Cove its name? Makenna did not dwell long on the speculation. The lives of others, past or present, were none of her concern.

Except for one, and then only because he had intruded himself into her world.

She took a sip of tea and a bite of toast, dutiful if not enthusiastic. To her surprise they both tasted wonderful, and she sampled them again as Mrs. Jarman beamed down at her. She even went so far as to consume the soft-boiled egg that had been determinedly set in front of her.

"You did a fine job getting the cottage ready for my arrival," she said, and meant it. "I wasn't sure what the solicitors would be able to arrange, handling everything by correspondence as they did. They had to use an agency not even on the island."

"Can't take credit where it's not due," Mrs. Jarman said. "Though there's work enough still to be done, Mr. Jarman and I found the place far cleaner than we'd been expecting. As if someone had been tending it, though not as careful-like as you'll get from the pair of us."

It was a peculiar piece of information. According to the solicitors, their hurried investigation indicated that Elysium had not been lived in for years. Who had done the tending? Makenna had no time to give the question consideration. Like an eager race horse, the housekeeper was off again, chattering about all she planned to get done that day, if, of course, Miss Lindsay was of the same mind.

When she could get a word in, Makenna ventured a new topic. "Do you know anything about Windward House?"

Mrs. Jarman frowned. "No more than anybody else. It's been boarded up until a month or so ago."

"But it's occupied now."

The woman nodded and freshened her tea.

Why wasn't she nattering on about who lived there? Her continued frown and silence struck Makenna as more ominous than words. Could the housekeeper possibly be afraid?

But that was absurd, and she hurried on. "I met the master of the house last night. At least, that's who I think it was."

The housekeeper set the teapot down with a sharp smack. "You've seen him?"

"On the beach. At dusk. I went down for a walk."

Mrs. Jarman looked past her toward the front of the house. "Mr. Jarman, come quick," she called out. "She's seen the captain."

The husband was in the room faster than Makenna would have thought possible.

"Now, now, wife, let's not be getting agitated. It's not good for your heart." He spoke as if he issued the warning several times a day, but the look he gave Makenna was as thoughtful as any of his wife's. "You've seen Captain Saintjohn?"

Makenna shifted uncomfortably. The couple was taking this far too seriously to provide the peace of mind she had been after.

"Last night on the beach. I went for a walk, and I suppose so did he. He did not introduce himself, nor did I. It seemed logical he came from Windward House, though it's only a guess."

She saw no purpose in relating the man's harsh words and insinuations, no purpose in describing her reaction. On this bright day she could not believe she had been so frightened, so angry, and, at the last, so intrigued.

"We were told he'd not be out," Mrs. Jarman said.

"By whom?"

"The vicar."

The husband spoke. "Reverend Coggshall also asked his flock not to speculate as to why."

"But you did," Makenna said, and could see by the pull of the woman's lips that she guessed right.

"It's only human," Mrs. Jarman said, avoiding her husband's eye. "But only to myself. He's not been the subject of gossip. Heaven above, we know little enough about him to speculate, coming by night as he did in a private boat. Any speculation that was done stayed in our minds, you understand, and was never spoken out loud."

Makenna should have nodded, pushed away from the table, and gone on with her day. To do otherwise only encouraged idle talk. But the memories of last night were too fresh in her mind to allow such sensible behavior.

"What did you speculate?" she asked.

Mrs. Jarman continued to ignore her husband's warning stare. Makenna got the idea that in following the vicar's request not to speculate, she had let ideas and questions build inside her like steam in a covered pot.

"We're a simple people hereabouts. We've few secrets. And here comes a stranger into our midst, arriving in the dark of night, keeping to his gloomy mansion which would serve half the village as shelter, scarce letting the light of day shine on his face. What's a body to think? Mark my words, there's mischief afoot in that house. I feel it in my bones."

So did Makenna. But that was more absurdity. One encounter, no matter how unsettling, provided no more facts about the man than Mrs. Jarman's maunderings.

She pushed back her chair, but the housekeeper, pale eyes glinting, was not about to let her go so easily.

"Now that you've seen him, it would do no harm to tell us what the man looks like."

Makenna had an image of sharp features, dark hair blowing wildly, a broad body holding strong against the wind. There was nothing she could bring herself to describe.

"The light was not good. The moon kept playing games with the clouds."

"Still and all, you must have seen something."

Makenna glanced at the husband, who seemed not quite so eager now to hush his wife's questions.

"He seemed tall," she said, then ventured another mild detail. "He went out without a coat."

"It's just as I feared," the housekeeper said. "The man's demented."

"Woman, how do you figure that?" Mr. Jarman said.

"It's cold on the beach when the sun's gone down. As my late mother used to say, madness in men and dogs can be found in the way they respond to the weather."

Makenna could have said the man did not look cold. On the contrary. In the midst of a swirling wind, she had felt his heat. But what sort of reaction that would have brought on, she refused to guess.

"You called him Captain Saintjohn."

"Captain Nicholas Saintjohn," Mrs. Jarman

said. "That's all we know, except that he spent some time at sea. The vicar said as much, and in a month there's little else that's been learned."

"As is only right," her husband said. "The captain has a right to his privacy."

Mrs. Jarman was not perturbed. "His man—"

"An old sailor, by the look of him," Mr. Jarman said, putting in his bit despite his criticism.

"—has come to the village once or twice a week for supplies. He says naught but what he wants and does not tarry."

"Following orders from his captain," Makenna said.

"That's the vicar's explanation," Mrs. Jarman said. "Following his own advice, the good man has said little more."

Makenna pictured a kindly old man with sympathetic eyes and a need to guide his flock down the right path.

Mrs. Jarman continued. "The Saintjohns built the house some forty years ago. Shipping family from Liverpool with more money than Queen Victoria herself, or so we're told. Must have forgotten about the place, since it's scarce been lived in over the past decade or so, though a few folks say that there was a time when visitors came. Not the Saintjohns, understand, not for a long while. And then the captain shows up."

She cleared her throat and stared meaningfully at Makenna. "Something happened to that family, you can be sure. Something bad."

Evelyn Rogers

"You're speculating again," Mr. Jarman said, then explained to Makenna, "We've been on the island scarce five years ourselves, which makes us strangers as much as you. No insult intended, you understand."

His wife took on an air of righteous indignation. "I'm telling the facts as I know them. A body can't help putting her mind to the why behind the what and the who. I planned to keep my silence, which you know is rightly true. But our mistress has the right to know who's wandering near her cottage, her being a female and living alone as she does. No one can call it gossiping. That's when you tell things you don't know are true."

Mr. Jarman threw his hands up in surrender. "I've work to do, and so do you." Shaking his head, he left the kitchen, and in a minute the sound of hammering drifted from the front of the house.

Somehow it reminded Makenna of last night's pitiful sobbing.

"Do you know if he came alone?" she asked Mrs. Jarman.

"If you're thinking of a wife, I doubt it. The supplies that're bought don't have a woman's touch, if you know what I mean. Though there's lots of milk ordered up to the house. And no liquor. He must have brought in his own bottles. I've never known a sailor didn't take a nip or two in the evening. That includes Mr. Jarman, though he be a sober man."

"Perhaps the milk means a child."

"Oh, I don't think so. Those two men and a child? Can't say that'd be proper. Besides, it would be hard to keep a child a secret. Unless you locked him in his room." She shuddered. "No, I'd say they eat lots o' pudding. Could be they're like Mr. Jarman, who has a sweet tooth the size of his foot. Don't know if you noticed or not, but the man wears boots big as boats."

"I hadn't noticed," was all Makenna could come up with. Sorry she had brought up the subject of a child, even sorrier she had mentioned Nicholas Saintjohn, she felt an oppression at odds with the bright day. Little she had learned explained anything. None of the information gave her peace of mind.

Was mischief afoot at Windward House? If so, it was none of her concern.

Excusing herself, she returned to the bedroom to face the boxes and the trunk. She threw herself at them with a vengeance, emptying the receptacles before coming up with a plan for organization. It wasn't until she had made her room a complete shambles that she remembered the second disturbance of the previous evening, the woman at the water's edge, the flash of white, the beckoning hand. As she had already decided, the vision was probably just that, a creation of her overactive imagination, unworthy of even a question or two for the Jarmans.

One thing was for sure. If she had brought up

the subject and if Mrs. Jarman knew anything about such a woman, she would have told all.

"A woman in white? On the beach at night? I'm sure I don't know what you're talking about."

Mrs. Jarman flapped one of Makenna's petticoats in the air and hung it over the line her husband had run from the back of the cottage to the small building that served as a stable and storage shed.

Makenna tossed a gown beside the petticoat, disappointed by the answer and relieved at the same time. She should not have brought up the subject. She was about to let it go when the housekeeper turned to her.

"You haven't been talking to Biddy Merton by any chance, have you?"

"No. Who is she?"

"She's a foolish old woman, that's who she is. Lives near here, though I'm not sure exactly where. As old as the dunes, they say. She's full of stories about strange goings-on. Not that she's paid any mind, you understand."

She spoke with finality, as if no one in her right mind would give credence to anything Biddy Merton said. With a sniff, she turned her attention to the clothes.

"An hour of airing in this breeze, and they'll be fresh as if they'd come from the laundry. A mite heavy, if you don't mind my saying so—for the island, you understand. They're fine for London.

Went there once when I was a child. Heavens, never saw such finery. Or such poverty. As my late mother said, there are only two kinds of folk in the city, the ones that are rich and the ones that are poor."

She paused only a second to catch her breath.

"We've got a fine dressmaker in the village if you're interested. Not up to date on the latest fashions, you understand, but she does right well for folks around here."

Makenna filed away the name Biddy Merton in the back of her mind, certain that if the woman could further disrupt her quest for peace, somehow, somewhere the two of them would meet.

"I'll let you know about the dressmaker." She studied the clothes on the line. They truly were inappropriate. But she didn't care. Suddenly she felt an uncontrollable urge to be alone.

"I can bring these in later. Why don't you and your husband go on home? You've been wonderful. We've accomplished far more than I thought we would. But we've got all the time we need to finish up."

A lifetime, she could have added, but it was not a comment the woman would have ignored.

Mrs. Jarman looked beyond her to the dark, rectangular shape that was Windward House, high on the cliff a half mile away.

"I'm not sure about leaving you alone out here at the end of nowhere."

"I insist. Believe me, Elysium is exactly what I

hoped it would be." She spoke with the authority of mistress of the house. It was a tone the house-keeper understood.

"There's a nice chicken stew bubbling on the stove. It'll taste right good, you can be sure. There's nobody can match my chicken stew."

With a smile as though she had won some kind of argument, the housekeeper went in search of her husband. Within a quarter hour, after advice from the man on securing the windows and doors at night and from the woman on the contrariness of the stove, Jarman had hitched their horse to the wagon that had brought them from the village and the couple was waving goodbye as they rode down the rutted lane leading to the main road.

Makenna felt as if the wheels had rolled over her. When the Jarmans were out of sight, she took down the clothes and carried them inside, tossing them onto the bed though she knew she would regret not putting them away. Airing them hadn't been her idea, anyway.

She had the rest of her life to get organized. She did not have to do it today. She had been expecting one more delivery and was grateful it had not come. A woman seeking peace and solitude could deal with only so much change at a time.

In the kitchen she removed the stew from the fire. She ought to eat. She ought to rest. But the sound of the ocean had been calling her all day. Tossing on her cloak, she gathered her sketch pad and pencils, threw a blanket over her shoulder, and after securing the cottage's two doors—Mr. Jarman's advice ringing in her ears—she hurried down the winding path to the beach. A half dozen yards from the water's edge, she spread the blanket on the sand, took off the cloak, and sat cross-legged, the pad in her lap.

She had come an hour earlier than the previous evening and rejoiced in both the superior light and the relative lightness of the breeze. Contrasts had always intrigued her. She planned to sketch the light and dark of the waves, the moving curves at odds with the rigid perpendicularity of the pier. But when her pencil touched the paper, the outline of a man began to form. Her memory was clear. The pencil flew, and she was soon rewarded with the shape and size of him.

She was about to start work on his features when she glanced up and saw her subject striding toward her along the water's edge. Her heart dropped. She was not glad to see him.

Neither was he glad to see her.

Chapter Three

Makenna felt at a disadvantage sitting on the blanket, like a sand crab caught at the edge of its burrow, but standing would make her seem even more imposed upon, as if he forced her to her feet.

Unfortunately, since she lacked the crab's hole in the ground, disappearing from sight was not an option.

There was only one thing to do. She returned her attention to the sketch pad and resumed her work. If the pencil did not move as quickly as it had before his approach, how was he to know?

He crouched in front of her, trousers stretched tight, arms resting on his thighs, his strong, blunt-fingered hands clasped loosely between his knees. The point of her pencil snapped. Without glancing up, she fumbled in her supply box for another.

"You didn't leave," he said, as if they had already dispensed with the standard greetings when people meet. He was not a man concerned with social amenities.

"You knew I wouldn't," she said, as casually as he, though she felt far from casual, not with a thundercloud crouching a few feet away.

"Aye, I knew."

She shaded in the hollows of his cheeks, using a fingertip to smooth the pencil marks.

"My presence bothers you," she said.

"As mine does you."

Why bother denying it? He could see the way she gripped the pencil.

Though she had bound her hair away from her face, the breeze whipped loose tendrils against her cheeks. They caught in her lips. She pulled them free, knowing he watched each movement. In a quieter setting, he could have heard the pounding of her heart.

Didn't the man ever wear a coat? Didn't he ever fasten all the buttons of his shirt?

"Maybe we could work out a schedule," she said with studied calm. "I could walk the beach from six to seven each evening, you from seven to eight. Or you take the evening, I'll take the morning." She looked toward the dark, restless water. "It's time I saw the sun rising over the sea."

"You're a stubborn woman."

I didn't use to be.

She forced her eyes to him. The sight of him so close, the harsh lines of his face, the tight eyes and mouth, the darkness so deep it absorbed the light—all took her breath away. No one feature stunned her. It was the total picture, the strong shoulders, the black fitted shirt, the trousers taut over his bent legs. He had strong thighs. Artist though she was, she had never paid attention to that part of a man's anatomy. She paid attention now.

Realizing what she was doing, where she was staring, she quickly looked at the sketch and hoped he did not see the burning in her cheeks.

"Captain Saintjohn, must you stare at me so?"

"Ah, my identity has been discovered."

"Was it supposed to be a secret?"

"Hardly. Saintjohns built Windward House two generations ago."

Ah, at least one of Mrs. Jarman's facts about the family was correct.

With light strokes of the pencil, she thickened his brows. "You were awake late." She did not know where the observation came from, except that it had been on her mind. As had everything else about him.

"Are you a clairvoyant as well as an artist?" he asked.

"I'm hardly either. A shutter pulled loose during the night. When I went out to secure it, I saw your light. Without moon or stars, it seemed very bright."

And ominous. She did not tell him that. Nor did she mention the sobbing.

"Yours seemed dim. Weak. Feminine."

So he had seen her lamp. She had wondered if he could. He must have been looking out the window in the direction of her cottage, else from such a distance he would have missed her small light.

Suddenly she realized exactly what he had said. Her eyes flew up. "Feminine? A dim light is feminine?"

"Insubstantial."

"That's as foolish a statement as I've ever heard. It's clear you know little about women."

She hoped to goad him to anger, as he was goading her. But his temper refused to rise, not the way it had done yesterday at his first sight of her.

"I make no claim to know the weaker sex," he said.

Makenna gritted her teeth. Concentrating on the sketch, she gave him small pig eyes and a very large nose. For good measure she put a hairy wart on the side. The grotesqueness did not satisfy. She had wanted to re-create not just the way he looked but the power of him, the force, the will. Caricature had not been her goal.

Tearing the paper from the pad, she thrust it beneath her supply box and began again. This time she was true to the vision before her as well as the vision in her mind. As if posing, he held still. She could hear his breathing over the breeze, over the splash of the waves as they slapped against the shore. A gull came from nowhere to sweep low across their crouched figures, searching for food, its caw sudden and shrill. She did not blink. Neither did he.

Something was wrong with her work. She could not get it right. The features were accurate enough, the size and impact of the body, yet the drawing lacked something important, something he carried within him that she could feel but not capture, a force she could not identify.

Perhaps when she got to know him better . . .

But that could not be.

Standing, he came around to look over her shoulder. He stared in silence.

"I'm not very good," she said.

"Do not be modest. It ill becomes you."

Before she could stop him, he pulled the first sketch from beneath the supply box and held it to the fading light.

"I think I prefer this one," he said. "Wart and all."

"It captures your spirit better."

Though he stood at her back, she could feel a change come over him, a darkness as black as his shirt.

"You would capture my spirit?" he asked. "I warn you not to try."

Reaching over her shoulder, he tore the second sketch from the pad and ripped them both in half. Scrambling to her feet, she grabbed the ruined drawings from him.

"There's no reason to destroy what doesn't belong to you," she snapped, truly angry.

"It's what I'm good at."

He sounded bitter, but she was too upset to give his feelings any attention.

"You had no right."

"Long ago I gave up worrying about right. I am a man without conscience. That is all you know of this spirit of mine that you speak of. It is all you need to know." His eyes trailed down her figure, rendering her far too aware of how the wind molded her gown against every curve. "Perhaps I know more about women than I've let on." He gave her no chance to reply. "Tell me the truth, Makenna Lindsay. How long do you plan to stay?"

Her name on his lips seemed intimate, unnerving.

"You know who I am," she said.

"How long?"

The man was impossible.

"Until my bones are buried beneath this sand."

"Which could be tomorrow."

"Possibly. Do you plan to do away with me? Do you want your solitude so much?"

His eyes bored into her until her blood thrummed. She stared at his lips, flat, taut, mocking.

"I have no plans for you at all. I have no wish for temptation."

"You think I'm trying to tempt you? Hardly. I keep telling you, all I want is to be left alone."

He laughed harshly. "I doubt you will keep that attitude long. You are a passionate woman."

She stared at him in disbelief. "If you mean what I think, the winds of Carnal Cove have rattled your brains."

"I am not a passionate man."

Makenna's heart continued to pound. Never could she have envisioned such a conversation with such a man.

"You have a temper," she said. "You are demanding. Are these not passionate traits?"

"I speak of carnality, and you know it."

The sands seemed to shift under her. She had to hold herself erect.

He moved closer and let his gaze roam over her face, pulling a strand of hair from her lips, brushing the tips of his fingers across her cheeks. She trembled but could not step away.

His hand fell and he gripped her shoulders. His hold burned through her gown.

"A man of carnal needs would not stop with a light touch, Makenna. Such a man would clasp you tight against him, would claim your lips, might even take you on that blanket at your feet and let the wild wind be the only witness."

Her head reeled, and she swayed toward him. Time stopped. Then he let her go as quickly as he had touched her, and she almost fell. But she remained upright, and her newfound toughness came to her rescue as she stepped away.

"We can both be grateful you are not such a

man. I do not take your condition as a challenge. You are safe from my wiles."

Was that a smile playing at his lips? Surely not.

"And your virgin flesh is safe from mine."

So why, she wondered, this tension passing between them like an electric arc? Why did the palms of her hands burn? What was this tightening in her abdomen? The swelling of her breasts?

Why the heat? In the darkest moment of her shame, she had never experienced anything like it. It made her feel newly aware of sexual arousal, almost like a virgin, something he had erroneously assumed her to be.

Hastily she gathered up her belongings, hugging the blanket and cloak against her body, not bothering to shake out the sand. With the wind propelling her forward, she ran awkwardly across the beach toward the dunes. He remained by the water. She could feel his watchful eyes on her back.

"You won't stay," he called out.

She ignored him and quickened her pace.

"Women grow tired of isolation."

Not this woman.

She repeated the phrase again and again. It was the litany that drove her up the path and into the protection of Elysium, where she bolted the doors and the windows as if locks and bars could keep him from her mind. Throughout the evening she felt the pull of the ocean, so strong it became an obsession to gaze through the misted window upon the cove. But she did not go out again.

*   *   *

At mid-morning the next day she received the delivery she had been expecting: her beloved piano. She doubted the humid island air would do the instrument much good, but she could not possibly have sold it, or stored it away. It was a part of her even more than her pencils and paints.

The lorry driver had brought two burly workers to manage the unloading and the shifting of parlor furniture until at last the piano rested in its rightful place.

In gratitude, she paid them generously and sighed with pure joy when they were gone. The Jarmans had been hired to work three days a week; Tuesday was not one of the days, for which she was grateful.

She had just settled upon the bench and begun to flex her fingers when a knock sounded at the back door.

"Miss Makenna, it's Reverend Coggshall," a man's voice called out.

Ah, the kindly vicar Mrs. Jarman had talked about. She pictured a graying head and sympathetic, failing eyes. His visit had been inevitable. Closing the piano and summoning patience, she went to the kitchen to let him in.

The man at the door took her by surprise: tall, well-built, with handsome, even features, his light brown hair attractively arranged, his observant eyes giving no sign of failing. She estimated his age at just past thirty, only a couple of years older than she. His clerical garb was the lone detail she had got right.

"I hope I've not come at an awkward time, but Mrs. Jarman insisted." His brown eyes twinkled. "You know how insistent Mrs. Jarman can be."

He spoke with the modulated voice of an educated man. No matter how much Makenna wanted to resent his intrusion, she could not do so. Bidding him enter, she heard herself offering him tea. While she made a fresh pot, muttering to herself over the contrariness of the stove, at her request he waited in the parlor. When she entered with the tray, she found him at the front door staring out at the cove.

"Terrible name, isn't it?" he said, turning to face her. "But not, I'm told, inappropriate. All those trysts were supposedly a long time ago, but then, the villagers would say that to their vicar, wouldn't they?"

"I've seen no sailors lurking about." *Though I've been accused of seeking them out.*

Technically, Captain Saintjohn could be considered a sailor, but she did not want to discuss her encounters with him. The vicar had been the one to request that the man's privacy be respected. Maybe she could get him to ask the captain to respect hers.

And to keep his hands to himself.

Then again, no. The captain was not a subject for conversation over tea.

Motioning to the vicar to take a seat on the small

sofa, she chose a chair opposite and poured.

"I've nothing else to offer by way of refreshment," she said.

"I suspect your cupboard will be overrunning with food before long."

"I suspect you're right."

Makenna was not used to feeling comfortable around men, especially strangers. Certainly she did not feel at ease around the captain. But Reverend Coggshall was different. As different as calm from storm.

While they drank, he described the village to her, talking a little about its people without indulging in more than a hint of gossip, lulling her into complacency until she was only half listening. Instead, she glanced longingly at the piano, hoping she did so unobtrusively.

"Would you play something?"

He had to repeat the question before she truly heard.

"Oh, I'm sorry."

"Don't apologize. You just had it delivered, isn't that so? It's natural you want to make sure it was not damaged in transit."

She would have preferred her initial playing be in private, but she knew far too well she did not always get her preferences.

Making no attempt at false modesty or shyness, she took her place at the bench and ran her fingers over the keys until she was satisfied that none was badly out of tune. Closing her eyes, she lost herself in a Beethoven bagatelle. When the short piece was done, she rested her hands in her lap and reveled in the first moment of pure pleasure she had felt in a long, long while.

"Exquisite."

She stirred and glanced at the vicar. He looked back with eyes that were far too admiring. She bounded to her feet.

"It's a piece I've practiced often. And it's not very long. You wouldn't want to hear my version of anything complex."

As if sensing her discomfort, he nodded and looked away. His eye fell on the art supplies and an easel resting in the corner.

"You paint?"

"Not well."

"No better than you play, right?" He glanced at a portrait of her mother, the only adornment on any of the parlor walls. "Yours?"

She nodded. She had hung it only this morning after carefully determining its appropriate place over the mantel. It was, in her opinion, the best thing she had ever done. Jenna Lindsay had not been a beauty, if one went by the standards of the world, but Makenna had thought her thick brown hair and deep-set brown eyes, her strong, even features, her erect stance, and most of all, the strength with which she faced the challenge of raising a child alone made her the most beautiful woman in the world.

Makenna knew she had captured on canvas the

woman's spirit, something she had been unable to do with the captain. This portrait, all that she had of her mother, was her most prized possession in the world.

"Who is she, if you don't mind my asking," the vicar said. "Obviously, someone you cared about very much."

"My mother. She died two years ago." Makenna still found the words hard to say.

"There's not much of a resemblance, except in the shape of the eyes."

"She always said I looked like my father. He died before I was born, at sea on his way to his holdings in the West Indies. My mother always regretted she had no portrait of him. That's why I painted her."

Makenna did not usually talk so much about herself, but her listener was sympathetic and she trusted he would not make her the subject of gossip.

"And you have no other family?"

"No."

"Please forgive me if I sound rude," he said, his words carefully chosen, "but you arouse my curiosity. What brings you to the island? To this cottage? Isolated as it is, few even know of its existence."

Makenna had not been so naive as to expect that such questions would not be asked. She was ready with her answers, most of them truthful.

"You are not rude. I grew weary of London and

found the deed to Elysium among papers left by my mother. Family solicitors investigated and found it available. I could not resist the call of an island retreat."

"I see," he said, but she knew he did not. He was a social man, devoted to being with others. He would not understand her need for solitude.

"Mrs. Jarman said the cottage looked as if it had been tending. Do you know anything about that? Who might have done so, I mean, and why."

Coggshall frowned. "This is news to me."

"I'm sure she will tell you whenever you see her again. Not tended well, she will say," Makenna added, hoping to add levity to the issue. "Not up to her standards."

But the vicar was not ready for levity.

"I can put questions about," he said.

"Please, don't do so. It's possible someone had been using the cottage illegally, but there was no harm done. I would not like to cause trouble."

"You are a kind young woman."

"Not really. I just want to get along."

An awkward silence fell between them. It was past time for the vicar to end his visit, but she was too unskilled in social intercourse to know how she might get him to leave.

"Tell me, Miss Lindsay," he said at last, "but only if you choose to do so. You have time on your hands, do you not? Have you ever considered sharing your talent with others?"

"What are you talking about?"

"I mean teaching. The village children have adequate instruction in reading and numbers and geography, though I fear their history lessons suffer on occasion. But outside of books and the natural excellence of their island, they have nothing of beauty in their lives. I speak of music and art, of course."

Makenna stiffened. "I know nothing about children. I've never been around them."

"They're really not beastly. Nor are they little adults. They have their own traits. Your music shows you to be a woman of great feeling. You would learn these traits soon enough."

A woman of great feeling, was she? Yesterday another man had called her passionate. Neither the vicar nor the captain understood her. If she had once been capable of passion, that time was long past.

Men killed passion, she could have told them, more permanently than they aroused it.

"I'm sorry," she said. "I couldn't possibly consider working with children. I came here to be alone. I can see you wish to protest. Please don't do so. I will not change my mind."

She was grateful when he did not argue, and after a short while he departed, leaving her with an invitation to attend services the following Sunday. Of course she would not do so. Eventually, perhaps. Perhaps not. She planned to be alone for a long, long while, though with all the visitors and passersby on her first two days at the cottage, she might as well be living on a busy London street.

She spent the rest of the day playing the piano, puttering around in search of the perfect locations for her scattered belongings, then playing again. Throwing open the windows and doors, she let the breeze blow through her three small rooms, bringing the scent and sound of the ocean to her since she chose not to go down to the beach.

But when night fell she could not resist standing in darkness on the narrow portico and, after a moment, sitting in the old rocking chair Mr. Jarman had found in the shed. Carved of driftwood, it went wonderfully with the rest of the house, though it would need a cushion to be truly comfortable.

She planned to stay outside only a minute. Then the sobbing returned.

She shivered. The sound was so heartbreaking, it brought tears to her eyes. Where did it come from? Impossible to tell, since it swirled around her on the wind.

Her gaze turned toward Windward House, to the lighted window on the top floor. What secrets lurked inside? What misery?

I am a man without conscience.

Of what depravity was such a man capable?

I am not a passionate man.

Did that mean he had no heart?

She could bear the sobbing no longer. Holding

her hands tightly against her ears, she stood. As if heralding her movement, the moon drifted into view and cast its light onto the water's edge.

When Makenna glanced downward, her gaze fell on a woman walking along the beach. Icy fingers stroked her skin. It was the woman of two nights ago, the woman in white, her long gown and pale hair flowing behind her. Though her figure was bathed in silver moonlight, a different kind of light came from within, a luminosity that glowed with eerie incandescence, as though she had captured a little of that moonlight and carried it inside her.

The woman walked away from Makenna, toward the rickety pier. As if in a trance, Makenna could not look away. From this distance the woman looked small, insubstantial, as though she were made of nothing but air. Glowing air. Which made no sense. But then, nothing about this night made sense.

Just as quickly as the woman had appeared, she was gone. As was the sobbing. The departure, and the silence, robbed Makenna of breath. She gripped a post supporting the overhang that formed the portico's roof. The moon slipped away, shrouding the cove in shadows. She looked toward Windward House. All the windows were dark.

Only the parlor lamp at her back provided illumination, but that was swallowed by the black of night in front of her. She stood unmoving, caught between the darkness and the light, for how long she had no idea. When she could finally pull herself inside, when she could breathe and feel a trace of human warmth, she quickly locked up, went to bed, and pulled the covers over her head, like the frightened child she had not been for a long, long while.

The next morning, little rested, she arose early hoping to view the sunrise over the water, but the day turned out cloudy and she saw nothing but a gray, rolling sea.

The Jarmans returned with their bounty of determined good cheer. After preparing breakfast, Mrs. Jarman set to scrubbing the parlor floor, though, except for a few sandy footprints, it looked perfectly clean to Makenna.

She kept her opinion to herself. Today was not meant for arguing. Today was meant for hard work. Today was meant for a mind occupied with ordinary thoughts.

She was behind the cottage discussing with the handyman the possibilities of a garden when another visitor arrived. He drove an open carriage pulled by a black horse that was high-stepping and sleek.

Not so the driver. He stopped in the lane just outside the back gate, let himself in without invitation, and, walking with a decided limp, brought his short, stocky frame in front of Makenna.

"Begging your pardon, you'd be Miss Lindsay, right?"

The man was a contrast to the fancy carriage and sleek horse. Her artist's eye picked out the details: square face, leathery skin, wrinkles etched deep just about anywhere a wrinkle could fit. His mouth was narrow, his pale eyes squinty, his nose large and veined, as if he had once been a heavy drinker. Or still was. His dark, bushy hair, extending out like tightly curled wires from beneath a sailor's cap, was heavily streaked with gray. He shifted his gaze from right to left, clearly ill at ease. He did not bother to remove the cap.

"See here, sir," Mr. Jarman began, but she waved him to silence.

"I'm Makenna Lindsay."

"Captain says I'm to offer greetings, or some such, and bid you come with me."

She couldn't have been more surprised if he had hit her with his cap.

"And you are . . . ?" she managed.

"Gibbs. The captain's first mate."

"Mr. Gibbs—"

"Just Gibbs. The one name'll do."

Makenna took a deep breath, trying to ignore the shiver of anticipation and dread that ran down her spine. Today was meant for ordinary thoughts, she reminded herself. Today was meant for hard work.

"Please tell the captain that while I appreciate his invitation—"

"He said you'd be stubborn."

Jarman muttered an expletive under his breath.

Gibbs was not deterred. "Saint Nick has something to say to you, miss. Begging your pardon, that's what we called him. Captain Saintjohn, I shoulda said. An offer of sorts, was the way he put it. Don't be asking what it is. The captain keeps his thoughts to himself."

A schedule for walks along the beach? She had mentioned such a thing as a joke. It would be best to remember not to joke with Captain Saintjohn.

Somehow she knew schedules were not on Nicholas Saintjohn's mind.

Mrs. Jarman came up behind her. "You run along now. Miss Makenna, being a lady, has no intention of calling on a man without a chaperone."

Unless she brings me with her. Makenna could read her thoughts.

Gibbs spat in the dirt and weeds of the forlorn garden, then shot a quick look of scorn at the older woman.

"We got us a housekeeper, if you're thinking it's all men at the house. She'll be right safe enough."

Would I? Makenna remembered last night, felt the desolation that had struck her when she'd looked out at the mysterious stroller by the water's edge, feared more than anything that the sensation would return again. Any danger offered by Saintjohn would be better than that. Or so she told herself, refusing to consider the possibility that

55

she wanted to see the man again, wanted to learn the reason for his summons.

"I'll get my bonnet and cloak and be right with you," she said. "In the meantime, Mrs. Jarman can get you a cup of tea."

"No, thank 'ee," Gibbs said over Mrs. Jarman's gasp. "Swill tastes like water from the bilge. Unless you've got a bit of rum to sweeten it. No, I can tell you don't. I'll be waiting outside the gate."

Makenna watched as he limped through the gate and back to the carriage. Without a glance at either of the Jarmans, refusing to read the censure in their eyes, she hurried inside to smooth her hair, settle her bonnet in place, and throw a cloak around her shoulders. The fact she debated changing her dress gave ample proof that she was demented in considering such a journey.

Sadly, dementia did little to squelch the curiosity with which she viewed the captain's invitation. No, it was more than curiosity. It was a burning need. From the moment Gibbs issued it, for all her shock, she knew she would accept.

Chapter Four

The ride took no more than ten minutes but it seemed an hour, the only sound the creak and grind of the carriage over the rough ground. They could have walked the distance almost as quickly. Then she remembered Gibbs's limp. Had the use of the carriage been his idea or Saint Nick's?

Winding upward from the cottage lane to the top of the cliff, across an almost barren heath, the main road showed signs of once having been wide and carefully graded. But it had been little used over the past years, perhaps not in two generations, since the time Windward House was built.

Or so she assumed. There was much she did not know about the strange new land she had chosen for asylum.

All the while, jouncing about, she stared at the Saintjohn mansion, which grew larger and more forbidding with each turn of the wheels. At times she could feel eyes on her, as if someone unseen watched her progress, watched and judged, but she brushed aside the feeling as the result of nerves.

Gibbs halted the carriage in the circular driveway, and she scrambled to the ground, craning her neck to study her destination. The three-story house was more massive than it had appeared from a distance, with gables and wings and windows shuttered as if to say *go away* to any uninvited visitors who might arrive.

But she was invited. The knowledge was not a comfort.

Windward House sat on the edge of a promontory, something she had not realized before. She had thought the island stretched on beyond the captain's home. Instead, the land ended with a drop-off far sharper than the one on the side of the cove.

It seemed to her the end of the world. With a shiver, she turned to the house itself.

The massive front door was unadorned, save for a bare-breasted wooden figurehead that hung on the brick wall above it, the carving's once-bright colors faded and chipped. She could picture it on the prow of a ship, glistening with sea spray as the vessel plowed through deep waves toward the horizon.

It did not seem suitable above the door of a family home.

But then, a family did not live inside.

Other than a few scattered weeds, the only vegetation at the front of the house was a lone tree at the corner away from the cove. Brave buds had begun to push through to daylight at the tips of the skeletal branches, which through years of being battered by the wind had grown slanted toward the brick wall, as if groping for comfort and safety.

Somehow the tree reminded her of the captain, though she could not have said why. Someday, she thought with equal foolishness, she would sketch that tree.

She whirled as she heard the crunch of wheels against the gravel drive. Without a glance in her direction, Gibbs was taking the carriage around the far side of the house, leaving her alone. He was, she decided, a suitable messenger for Nicholas Saintjohn.

A sudden stillness unnerved her. How quickly she had grown used to the sounds of the sea. Turning toward the door, she was prepared to knock when it slowly creaked open.

Darkness greeted her. This was ridiculous. Did Saintjohn always have to intimidate her? Sighing impatiently, she walked inside. The door closed with a slam.

"Welcome to Windward House."

"Oh," Makenna said with a yip, hand on her

pounding heart. As her eyes adjusted to the dimness, she made out the figure of a woman, tall and impossibly thin, her dark hair pulled back from a pale, unsmiling face. She wore the gray gown of a housekeeper. The only relief from the dark was a white apron tied at her waist, and, of course, her white face.

"I'm sorry," Makenna said when she found her voice. "You startled me."

She got no apology.

"I'll tell the captain you're here," the woman said and disappeared into the gloom.

Makenna took a deep breath. The musty interior held a hint of sea air and the odor of baking bread, smells that should have comforted her, but they could not overcome the effect of the dimness. If the captain was really trying to intimidate her, he was succeeding. She opened the front door to let in light and looked around at the wide entryway with closed doors to right and left, and straight ahead a wooden stairway that wound upward into more darkness.

Footsteps sounded on the stairs. She watched as Nicholas Saintjohn came into view. He was wearing light brown trousers and the ubiquitous black shirt, over which he had added a black coat. The shirt was unbuttoned at the throat. His hair, unmolested by the wind, was combed back from his face. He was a handsome man, she realized with a start; handsome in a worldly sort of way. On the beach, she had thought him too rugged.

But he wasn't too rugged at all. He was strong. And intimidating.

She rubbed her burning palms against her cloak.

"Mrs. Loddington has it in her head we must conserve lamp oil." He nodded toward the open front door. "Were you about to flee?"

"It's still a possibility."

"Then I'll make sure you always have access to a way out."

Always? Did that mean he expected her to be here often?

He turned from her. "Come," he said and started up the stairs. He did not look back to see if she followed.

She did. But she would allow herself ten minutes with him and not a second longer. If in that time he did not reveal his purpose in asking her here, she was headed for the promised way out.

He led her up one flight of stairs, and she half expected him to continue upward, to the top-floor room whose light she had seen in the night. Instead, he strode down a long hall, only slightly better lit than the entryway, threw open one of the corridor's many closed doors, and gestured for her to enter. She walked into a room that was surprisingly well furnished with a lovely marble fireplace at one side and a magnificent seascape over the mantel.

Bookshelves lined most of the walls, each shelf

61

filled with leather tomes that appeared at a glance to be well read. Ever the artist, she went immediately to the seascape, a painter's version of a schooner caught in a violent storm.

"It's a Turner," she said in surprise.

"Ah, an educated woman. I thought as much."

She ignored him, so lost was she in the beauty of the work. "I've never seen it before."

"You're a visitor to museums and galleries?"

"I was." It was all she would say on the subject, all she would ever say. She turned to him. "Where did you get it?"

"My grandfather purchased it when he built the house." He spoke brusquely, his eyes on her instead of the painting.

"Your grandfather had exquisite taste."

"Yes. He was not rude and crude and bumptious like his grandson."

Nicholas Saintjohn might be rude and sometimes crude, but he was not bumptious. No man of that description would have looked so at home in this inviting room.

"Aren't you going to ask what a valuable work such as this is doing out here in such desolation?" he said.

Why was it that everything he said came out a challenge? She would have preferred a civilized exchange, but he gave her no choice except to answer in kind.

"I could ask what it's worth, or give my own estimate. That's what you expect, isn't it? In their

weakness, women put a monetary value on everything."

"A clever woman as well as educated."

Makenna stirred restlessly. "Clever enough to
know you're judging me, studying me, as if you
had me under a microscope."

"I am not a man of science."

"You keep telling me what you're not. If you're
so fond of self-revelation, you ought to tell me
what you are."

Mrs. Loddington chose that moment to enter
with a tea tray; she set it on the table in front of
the fire.

"The biscuits aren't as fresh as they could be,
begging your pardon, but the tea's newly steeped.
Ring if you'll be wanting anything more. There
will be warm bread before long."

She spoke bluntly, then left, closing the door,
leaving both Makenna and Saintjohn to stare after
her. Despite her uneasiness, Makenna laughed,
then swallowed hard, embarrassed. She glanced
at the captain and was surprised to see him smiling at her. When their eyes met, the smile died and
the laughter caught in her throat.

Neither moved for what seemed an eternity. He
was the one to break the silence, his voice
brusque, his words bordering on rudeness.

"Sit. I'm sure you don't have all day, and neither
do I."

Oh, but she did, and she suspected he did, too.
Perverseness made her take her time selecting a

chair, one next to the tea tray. Taking off her bonnet and cloak, she smoothed her hair and looked innocently up at him. "Shall I pour?"

He chose to stand next to the fireplace, his arm resting on the mantel. His look was stern, his tall, hard body rigid. She could see him in command on the deck of a ship, buffeted by winds that would sway a weaker man. He would have the respect of his crew. He would exercise complete control.

On shore, with his aura of danger and dark masculinity, he would have his pick of women. A woman would want to stroke his hair, touch his face, rub her hands against his strong, broad shoulders. A woman would want to bring a smile to his lips and a light to his dark, watchful eyes. She would want to press her lips against his throat. She would want her tongue to taste him.

Makenna could not believe she was thinking such things. They made her stomach tighten and her mouth go dry. Whatever a woman did with him, their relationship would not be a permanent one. Captain Nicholas Saintjohn would never be content with one sexual companion. And sexual was all the relationship could be.

"None for me," he said.

"None what?" she said, then felt stupid. Worse, she felt obvious. And weak. And far too vulnerable to isolate herself in the room with such a man. Her wounds from the past were too fresh. The scars had not yet healed.

With leisurely deliberation, willing the trembling from her hands, she prepared her tea, added great dollops of cream though she rarely used it, then chose a biscuit with the care she might have given to choosing a work of art.

She took a small bite. The crumbs were dry on her tongue. She had a hard time swallowing.

"Mrs. Loddington was right. They're not as fresh as they could be. I could have Mrs. Jarman—"

"Stop it, Makenna."

"Stop what?"

"Pretending there is nothing passing between us."

If he could be blunt, so could she. "Nothing can."

"I agree."

"Then don't call me by my first name. You are too familiar, Captain Saintjohn."

"Then match me. Call me Nicholas. I'd like to hear you say my name. Just once, if you can manage no more. Since nothing can pass between us."

She took a deep breath. "Nicholas. There. Are you satisfied?"

"Satisfaction is not what I seek."

She could not be coy and pretend she did not understand what he meant. Coyness had never been part of her nature. It would be impossible to fake it now, not with the tension that crackled in the air between them.

"Again you speak in negatives. What is it you do want?"

"Oh, I want satisfaction, damn me to hell. I said it wasn't what I seek."

I am not a passionate man.

Could he possibly believe his own words? If she began to unbutton her gown, she knew he would not stop her. In an instant they would both be lying in a tangle of discarded clothing and all the past hurt and the firm resolutions would be as naught the moment he pressed his hands and lips to her bare flesh.

The cup rattled. She set it aside and stood.

"Thank you for the tea. I'll let myself out."

He moved quickly to stand in front of the library door.

"Sit."

"No."

"Please."

He ran a hand through his hair, destroying the careful grooming, making him look more like the stranger on the beach. And all the more endearing, which was about the last word she would have chosen to describe him. Yet somehow it fit.

"I'm handling this badly," he said. "I want to talk to you about something important. To me, at least. Hear me out."

Crossing the room in a few strides, he went to the desk in front of the window and took a seat. "I promise not to leap over at you. I'm out of practice. I don't think I could."

It was a poor attempt to placate her. If Nicholas

Saintjohn wished to jump across the desk at her, he would manage it with little effort.

She turned to leave.

"You play the piano very well."

If he had spoken to her in Arabic, she could not have been more surprised.

"Sound carries on the wind," she said, and thought of the sobbing. She must not forget that plaintive cry, though she had almost done so. It was why she was here.

"And your sketches—"

"The ones you destroyed."

"—were quite good."

"For a woman."

"For anyone."

"Why the compliments? They are not like you."

"I have my moments. Or I used to."

Again she could feel the darkness roiling inside him. He was a complicated man. Without doing anything more than simply being whatever he was, he terrified her.

"Does all this have a point?" she asked.

To her surprise, he came from behind the desk, went to the wall beside the door, and rang the bell. Mrs. Loddington must have been standing in the hallway outside, for she entered immediately.

"He's ready," she said.

"Bring him in."

The housekeeper disappeared for a moment, then returned, a small boy of no more than six in front of her. He was dressed in the formal attire of a public schoolboy, jacket and full tie, white shirt, knickers, dark socks, and polished shoes. His dark hair was combed neatly in place and he looked well scrubbed. Wide, dark eyes stared up at her out of a thin, pale face, then looked quickly away, as though he knew he was being rude.

"My son Jonathan," Nicholas said. "Jonathan, this is Miss Lindsay. The lady I was telling you about."

"I am happy to make your acquaintance," Jonathan said with a slight bow.

He spoke much too formally for such a young child. Whoever had raised him—it could not have been his seafaring father—had been very strict indeed.

Makenna's heart twisted. Was this boy the source of the sobbing she heard on the night wind? He seemed much too small to let out such a far-reaching cry.

She put out a hand, sorry she was not wearing gloves. The child's appearance and manner demanded formality. He looked at his father as if seeking advice on what to do. He got a nod and put his small hand in hers.

Makenna could not remember when she had last touched a child, if ever. She was not prepared for the delicacy of his bones. For some inexplicable reason his fragility made her want to cry.

She knelt before him. "I've not seen you playing on the beach."

He kept his eyes downcast. "I prefer to stay inside."

As little as she understood children, she knew that was not right. Unless he was in ill health, no six-year-old could resist splashing in the surf or building castles in the sand. While Jonathan looked frail, he did not look sick.

She stood, and the boy looked past her to his father, who had returned to the chair behind his desk.

"May I go now, Papa?"

Nicholas nodded impatiently. "Of course. Mrs. Loddington, take the boy to his room," he said, dismissing his son as if he had served his purpose and was best removed from view as soon as possible.

When Makenna and Nicholas were again alone, she turned to face him.

"Where is the mother?" she asked.

"My wife is dead."

He spoke in a way that showed no sign of emotion, no grief or, God forbid, relief, no feeling of any kind.

"When did she die?" she asked, thinking the loss had been years past.

"Six months ago," he said.

Not long, not long at all.

"I'm sorry," she said, but he hurried on as if he had not heard her, forcing her to swallow the questions that rose to her lips.

"I can teach the boy to read and to cipher, and

more than he would ever want to know about geography, of course, but little else. When I heard you yesterday, I knew what I had to do."

"And what is that?" Makenna said, suspecting the answer, incredible though it might be.

"I want you to instruct him in music and art. I will pay you well."

She stared at him in disbelief. He and the Reverend Coggshall were as different as two men could be, yet they had come up with the same proposal. Each of them must have seen something in her she did not see, something that was not there.

"I live in a small, rather run-down cottage, Captain Saintjohn, which might have misled you about my finances. I am fairly well off. I do not need your money."

"Since you plan to remain here until your bones are planted in the sand, you might very well need something to pass the time."

"Besides walking the beach and interrupting your solitude."

"I was not thinking of my solitude. My concern is for the boy."

"Your son."

"And the only one I'll ever have."

"So you want him to turn out right. Able to read and handle mathematics and to understand at least the rudiments of the piano and of sketching."

"You make that sound wrong."

"It's not wrong." *If you don't make him cry.*

"Then you'll do it."

70

"No."

He stared sharply at her. He had not expected that response.

"Why not?"

"I've never taught."

"Which doesn't mean you can't."

"I've never been around children. I do not understand them."

"They're little adults."

"No, they are not." It was something she had learned yesterday from the vicar.

"So you do understand them."

She sighed. "Captain Saintjohn, your experience aboard ship has conditioned you to command. But you're on land now. I am not a member of your crew."

He shoved his chair away from the desk and rose to his feet. It was an explosive move. She expected further verbal assault. Instead, he turned his back to her and stared out the window at the water far below his cliff-top house. On this side of the house, he would be looking down at the jagged, rocky edge of his land. If the window were open, he would feel the sting of the north wind.

"Leave," he said.

The order was not graciously said, but graciousness was not a quality she expected from him.

Even he must have realized his rudeness. "I have kept you far too long," he said. "Thank you for listening to my request." The thanks sounded forced and insincere, but at least he had made the effort to give them.

She stared at his back, at the way his hair lay straight and thick against the collar of his coat, everything black, everything strong, everything unapproachable. So why did she want to go to him and offer consolation? He gave no sign he needed or wanted it.

And yet he did. She knew it in her heart.

In that instant, she knew he was far more dangerous than he had ever seemed before. Without a word she grabbed up her cloak and bonnet and let herself out, hurrying down the stairs and out the door without seeing Gibbs or the housekeeper or the boy. She ran across the gravel driveway and down the winding road, not stopping until she was through the back gate and inside the sanctuary of her kitchen.

"You've returned," Mrs. Jarman said with a loud sigh. "There's pink in your cheeks. You must have run all the way."

Makenna did not want to think about what Mrs. Jarman would make of that. Already the housekeeper looked eaten with curiosity, her eyes eager, an encouraging smile on her lips.

"I am fine. Captain Saintjohn invited me for tea, that is all."

It wasn't a total lie.

"But it seems I've come down with a ferocious headache."

Also not a lie.

"I'll skip lunch today."

Mrs. Jarman sniffed her disappointment. "I've made a special meat pie for you."

"It'll make a wonderful supper. Right now I want to lie down for a spell. You and Mr. Jarman are free to leave whenever you wish. I'll see you in two days."

Forestalling any further protest, she hurried to her room and sat on the side of the bed, looking out the window at the narrow view of the water and the dunes, grateful this side of the cottage did not open onto the sight of Windward House.

It was a long time before she remembered to take off her bonnet and cloak.

The quiet of a moonlit evening came as a blessed relief. Makenna took her sketch pad and went down to the water's edge, somehow certain Nicholas Saintjohn would not join her. When he'd turned from her, she had sensed a withdrawal so complete, she wondered if he would ever speak to her again.

Of course such a thing did not make sense. Nothing about him did. All she had done, as best she could recall, was mention his time at sea. Then the explosion had come.

His anger did not bear dwelling upon, and she threw herself into her drawing. She soon grew tired of re-creating waves splashing against the shore, especially in the soft light. She was preparing to leave when the wind died, leaving an emptiness that seemed to rob the air of oxygen. She struggled to breathe. Panic fluttered in her breast. She had to get away, back to the cottage, yet her feet would not respond to her urging.

As suddenly as it had died, the wind returned with a rush, and she saw the familiar figure of a woman walking away from her down the beach. The sight chilled her, far more than the evening air. She felt pulled to run after the woman, and at the same time to fling herself in the opposite direction.

Again, she could not make herself move. It was as if an invisible barrier surrounded her, an iron fence constructed without a way to get in or out.

She had to capture this moment, just as she was captured. Taking up her sketch pad, she drew the beach and the water's edge as she had been doing, but in the center she added an outline of what seemed almost an apparition, its long, flowing gown pale as the moon, its equally long and pale hair, capturing as best she could the otherworldliness of the creature.

What she could not capture was the luminosity that issued from within the vision. There was no way with pencil and paper to re-create the mystery of where she came from and where she went. Indeed, Rembrandt himself might have puzzled over the transference onto canvas of such a mysterious light.

Mrs. Jarman had denied knowledge of the apparition. In the same breath she had mentioned one of the village women. Makenna thought hard to remember the woman's name. Biddy Merton, that was it. At the time the name had seemed important, and it still did. Perhaps she was the person who could help her understand what she saw.

When the apparition was out of sight, gone too was the restraint that had held Makenna in place. She listened to the roar of the ocean, trying to make sense of this supposedly isolated part of the island that she had hoped would be her refuge. All she got was a chill from the cold night air.

A deep resentment welled within her. She asked so little of life—at one time love and now solitude, both as elusive as the mist that blew in off the sea.

Slowly she made her way back up to the cottage. After placing her drawing on the easel in a corner of the parlor, she changed into her nightgown, braided her hair, and crawled into bed. But she could not sleep. Too many visions crowded inside her head: a formidable man beside a fireplace, a small boy with solemn eyes, a wisp of a woman in a place she could not be.

Giving up any hope of rest, she pulled on her wrapper and sought her one source of consolation, the piano. In the silvery moonlight filtering through the window, she let her fingers wander over the keys, then turned, as she always did in troubled times, to Beethoven.

She had no doubt Nicholas Saintjohn listened. On this strange night, after a stranger day, she felt linked to him through the music. She had never felt like that about any other human being, not her mother, and not . . .

She refused to think of the name.

Another image came to mind, the unsmiling face of the captain's son. She gave thanks that she heard no sobbing tonight. Pouring herself into her playing, she was able to forget time and place for a while. When the music ended, as it always had to, she sat in the shadows, unwilling to move, knowing sleep still would not come.

A movement made her turn her head. Nicholas Saintjohn stood in the open doorway, dark as the night behind him. Somehow his presence seemed as inevitable as it was forbidding. When he took a step into the parlor, a cry of protest died in her throat.

She stood to face him, wondering if he would harm her, and wondering, too, though the possibility lay beyond all reason, if she had the power to harm him.

Chapter Five

"Who are you, Makenna Lindsay? Someone sent to torment me?"

Makenna had been prepared for almost anything but accusation. It took her a minute and several deep breaths to find her voice.

"I can only tell you what you told me on this same day," she said over a pounding heart. "Leave."

"No."

She had expected no other response.

"Since you choose to stay, I can only assume you enjoy torment," she said.

"Like the air, it is a part of my days. And my nights."

"I don't understand you. Why are you here in the middle of the night?"

The question was genuine. He would not ravish her—she knew it though she knew little else about him—but that did not mean he would not bring her harm. There were many ways a man could hurt a woman. And Nicholas Saintjohn would know them.

"You know why," he said, running a hand through his unkempt hair. "I couldn't sleep any more than you. On the beach I heard your music and knew you were calling to me."

"That's ab—"

Before she could finish, he crossed the room and put his hands on her shoulders. His touch burned through her thin wrapper and gown. She could have stepped away, turned from him, and hurried from the room. Instead, she held her place and stared into his burning eyes.

"We may not like it, and we may not want it," he said, "but there's something between us. You feel it, too."

He bent his dark head and brushed his lips against hers, a light touch that filled her senses and seared its way to her bones.

The gentleness did not last. With an animal growl, he opened his mouth and forced his tongue between her lips. Startled, she tried to pull away, but his hold was strong; a moment later she no longer wished to free herself. Instead of less of him, she wanted more, her weak protest transforming itself into a wild hunger she could not contain. She let her tongue dance with his, her fingers gripping the front of his shirt to hold him close lest he disappear and his presence become a dream.

He tasted of a sea, storm-tossed and endless, his lips sweet, tender, and hot, but his body, pressed tight against hers, was as hard as the cliff on which he lived.

She kept her eyes closed, knowing that to open them would let in reality. She wanted darkness, the velvet void that swirled around them and kept them clinging to one another, as if to let go would be to drown in emptiness. Nothing was real in such a darkness, nothing that would remain beyond the moment. She managed one rational thought: This could not hurt; it felt too good.

One hand slipped from her shoulder and caressed her breast. His thumb stroked the hardened tip, a touch both light and electric, letting her know what he wanted, and what he could bring to her. Arousal, excitement, all the passions inherent in the flesh, he offered in abundance. They flashed through her like a sudden storm.

Startled, she opened her eyes and saw the shape of his cheek, the thick brows and the shadow of lashes against his dark skin. Oh yes, he offered more than her shabby past experience had ever provided. But if the pleasure was greater, so was the cost. Even in this quick, wild taste of ecstasy, she saw the truth.

Trembling, she found the strength to push him away. He dropped his hands to his sides, his breathing as ragged as hers.

Her humiliation was complete. She could not look into his eyes. Instead, she stared at the open throat of his shirt. Fine black hair curled against his taut skin. Her curse, now and always, was to notice the particulars of him. In a thousand ways, he was like no one she had ever met.

"This cannot happen again," she whispered.

"It shouldn't." His voice was as low as hers, but thick and uneven. "I want it no more than you. And yet we both know it will."

She shook her head. "No, no, no."

"You protest too much."

He was wrong. Her protest was weak, unsure, spoken to convince herself as well as him of the way things had to be. She needed to protest with all the power and emotion she had thrown into her music. She needed to scream, to rant, to cry. Instead, she had to force herself to look into his eyes. Intensity burned in their depths, the torment that he lived with day and night. She did not want to know its cause. She had torments of her own.

"You dishonor me," she said.

She expected further argument. Instead, he held silent and still, his reaction as stark as if she had slapped him, when all she had done was tell him something he should have known.

"It was not my intent," he said stiffly, as if somehow she had wronged him.

An urge to brush his hair from his forehead took hold. Stupidly. What had come over her?

She took refuge in anger. He had no right to stir her in such a way. He had no right to destroy her fragile hold on peace.

"What exactly was your intent, Captain?" she asked. "You were lonely? You wanted sex?"

In another life such crudeness would have been impossible for her. But not in this one. Not now. Not here.

He stroked her face. She brushed his hand away. "I am no more lonely than you," he said. "And no more aroused."

"You are not a passionate man."

"So I believed."

And I am not a passionate woman. He would laugh if she said the words. Had she not on this night proven they were a lie?

They stood close, their bodies separate yet linked by an invisible bond of heat. Cupping her face, he brushed his lips once more against hers. She trembled. He had to feel it. But he held his silence and, stepping away, let his eyes caress her instead of his hands. The caress was devastating in its gentleness, a kind of ravishment she could not fight or forget.

At last he turned from her and walked to the door. Pausing, he looked back as if he would say more. After a moment he left, disappearing into the night from which he had come. She stood in darkness, her arms wrapped around her, not so much for protection as, God help her, a foolish attempt to hold in the feelings he had aroused.

An eternity passed before she locked the door, as if such a gesture would keep him from her. She went to bed, to a night of sleeplessness and unwanted contemplation of her strange new life on the Isle of Wight, and worse, memories of what had brought her here.

It was time she let herself remember another man, one she could not compare to Nicholas Saintjohn except for his gender. For the first time in weeks she allowed herself to think of that man, of what she had given to him, of what he had done to her.

Ascot Chilton had been gentle, artistic, the owner of a gallery she had liked to visit. After her mother's death, she sought comfort in his sympathy. That sympathy had led to what she once believed was an everlasting love. She knew he made a poor living at the gallery, but she had money. Assuring him she would help as best she could, she put a portion of that money into his open hands.

She also let him make love to her. She was not a child. They were to be married. She could see no harm.

She had been blind, groping for acceptance in a dark world whose cruelty she could not see. The arrival of a distant cousin, wealthy and beautiful, dragged her into the light. Chilton had chosen the cousin. And she had chosen to leave, without asking for an apology, without demanding repayment of any kind.

All she had wanted was solitude and, like a wounded animal, a chance to lick her wounds.

Instead, she had met Nicholas Saintjohn on a windy stretch of beach known as Carnal Cove. In her innocence—it was hard to believe she could still be innocent—she had not known how prophetic the name of the cove could be.

His visit tonight was more than strange; it was as otherworldly as her vision of the woman in white.

Worst of all, he had left his mark upon her. She could still feel his lips and his hands, could still taste his tongue. The memories of him burned inside her with far more intensity than Ascot Chilton had ever aroused.

And all he had done was kiss her, and touch one breast.

She thought about that kiss and that touch through most of the night. The next morning, half drugged from lack of sleep, she decided to sit on the portico and watch the sun on the water. The Jarmans would not be here today, a fact that brought no satisfaction. They were the most normal people she had met in her new world. They acted as a buffer against facets of her new life she could not understand.

Preparing herself a cup of much-needed tea, she carried it into the parlor. As she made her way toward the door, she glanced at the easel in the corner. It held the drawing she had made yesterday evening on the beach, when she had seen the mysterious woman walking away from her toward the pier, before she had come inside to sit at the piano, before her life had been turned upside down.

Staring at the easel, she dropped the cup. It shattered on the floor.

Much of the sketch was as she remembered it, the background of water, the foreground of sandy shore. But the middle was blank, as if a hole had been cut out of the drawing, though the paper was untouched.

In the place where she had drawn the woman walking past the pier, she saw only a white void. The image of her night stroller had disappeared.

The village of East Hartsbridge lay a brisk hour's walk from the cottage, over a high, rutted road from which could be seen the rolling landscape of her corner of the island. Few houses greeted Makenna as she hurried along, and only a half dozen men and women, who stared at her in curiosity as she passed.

The friendliest reception she got came from a tawny, shaggy-haired dog who came bounding out of nowhere and circled her for half the journey, barking and jumping as if walking with her was some kind of game. No one called him or whistled, and she decided he must be a stray.

Having had no more experience with dogs than

with children, she did not give him encouragement, though he seemed not to need it. At last, as she topped a rise that overlooked the seaside village, he disappeared, and she hurried toward the church steeple visible above the cluster of cottages, shops, and one pub—the Crown and Anchor—that lay along East Hartsbridge's main street. She could see the dock with its row of fishing boats and the ferry landing site. She had been on the island only five days, yet her arrival seemed a lifetime ago.

A small house lay to the east of the stone chapel, a graveyard to the west. A flower-lined walkway connected the buildings. The vicar waved to her in welcome from the house.

She hesitated. He was not alone. Beside him stood a portly, gray-haired man of middle years, the kindness in his face offset by the glint of curiosity in his eyes as she slowly walked down the hill. He wore the suit of a gentleman, though, like him, it showed signs of age.

"Miss Lindsay," the vicar said, smiling at her approach. "What a delightful surprise."

He introduced his companion as Dr. William Beaumont, the village doctor. "We've just concluded our weekly chess game," he added. "Perhaps the two of you will join me for a cup of tea."

"Thank you, Edward," Dr. Beaumont said, "but I suspect Miss Lindsay would prefer a private visit. Pardon my bluntness," he said to her, "but the vicar will tell you it's my way. Besides, I must celebrate my victory at the Crown and Anchor."

With a doff of his hat, he was gone, leaving Makenna to accept the vicar's offer alone. They stood in the street watching the doctor's departure.

"He does like his pint," the vicar said. "He's a good man, a widower for many years, childless. He's devoted his life to the villagers, and to the study of his profession, I might add. East Hartsbridge is fortunate to have such a clever doctor. I suspect he could have enjoyed a much more successful practice in a city."

As he led her inside, Makenna was only half listening. Her heart pounded, not only from the walk. She had much to ask the vicar, yet knew not which words to choose. It would not do to present herself as a foolish flibbertigibbet or, worse, a lonely creature grown demented through the trials of her life.

He did not know why she had moved to the island, her explanation having been weak as well as vague, but he must have guessed a man had been involved.

His housekeeper, a quieter version of Mrs. Jarman, brought tea and cakes into the parlor, then left after receiving permission to complete her morning's shopping. Setting her cloak and bonnet aside, Makenna took a chair and accepted a cup of sweetened tea.

"You must have walked quickly," Reverend Coggshall said. "There's a pinkness to your cheeks from the morning air."

The pinkness could have come as well from her memory of the captain's kiss. Stirring her tea, she lectured herself against remembering too much. She knew of only one way to get Nicholas Saint-john from her thoughts, and that was to think of a topic more startling. She knew of only one.

"Does the church believe in ghosts?"

Her last word hung in the air of the vicar's neatly appointed parlor. She hadn't meant to be so blunt, but the events of last night and this morning had left her too rattled for subtlety.

Coggshall set his cup aside. He barely registered surprise, though she had not missed the quick, slight tightening around his mouth. When he finally answered, she credited him with treating the question seriously. And for not asking why she wanted to know.

"Yes, if you're talking about the sense one can have of a departed loved one lingering in spirit. Though the issue is much less clear, most of us in the clergy cannot deny the existence of evil spirits as well. Too much suffering in the world keeps us from doing so."

"How can you tell the difference?"

"A good question. Good and evil can best be differentiated in the heart and soul. Whoever senses the presence of a spirit is the one most capable of sensing the truth. If such a truth exists." He paused a moment. "You've experienced the presence of something unseen, I take it."

"Not exactly unseen."

She shifted under the watchful gaze of his clear blue eyes. She owed him some sort of explanation, but she could not tell him everything.

"In the cove I thought there was something, a woman in white walking at the water's edge."

"In the night?"

"No, in the evening, when the moon is on the rise. It's been full, or close to it, ever since I arrived. I've seen her more than once."

"Ah, moonlight."

As if that explained the situation, as if in such circumstances a woman alone, isolated from others, might hallucinate such a creature as she described, suffering the kind of lunacy brought on by the presence of the moon.

Makenna stopped herself. She must not judge him harshly. Perhaps his comment had not been so critical.

"Has there been any talk of such a vision?" she asked.

"None that I have heard, but I've been here less than two years. That makes me a stranger, you understand. An accepted stranger, given my assignment at the church and the ready friendship of Dr. Beaumont. I have been told stories of the past, mostly of festivals and hard times and storms. And, yes, even a hint of the events that gave Carnal Cove its name. And a drowning or two as well, the tide being particularly strong in the cove."

"But no stories of ghosts? Or anything else amiss at the cottage?"

"Idle talk, nothing more. And nothing about ghosts. Oh, we have our odd villagers who tell a tale or two about dead souls who have not completely departed. You'll hear such stories throughout the country, most especially in an isolated village such as this."

She thought of Biddy Merton, a teller of strange tales, according to Mrs. Jarman.

"But the church ignores them," she said.

"Not always. In each diocese you can find three or four clergy who will perform exorcism, although a requiem is preferred if the soul is seeking rest."

"Would you perform such an exorcism? Or a requiem?"

"It is something I would have to study upon."

She gave him silent thanks for continuing to answer her forthrightly, avoiding an outright accusation of an unwell mind. He deserved a respite from the far-fetched subject she had introduced. After all, he had not seen the woman. Nor had he seen the sketch.

Nodding, she managed a smile. "I'm sure what I saw was the moonlight and the wind and my own imagination."

To her surprise, Coggshall persisted. "Did you hear this ghost call to you?"

The question was not easily answered. How could she describe the beckoning she had felt in her soul, the compelling urge to leave the cottage and hurry down to the beach that came before each sighting? And what of the cry of that first time at the cove, the plaintive keening that still echoed in her mind?

There was, too, the sobbing, the memory of which tormented her heart.

She could not bring herself to tell him of any of these.

"No, I have not been called."

He smiled, she thought somewhat patronizingly, and she felt a stirring of irritation. For a while she had thought him sympathetic, open to possibilities out of the ordinary. She wondered about his sympathy now.

I sketched her, but the pencil marks vanished from the paper overnight.

What would he say to that?

My dear Miss Lindsay, your move from London has exhausted you.

He might very well be right. But her exhaustion had nothing to do with the altered drawing.

As far as she was concerned, the subject of spirits, both good and evil, was exhausted. She tried another, one that was no more comforting, one that weighed equally on her mind.

"I've met my neighbor."

He looked up sharply from his plate of cakes, obviously more interested than he had been in ghosts.

"Captain Saintjohn?"

"He sometimes walks on the beach. Never, I should add, when the apparition or whatever it is makes an appearance."

"You've talked to one another?"

That's not all we've done.

"Briefly." She spoke the truth. Their conversations tended to be short-lived.

"I had hoped . . . well, never mind. Your meeting was inevitable, given that you both live on the cove."

"He's not been here long, has he?" she asked.

"A few weeks longer than you."

"This seems a strange place for a sea captain still in his prime."

And how do you know he's in his prime? the vicar might ask.

He has held me in his arms.

"Even the Queen takes her holiday here," Coggshall said.

"He doesn't appear to be on holiday."

"How does he appear?"

There was definite alarm in the vicar's eyes. Makenna wished she had never brought up the subject. She wasn't learning anything about the captain, and she was revealing far too much about herself.

"Brooding."

"You've had trouble with him?"

"I meant no such thing. It's just that he always seems deep in thought. And he never says much."

In truth, the most he had talked was when he

asked her to instruct his son. It was a topic she would not bring up. The vicar would take the opportunity to press his own request in that regard.

Coggshall took a moment to respond, as if he had to choose his words carefully.

"He has a son."

She tried to act as if she had not known.

"I've never seen him on the beach."

How easy it was, she found, to lie by omission.

"The boy has recently suffered the loss of his mother."

"So they are both in mourning."

"Captain Saintjohn was at sea much of the boy's life. I believe he wants to get to know his son better."

She recognized the evasion for what it was. Nicholas Saintjohn was not grief-stricken over the death of his wife, a fact she had already determined for herself.

"I'm surprised he told you this," she said. "He seems so uncommunicative."

At least in words.

"We've barely spoken. My information comes from a fellow clergyman in Liverpool, where the Saintjohn family home is. At the wishes of the boy's grandparents, he wrote to tell me of the captain's arrival."

He must have written more, otherwise Coggshall would not have warned the villagers against gossiping about the newcomers.

"Was the mother ill for long?" she asked.

"The late Mrs. Saintjohn suffered a tragic death, an accident, I was told."

Abruptly he stood and walked to the door leading to the back of the house, glancing down the hallway before turning to her.

"I would like to tell you something in confidence. A bit of advice, actually."

"You can trust in my silence."

"You would be better served to keep your distance from the captain and from Windward House."

"Why?"

"I can only say he is a troubled man. There were rumors . . . well, never mind."

"What kind of rumors?"

"It would do you little good to know. Rumors are, after all, not necessarily related to fact."

"But I'm to keep my distance from the captain."

"There is no reason for you to do otherwise."

Unless I want to be kissed until my toes curl under and my blood boils.

Which she didn't.

"I'll remember your advice." She stood. "Thank you for the tea and for giving me your time."

"Never hesitate to seek me out when you are troubled. Or when you are not." His eyes warmed. "I would like to call on you again."

Here was a complication she did not welcome.

"Give me some time, Reverend Coggshall. As you might imagine, my moving here has been tiring."

"Of course." He hesitated. "Have you given any

thought to my suggestion about the village children?"

"About teaching them, you mean? Not really. I do not believe I am qualified."

Gathering up her cloak and bonnet, she asked for directions to the shop of the East Hartsbridge dressmaker, thanked him again for his time, and departed, mulling over what she had learned: The church recognized the presence of ghosts, although hers evidently existed only in her exhausted mind; the captain was not long a widower, his wife had suffered a tragic death, and he'd left his home under some sort of cloud.

Nothing the vicar had said explained anything. Indeed, his words had only raised more questions.

The housekeeper at the vicarage met her on the walkway with a basket of biscuits.

"The vicar thought you might be wanting these. I baked them myself and they're still warm."

Makenna was sincere in her thanks. Reverend Coggshall was treating her with kindness and consideration. She ought to be more grateful. Instead, he made her ill at ease.

Next came a visit to the dressmaker, Mrs. Tobias Bent, as she proudly introduced herself, wife of the village constable. Makenna, grateful the husband was nowhere in sight, ordered a half dozen dresses that ought to see her through several springs and summers, then set out on her return walk to Elysium. The shaggy-haired dog met her when she was no more than halfway home.

She tossed him one of the biscuits and then another. He wolfed them down so quickly, she finally fed him everything in the basket, down to the last crumbs.

In gratitude, he danced around her, darting up the road and back again, circling and barking, then dashing off again. He disappeared over a rise, and she thought he had abandoned her. Not so. He waited for her at a narrow trail that dropped down off the road in a westward direction, away from the water. She stopped in front of him. He yipped, ran down the trail, and stopped to pant expectantly at her.

"I'm supposed to follow you?" she asked.

As if he understood, he yipped again, ran a little farther on, then stopped and waited for her to catch up. Intrigued, she followed him. The trail, descending sharply from the high point of the road, led to a dense line of trees not visible to passersby. She walked through the growth, enjoying the shade on the sunny spring day.

Her progress ended when she came to a clearing, at its center a rectangle of unstable wooden fencing some twenty yards square. In the middle of the rectangle was a hodgepodge of headstones, some broken, others leaning at such an angle they almost touched the ground.

It was a graveyard that far predated the one beside the village church. A chill went through her, and she pulled her cloak tight.

It wasn't the graveyard itself that chilled her. It

was the woman standing in its midst, bent and gray-headed, a threadbare shawl pulled over her thin shoulders.

"I've been waiting for you, Makenna Lindsay," she said in a voice as cracked as the headstones. "It's long past time we had our talk."

Chapter Six

"You're Biddy Merton, aren't you?"

Biddy Merton, the woman who told tales. Makenna felt an unexpected urge to smile. She wanted very much to hear those tales, but not here, not surrounded by the dead. She had pictured their meeting in a safe and open place.

The woman kept her silence and her position in the midst of the weed-choked graveyard, as if waiting for Makenna to join her. Her skin was pale and etched by wrinkles, her eyes so narrow Makenna could not make out their color. Her nose was large, her lips thin, her brows as gray as the hair loosely bound in a bun at her nape.

Small and bent and as still as a headstone, she looked as if she had been waiting for years in this eerie, isolated place. Makenna almost expected to see cobwebs connecting her shawl to her faded skirt.

"You sent the dog for me. He belongs to you."

"The dog's a stray. He is not mine."

"Still, he is not a stranger to you. Not like me. How did you know my name?"

"Old bones know things." A gnarled hand waved over the graves. "As do those buried in this unsanctified ground. What things they could tell us if they could only talk."

The gate creaked as Makenna let herself inside the fence. Behind her the branches of the trees scraped together in a sudden gust of wind. A dark cloud rolled over the sun.

She swayed from the force of the wind; it blew against her back, pushing her forward. Biddy Merton remained unmoving, scarcely ruffled by the gust.

Makenna's heart pounded in her throat. She glanced at the circling canopy of trees. The dog was gone. She and Biddy Merton were alone. Except for the old bones beneath the untended ground. The situation did not frighten her so much as bring on an easiness that killed the urge to smile.

"What have we to say to one another?" she asked.

"You've seen her."

Makenna's skin prickled, as if invisible hands stroked beneath her clothes.

"Who are you talking about?"

"Do not pretend ignorance. I speak of the ghost of Carnal Cove."

Thunder rolled in the distance. Makenna ran her hands over her arms but stirred no warmth.

"If there is a ghost," she said, "you and I are the only two who seem aware of it."

"Ghosts have their peculiar ways."

"So you've seen it."

"Her. Our ghost was once a woman. But no. I've not seen her."

"How do you know she exists?"

"Old bones know things."

Even in her shaken condition, Makenna was far too sensible to accept such an answer.

"That doesn't make sense. No one else I've talked to is aware of this ghostly woman's existence."

"You claim Carnal Cove as your home. You have stirred up the past."

"So the ghost is my fault. What about Nicholas Saintjohn? He lives at the cove, too."

"The captain's view is inward. He sees little of his new world. Except you."

"What do you know of my relationship with him? No, don't answer. I already know what you will say."

She listened for a moment to the wind, circling and isolating the two of them. For all the attention they could attract from the outside world, they might as well be on the dark side of the moon.

Despite herself, Makenna shivered. "What else do your bones tell you?"

"That trouble lies ahead."

"Trouble for whom?"

"For us all."

"Because of the ghost?"

"It is possible."

"Or is it the captain who threatens us?"

"Again, a possibility."

"Are you warning me against him? If so, you are the second one today to do so."

"I warn you to have courage. You must also open your mind to mysteries few on this earth can explain."

"That's what you wanted to tell me? That's why you waited in this godforsaken place on the off chance I might come strolling by?"

"Little happens by chance."

"Then by whose design? Yours, of course."

"I have no such power. The answer is one of the mysteries."

Heavy splats of rain disturbed the weeds and hard-packed dirt around them. The sky had darkened to the color of night, though the hour could be no later than three. Makenna pulled the hood of her cloak over her head, but the frail-looking old woman stood rigid and unperturbed.

The two women stared at one another. Makenna was overtaken by the sense she had known Biddy Merton sometime in the past, perhaps in another life. But Makenna did not believe in reincarnation, any more than she believed in ghosts.

Biddy Merton broke the silence. "We will talk again," she said, then turned and disappeared into the deepening gloom, leaving Makenna in a confused state of curiosity mixed with fear, wanting to run after the strange old woman, wanting equally to flee.

The rain became a downpour and determined her course. She took refuge under the trees. When the storm gave no sign of easing, she ran straight into its fury, up the graveyard trail to the main road, then northward to the lane that led to Elysium.

Bolting herself inside, she threw logs onto the fire, then changed into dry clothes, brushing her hair until it crackled with electricity, tending to necessary chores, keeping her mind a blank as best she could. She moved by rote, each movement determined, the only sign of stress the trembling of her hands.

She heated the last of the food left by Mrs. Jarman and ate it, but it brought no warmth. Neither did the fire she continued to feed in the parlor, though she huddled close to it for much of the night, stirring the embers with a poker to keep the flames alive. Around her the latched windows and doors rattled in the storm. At midnight she tried going to bed, but eventually took blankets and pillow into the parlor and bundled herself in a makeshift bed in front of the hearth.

Here she could let the portrait of her mother

look down on her. The portrait always brought her a sense of peace. It did not fail her tonight.

Eventually she allowed herself to remember all that the day had held. Not once did she glance at the altered sketch on the easel, nor did she need to do so. The details were etched in her mind.

Exorcism, mysteries, the certitude of Biddy Merton that the ghost truly did exist—so much to think about and nothing to understand.

At last her thoughts centered on Nicholas Saintjohn. The captain was as much a mystery to her as her spectral visitor at the water's edge. The vicar had talked of rumors surrounding him. She gathered they had something to do with the death of his wife.

Biddy Merton, too, suggested he would bring her trouble. There was no doubt of that. She had not been able to get his late-night visit from her mind.

Nicholas had said there was something between them, something they could not deny. She did not attempt to do so. The taste of him was still on her tongue.

If Ascot Chilton had possessed a taste, it was of weak tea. Nicholas Saintjohn tasted of heady wine.

And she had thought herself in love with the gallery owner. What was her feeling for the captain? Arousal, certainly, a primal urge to debase herself in the pleasures of the flesh. But he could not, did not, would not ever stir her heart.

Eventually she thought of the boy. Jonathan must be as bereft in that dark and lonely mansion as she had been in the storm. Repeatedly she had been warned away from his father. No one had mentioned keeping her distance from the child. Though she felt no stirring of a latent maternal urge buried within her, she could not forget the pair of wide, unsmiling eyes that had stared up at her.

Nor could she allow herself to cower in fear and trembling. The cottage had not become the place of peaceful refuge she had envisioned, but that did not mean she could let it be her prison.

In the morning, with the sun glistening on the outside pools of water left by the rain, she waited at the back door for the Jarmans to arrive. Declining tea, she pulled on her cloak and made an announcement.

"I will be gone for a while." There was no keeping her resolve a secret. "I'm going up to Windward House. Captain Saintjohn has requested I teach his son music and drawing. I have decided to accept."

By the time Makenna stood in front of the captain's desk, staring at his rigid, rugged face, all determination had fled, and with it all courage.

She had taken the walk quickly, without hesitation, ignoring the feeling she was being watched, had even followed the housekeeper Mrs. Loddington up the dark stairway to the captain's door with no more than a flutter of concern, entering the library with a steady step, gesturing for him to keep his seat.

But she had forgotten what it was like to look down at Nicholas Saintjohn, to look at the firm set of his lips, to study the open throat of his shirt.

And she had forgotten the way he returned those looks. As if she were here for more of what he had given her two nights ago. She wasn't. Not in the least. Once she found her voice, she needed to tell him so.

Looking away from him, she studied the Turner seascape over the mantel.

"Turner painted storms well," she said, remembering her dash through the rain.

"Without a doubt."

"It is very important in life to understand art."

"So some believe."

An edge to his voice made her turn to him.

"But not you?"

His eyes were dark, unreadable.

"I do not always find paintings, or music, soothing. They stir emotions sometimes best left alone." He paused a moment, as if his words needed emphasis. "But this is something you already know."

Makenna could hear music vibrating around her, the passionate music that had enticed an aroused man to her door. Music innocently played, or so she told herself.

She stiffened. "A gentleman would not mention such things."

"A gentleman would not have visited you in the night. A gentleman would not have—"

"Please, Captain Saintjohn, do not mention things I am trying hard to forget."

"Have you succeeded? I think not. No more than I."

He leaned back in the chair and waited. He wore no coat on this day, just the dark, unbuttoned shirt and trousers, his hair carelessly combed. He looked as if he were not long out of bed.

Her stomach knotted.

"You asked if I would teach your son art and music. I told you no."

"You said you had never done such a thing. That you know little of children."

"Those things are still true. I also do not understand your wish that he be educated in such areas, since you claim they stir unwanted emotions."

"Have you not discovered I am seldom a reasonable man?"

To answer truthfully would be to say she understood little about him or her reaction to everything he said and did. But this was a time for only partial truth.

"I do not guarantee success at even the most rudimentary level. But if you wish to entrust part of Jonathan's education to me, I will do what I can to share with him what I know."

He did not speak right away, but she could feel his heat from across the desk. It came at her like tentacles from a creature of the deep.

"What changed your mind?" he asked.

Not your visit. Not your kiss.

"Nothing I can explain."

How to tell him that people kept warning her away from this house? How to describe the lingering sounds of sobbing? What words could convey the image of sad brown eyes in a face too young to show such depth of emotion? How to tell him she could still feel the boy's small hand in hers?

"Perhaps it is as you said. I have time on my hands and need something to fill the hours. Or perhaps Jonathan offers a challenge I cannot resist."

"Teaching my son is not a game."

"You insult me. I do not look upon it as such. Although it probably wouldn't hurt for him to look upon our time together in such a light."

"First I dishonor you, and now I insult you. What else do I do to you, Makenna? Do you dare put it into words? Or is that too much of a challenge?"

He stood and came around the desk, halting scant inches away from her. Her heart stopped. She stepped backward, hating herself for doing so. It took all her courage not to run from the room.

And all her will not to rest her hands on his chest, to seek out the beating of his heart, to feel the warmth of his body.

"You're making this very hard," she said.

"I could say the same of you."

He seemed to be saying something she did not understand.

"In what way?" she asked. "All I did was walk into the room and state my purpose."

"You are an innocent."

"You did not think so two nights ago."

"If I had thought otherwise, we would have been in your bed."

"So my innocence, my virginity if you will, kept you from assaulting me."

"Do not lie to yourself. I would have been there by your invitation."

She closed her eyes. He knew nothing about her, yet he understood far too much. She had wanted more than his kisses, yet dreaded his touch more than she had dreaded anything in her life. He read the former far too clearly, but the latter he could never comprehend.

She turned to leave. "This is a mistake."

His hand rested on her arm. It was a link as powerful as a chain.

"I am a fool, Miss Lindsay," he said stiffly. "I risk the well-being of my son. Believe it or not, it is much of the reason I am here."

She wanted to believe him. Until she could do so, she would have to pretend.

"So you accept my offer?"

"I do."

"There is one condition," she said.

"I would not have expected otherwise."

"I will teach him at the cottage."

His hand dropped. "No."

"I have to. For one thing, there's the piano."

"Windward House has many amenities, not the least being a music room complete with several instruments, including a piano. It is well lighted, overlooking the water on the side of the house away from the cove. You can teach him both music and drawing. I promise not to intrude while the two of you are there."

"I would be more comfortable in my own surroundings."

"Jonathan must remain under my protection."

"That's ridiculous. I would not harm the boy."

"I never thought otherwise, else I would not have asked you to be his teacher. But there are things you do not know. Things you do not want to know."

As always, matters between them that should have been simple became layered with complications. With mystery. With intrigue.

An image of yesterday's graveyard flashed in her mind. Somehow Biddy Merton's warnings of trouble seemed far more ominous than anything the vicar had said.

"If you insist, you can take him to the cove so that he may learn to draw the water and the birds and clouds."

"But you will be watching."

"Probably."

She knew there was no *probably* to it.

What if she told him a ghost haunted the cove?

What if she told him about the inexplicable change in her drawing? What if she described the chilling obsession that drew her to the water's edge on moonlit nights?

He had secrets. But so did she.

"The music room it is," she said. "We do not need the cove."

"I expected greater argument."

"It does me good to know I can surprise you."

"You surprise me every time we meet."

His voice had thickened. "Don't tell me how," she said, but she might as well have ordered the waves not to crash on the shore.

"You already know. I plan to resist you, yet in an instant, right here and now, I could strip the clothes from your body and take you on the rug, letting the firelight flicker across your skin, learning the contours, the shades of dark and light."

His words alone seemed to rob her of clothing, to render her naked before his dark gaze, to expose her swelling breasts with their taut tips and her pulsing intimate parts, all of her aroused by no more than the sound of his voice.

She covered her ears. "Please, no."

She could not shut out the penetration of his words.

"I sound like an artist, but I am not. Nor am I a musician, yet I would play your body the way your fingers caress piano keys."

She should slap him—any decent woman would, then run from the room—but if she raised her hand to him, it would be for a caress. Around Nicholas Saintjohn, decency fled.

"You call me an innocent, yet you do not talk to me as if you believe it."

"Talk is all I can allow myself. Please note I have not torn off your clothes."

"The mark of a true gentleman," she said, trying for scorn, though she could apply the emotion to herself as well as to him.

"We're back to that again."

He stepped away and to her surprise went to the window and stared out at the vast, dark, rolling water.

"I have spent my life at sea. My days in port offered little opportunity for subtlety. When I wanted a woman, there was always one available. Sometimes more than one. Often I chose to be alone. I planned such an existence here at Windward House. After only a few weeks here, I took a walk onto the beach. It was not my first. But it was the most memorable one."

He shifted to face her, and her heart caught in her throat. She stood on ground that moved beneath her. She had to steady herself.

"What of your wife? Do you not still mourn her?"

Already she had guessed the answer, but she threw out the words to break his hold on her. She wanted to ask more, to invade his privacy as he had invaded hers. What kind of tragic accident had taken the mother from her son? Did the women in the ports come before his marriage, during, after? She suspected all three.

Instead of answering, he simply stared at her, his eyes shuttered, and an invisible door closed between them. It was as she had wished, yet she felt a sharp disappointment. Walking around her, he opened the door to the hallway. Mrs. Loddington, lurking outside, jumped away.

"Please escort Miss Lindsay to the music room, then take my son to her." He spoke briskly, snapping orders as he once had done on the bow of a ship. "Beginning today, she will be instructing Jonathan."

He looked back at Makenna. "Are there any other conditions you would like to discuss?"

"I had not planned to start so soon. Since it's Friday, I assumed Monday would be the first lesson. Besides, I'll need drawing supplies and music."

"They await you."

She sighed. "You knew I would accept."

"I hoped."

He more than hoped. He had judged her well.

She walked past him, then paused in the hallway.

"There is one condition I insist upon. No, two. I will teach Jonathan here, as you wanted, but we must be left alone. And you cannot question my methods." Whatever they turned out to be.

He studied her for so long, she began to think he had decided to dismiss her before her work had begun. As always, he looked at her in a way that bound her to him and at the same time thrust her away.

"Agreed," he said, then closed the door, leaving her to follow Mrs. Loddington down the stairs to the ground floor, to a far room at the end of another hallway, a long, wide room with windows opening onto the sea. The housekeeper immediately left, and Makenna was free to study her new surroundings.

Expensive carpets covered large sections of the polished hardwood floor, and there was an equally expensive set of sofa and chairs arranged close to the door. A table and chair meant for a child rested in front of the windows, the panes clean and sparkling in the bright sunlight that fell inside.

On the opposite side of the room was a grand piano already open and waiting for a pianist to arrive. The music stand held a sheaf of musical exercises appropriate for a beginning student. In a cabinet next to the small table she found stacks of drawing paper and a box of pencils and pens. There were even charcoal, watercolors, and brushes, all of excellent quality. She touched the latter as if they would tell her something about the man who had ordered them.

The door opened behind her and she turned, expecting to see the housekeeper and her young pupil. Instead, the captain's man Gibbs came into the room, his uneven gait and rough clothes and features at odds with the elegant furnishings. He looked at her with evident disapproval.

"I feared you'd accept. Not many women can turn down Saint Nick."

Stunned, she could do no more than point out the obvious. "You don't think I should be here." It was an understatement. From the look in his eye, the old sailor wanted to pitch her out the window.

"He don't need more trouble. Not now."

Here was an injustice if she'd ever heard one.

"I have no intention of being trouble. No more than I want trouble in return."

"Maybe. Maybe not."

"Does Nicholas know you're here?"

Purposefully she used Saintjohn's first name, making it sound natural on her tongue. If Gibbs could rankle her, she could rankle him.

"Soon will, I expect. When you tell him."

"I have no intention of doing any such thing."

"So you say. Never knew a woman could hold her tongue."

"You don't know me."

Whatever Gibbs planned to retort was lost when the door opened once again and Mrs. Loddington led Jonathan into the room. The boy, dressed formally as he had been before, looked past her around the room, as if he had never seen it before. Did he not explore his new home? Again she wondered what sort of life he led.

Without a word, Gibbs and the housekeeper departed, closing the door behind them, leaving teacher and pupil alone in an uneasy silence.

"Hello, Jonathan. Remember me? I'm Miss Lindsay."

The boy nodded but did not meet her eye.

"I'm to be your teacher," she said.

His young, round face seemed to brighten.

"Are you taking Papa's place?"

"Oh, no." The brightness faded, and she felt a sudden kinship with him. "I'll teach you music and drawing."

She got no reaction to tell her what he thought of the news. Instead, he stood in place, his hands at his sides, as if waiting for whatever shift in his life fate chose to place before him. Far too recently he had lost his mother and been taken from his home by a seafaring father he scarcely knew. He ought to cry or whine or complain, but all he did was remain in place without expression and await the next blow.

Six years of age was far too young to be so stoical.

A sense of desperation took hold of her. The boy needed something, but she had no idea what. Nor did she have any idea where to begin. Silently she cursed the captain for putting her into this strange situation, then cursed herself for agreeing to his request.

Taking off her cloak and bonnet, she tossed them on a chair and guided the boy to the supply cabinet. Kneeling, she put herself at his level.

"First," she said, "let's empty this and see what's inside."

"Mrs. Loddington says I'm not supposed to disturb anything in the house."

"Does she really?" Anger replaced the desperation. "Artists disturb things. It's what we do best."

Lifting out a stack of sketch pads, she dropped them on the floor, not caring that they scattered as they fell. "Now then, you take the pencils and the pens and I'll get the paints. We'll look the whole thing over and decide where we want to start."

At last the boy's small hand reached inside the cabinet for the pencil box. He looked as if he thought the thing might bite him, but her warm smile encouraged him to continue.

In her mind's eye she could see the captain watching and frowning. He probably wouldn't approve of the way she began. She wasn't sure she did, either, but she had only her instinct to guide her, and a sense that if what she did bothered the man, it could not be totally wrong.

Chapter Seven

Throughout the weekend and into the next week, the days were cloudy, the nights moonless. Each morning she walked to Windward House, spent two hours with Jonathan, then walked home, though Gibbs was always present with the carriage to offer her a ride.

Not once did she see Nicholas Saintjohn, though she knew he was behind the offer from Gibbs.

On each of her journeys, both coming and going, she had a companion: the shaggy dog that had led her to the graveyard and to the strange talk with Biddy Merton. She got into the habit of bringing him food, though she doubted her meager offerings could account for his presence. Curiously, he seemed to like her company.

Occasionally during a lesson the sound of hammering came through the window, sometimes steady, at other times uneven, as if whoever wielded the tool was struck by bouts of uncertainty. She did not ask her pupil the source of the noise, preferring to concentrate on the tasks at hand, and he never ventured an explanation, acting instead as if he heard nothing more than the sounds inside the music room.

On Friday, seven days after the first lesson, she found an envelope awaiting her on the music room table. No note was inside, just a generous amount of cash. She had not asked for money, nor did she want it. But the payment put her relationship with the captain on a business level, and for that reason alone she thrust it in her pocket and went about showing her young pupil how to sketch the wind-shaped tree visible in part from the window of the ground-floor music room.

When the sketching was done—when they had both reached their separate levels of frustration— they moved to the piano, where she watched his small fingers seek out the keys of a simple song. He seemed to show more pleasure in the music than the drawing, hence they stayed at the piano twice as long as they did the sketch pad.

Later, sipping tea served by the solemn-faced Mrs. Loddington and sharing with Jonathan biscuits baked by Mrs. Jarman that she'd brought, she announced she would not return until Monday, when they would continue their lessons.

"You've worked very hard, and you've earned two days of rest."

Jonathan's eyes widened; then he looked away, as if to hide the distress she had seen in his expression. For the first time she realized he found pleasure in their time together, or at least he preferred it to however he'd spent his mornings before the lessons had begun.

Her heart warmed, and she realized she felt the same about her own mornings. She sought a way to ease their distress.

"Will you promise to practice on the piano?"

He nodded.

"If you don't mind, I would forget about the drawing we started today. We can throw it away and put the tree out of its misery."

He started to nod, his usual reaction to everything she said, then stopped.

"The tree is unhappy?"

"It has to be. Look at the way you drew it."

He began a laugh, then clamped his hand over his mouth.

"Trees don't feel," he said, full of worldly skepticism.

"Who says?"

"Papa would, if I asked him. And Mrs. Loddington." He thought a minute. "I'm not so sure about Gibbs."

"Have you asked the tree?"

"Trees don't talk, either."

"Let's go find out," she said, and at his frown, added, "It's what we artists do. We explore unusual things."

Makenna knew she was talking nonsense, yet somehow it seemed right for the moment and for her companion. Neither she nor the boy had experienced much nonsense in their lives. Just now a touch or two could not hurt.

She stood. The boy looked up at her as if she had lost her mind. She extended her hand. He hesitated, then put his hand in hers, and she was struck once again by his fragility.

Old bones know things.

What about young bones? Did they know things not understood by those around them, the people who had supposedly reached maturity? She sometimes thought that in his solemnity Jonathan possessed a wisdom she had not reached. She reminded herself that only six months ago his mother had died. He was not only solemn and wise, he was incredibly brave.

Letting go of her hand, he reached for his jacket.

"You can go in your shirt sleeves," she said. "The sun is warm outside. I'm not going to bother with my cloak."

"I'm supposed to wear it," he said.

She did not argue as he slipped into the garment, which seemed perfectly tailored for him. Laboriously he fastened each button before accompanying her out the door and into Windward House's wide, dark entryway.

As they emerged onto the front drive, after her eyes adjusted to the bright sun, she glanced up at the bare-breasted figurehead over the front door and wondered what the boy thought of it. Had his father explained how sailors put such carvings onto the prows of their ships to lead them safely through the stormy waters?

She would have bet her cottage he had not.

To her surprise, the dog greeted them with a bark and a wag of his tail. He seemed especially joyous at the sight of the boy, prancing around him with more energy than he had shown Makenna, then stretching out his front paws and lowering his head, as if begging to be petted.

Jonathan clenched his fists, his dark eyes rounded.

"You can touch him," she said. "He won't bite."

"Mama said dogs have fleas."

What a curious time for him to mention his mother. He had not done so before. She would have liked, more than was decent, to ask questions about the woman. But she did not.

She would have also liked to give him a hug but feared she would be awkward and do the boy more harm than good.

"What does your papa say?"

"He's never mentioned dogs."

"So you'll have to trust my advice. This dog is a friend of mine. No friend could possibly have fleas. Human or otherwise."

The boy's lips twisted into an almost-smile. It was, she decided, as good as a hug.

She knelt beside him and stroked the animal behind his ears. His long tail fanned the air, but Jonathan's hands remained clenched at his side.

"Maybe later," she said, "when you get to know him better."

They stood, and the dog, as if knowing he had been dismissed, trotted away from the house, taking his place at the side of the road as a sentry might have done.

Crossing the drive, Makenna and the boy stopped at the corner of the house, by the tall tree with its budding branches bent by the north wind toward the brick, away from the water and the edge of the cliff.

"What do we do now?" Jonathan asked in a doubtful voice. "Does the tree know we're here?"

Being unused to nonsense, Makenna had no answer to either question. But she was in no position to change her course, not with his opinion of her at stake.

Taking one of his hands firmly in hers, she touched the tree's trunk and placed her ear against the rough bark.

"I think he sighed."

"How do you know the tree's a he?"

Jonathan sounded far too much like his father.

"It's sturdy and strong and rough on the outside but smooth and softer inside."

The boy thought that one over for a minute.

121

"Papa's not smooth and soft."

"Maybe he just doesn't want you to know. Men think they have to be hard."

Suddenly she understood Saintjohn's reference to hardness when he had stood close to her in his study. If he could hear her now, what a look of scorn and enticement she would get.

She blushed, grateful the boy was as innocent as she was supposed to be.

Kneeling beside him, she placed his hand on the tree. "Put your ear beside your hand. Don't you hear a sigh?"

The boy did as she asked. "No," he said. "That's just the wind."

A practical lad. She would have to work on his imagination.

"What are you doing?" a harsh, familiar voice asked. Both she and the boy started, then jumped up to face the captain.

"We're listening to the tree," Jonathan said, then added, as if that weren't bad enough, "It's what we artists do."

Makenna's cheeks stung. It was unfortunate that the boy had chosen this opportunity to answer his father so readily. At least he had not mentioned the other characteristic of artists she'd told him the day of their first lesson, that artists disturbed things. It might have been grounds for dismissal on the spot.

"I see," Saintjohn said, his gaze on Makenna.

She knew he did not see at all. "Is my son an artist so soon?"

She tilted her chin against his coolness. "We're working on it." As she spoke the words, she realized how true they were.

His dark, unreadable eyes unnerved her, but she refused to look away, even when he let those eyes trail down the sky-blue gown that had been tailored for her by the village dressmaker. He seemed particularly interested in the bodice.

Her pulse quickened. Why, today of all days, had she chosen to wear clothes that conformed to her figure so well?

"Go inside, Jonathan," he said. "Mrs. Loddington is waiting in the dining room with your midday meal."

The boy offered no protest. Making a wide berth around his father, he hurried inside and closed the door behind him.

Makenna had glimpsed into the room that was his destination. It was long and wide and dark, centered by a trestle table that could easily accommodate twenty guests. Jonathan would be sitting there alone. She almost hurried after him.

Nicholas Saintjohn stopped her. "Tell me, Makenna, what did you expect the tree to say?"

The man had a way of using words as a weapon. Did he really expect an answer?

She gave him one anyway.

"That's hard to know. I'm not familiar with this particular species."

123

"Then your ignorance is understandable."

He made ignorance sound like a terrible flaw. She doubted he spoke of her knowledge of botany, but of something beyond, ignorance of a subject profoundly important to him. Was she supposed to ask his true meaning? She would not, suddenly finding herself too exhausted to engage in his game of words.

"Thank you," she said in all sincerity, "for not mocking me in front of the boy."

"You would rather I mock you in private?"

"I would rather—"

She stopped herself. What she might have said shocked her and sent the blood pounding faster than ever in her veins.

"I am trying to stir your son's imagination." But it was hers that had flamed into the lascivious image of her body pressed to his, naked flesh to naked flesh. She could gaze into those probing eyes no longer without telling him the truth. She looked away and said, "The lesson is done for the day. If you wish me to return Monday, I will do so."

"What about tomorrow and the next day?"

"Your son needs to play. I don't know if he ever does so. I'm not sure he knows how."

"Be careful, Makenna."

But she could not heed his warning. "He's far too pale. He needs to get out more often and listen to trees."

"We have only the one."

"You take me too literally."

"I would take you anyway I could."

Her cheeks burned. The wind whipped at her hair, loosening far too many strands for the dignity she was trying to maintain.

"You make sport of me. Find a kinder way to do so with your son."

With the dog falling in behind her, she fairly ran from him, down the winding road that connected Windward House to Elysium, not looking back or stopping until she reached the cottage. To her regret, the Jarmans were still there, but she could not send them on their way without arousing questions over what went on at the mansion of Captain Saintjohn.

Nothing out of the ordinary, she would have told them. But, oh, the things that went on in her mind.

Changing out of the new gown, her favorite, regretting once again that she had worn it this day, she went to the garden to help the handyman dig in the dirt, half listening to his talk about bugs and worms and about plants that should be put out soon. Allowed inside the fence for the first time, the dog lay in the shade and promptly fell asleep.

In an imaginative mood, and remembering the suggestion she had made about the tree, she half expected the shrubs to speak to her as she attempted to study them. They did not, nor did the weeds she pulled up by the roots. If they had, she knew what they would say:

You are a foolish woman, Makenna Lindsay.
They would be right.

Hours later, when the Jarmans had gone, she bathed her face and hands but found herself too weary to change out of the soiled black gown she had chosen for gardening. After toying with her meal of roasted beef and potatoes, she banked the fire in the parlor—on this warm night there was no need for flames—and, placing the poker upright on the hearth, prepared to read a book on spiritual mysteries sent to her by the vicar and delivered by a far-too-curious housekeeper.

She had done no more than settle in a chair by the parlor lamp when the sobbing returned.

Soft though it was, it screamed in her ears. A chill penetrated her bones, a sensation so cold no fire could bring her comfort. Dropping the book, she had no choice but to walk to the door, to step onto the portico, to look at the flood of moonlight on the beach. And to stare at the luminous figure of a woman walking at the water's edge, away from Makenna, her long, white, flowing gown trailing in the dying waves.

Something stirred beside her. She jumped, then saw it was the dog, who had to her surprise found a resting place beside the rocker. He, too, stared toward the water, his tawny hair standing up like quills along his arched back, a growl deep in his throat.

Fear gripped her, but it was no more powerful

than the desire to join the woman, to touch her gown, to grope for something solid, to listen to whatever she might have to say. Was she good or evil? A restless soul unable to find peace, or a vengeful wraith determined to wreak mischief wherever she could?

Most of all, why did she appear only to Makenna? It was the most terrible question of them all.

A sob caught in her throat, a muted version of the crying she had heard moments ago on the night wind. Drawing a ragged breath, she discovered a new odor mingling with the salty dampness of the sea; it was the smell of lilies and hyacinths and roses, the flowers of a funeral bouquet. The air grew thick with the unwelcome sweetness, and she could barely breathe.

In desperation she motioned the dog to draw nearer, but he kept in his place. Compulsion pulsed in her blood and reason fled. Alone, she threw herself down the path to the cove, stumbling across the sand, hurling herself forward as fast as she could but never seeming to close the gap separating her and her ghost.

If that was what the woman truly was. On this night, she could believe nothing less.

"Stop!" she cried out, and the creature slowed, allowing her to draw close, but only for a moment before quickening the pace, drawing Makenna close to the rickety pier.

To her surprise, the ghostly figure glided up the

broken steps and onto the pier itself, moving out over the deepening water without hesitation, without a backward glance. Whatever protective railing had once been on the long, narrow structure was long since gone, leaving only the uneven planks and the unstable supporting columns that sank into the restless deep.

Makenna's head reeled. A harsh wind struck at her back, as if the elements themselves drove her onward, giving her no choice but to follow the flowing white folds of the vision's gown. It made no difference if the vision was good or evil. Judgment and caution were lost in the swirling mists of the night.

The first step of the pier groaned under her weight, and then the second, and the third. She scarcely heard them. An invisible bond linked her to the creature; she must follow wherever the specter chose to lead.

Vaguely she was aware of a voice calling, but the urgent, shouted words were lost on the wind. Poised to walk onto the pier itself, she felt a strong, whip-like arm wrap around her middle and pull her back down the steps and onto the sand.

"What the hell are you doing?" the voice growled.

She fought to get away, lashing out with her fists, twisting in frantic jerks, but Nicholas Saintjohn's arm was made of iron and held her fast against his hard, unyielding body. Not quite sane, she stared frantically down the length of the pier, but the woman had disappeared.

"Didn't you see her?" she cried.

"See whom? What are you talking about? There's only you, Makenna. Only you."

She shook her head violently. "No, no, she's there," she said, and then, less insistently, in more of a sob, "Or she was. I know she was."

His answer was a tightening of his hold. He was so solid, so truly real, like an anchor keeping her from the ethereal mist.

Gradually sanity returned, if a mind as jangled as hers could be considered sane. Raggedly drawing the damp night air into her lungs, she let her struggles subside. The scent of flowers was gone, as suddenly and completely as her view of the vision's robes. Reality became a man's arm around her waist and a man's warm breath on her cheek.

His hold loosened, but before she could free herself, he picked her up and cradled her against his chest, one arm beneath her legs, the other tight around her shoulders. In the comfort of his arms she began to shake, her whole body beset not with the tremors that came from exposure to cold nor even the ones that might accompany fear, but bone-deep quavers that defied explanation, that came from beyond rationality, quavers that came from the center of a disturbed soul.

Her soul. She would have wept, but the bleakness of her condition had dried her tears.

She was barely aware of the ground they covered as his long, strong legs took them across the sand and up the path to the cottage. The door slammed behind them, and suddenly they were in Elysium's small bedroom and he was placing her on the bed and wrapping the covers around her, as if their warmth would soothe her body into calm.

If that was what he thought, he guessed wrong. She needed more comfort than any blanket could provide. Reacting quickly, taking him by surprise, she threw off the restrictive covers and pulled him down to her, fingers clutching his shirt as she covered his mouth with hers and thrust her tongue past his lips and teeth.

He reacted as quickly as she. With a moan, he sucked her deeper inside him. His hands tore at her clothes, and she could feel the buttons give way. Each action of his was quick, efficient, as he pulled the gown from her shoulders, breaking the kiss to strip away the offending garment and toss it aside, leaving her in the thin undergarments that scarcely concealed her nakedness.

When one hand covered her breast, she realized the shaking had at last subsided, replaced by far sweeter tremors of pleasure. Her thoughts had turned to only the places he touched and the yearnings he aroused.

"Nicholas," she whispered and sensed the satisfaction he took in the sound of his name, as if no woman had ever done anything to him half so intimate.

Bending her head, she kissed the hollow of his throat, a particularly delectable place that had so often caught her attention. It tasted as good as it looked.

"Good God," he whispered.

Abandoning her breast, his hand found its way to the hem of her petticoat. When it was bunched around her waist, he moved his hand between her legs to the opening slit in her underdrawers.

She expected him to caress her flesh. Instead, he pulled away to look down at her. A lamp in the parlor provided their sole source of light. What could he see in the dimness? She hoped not much. Sight gave rise to thought, thought to hesitation. And in the latter would come the return of memory.

She wanted knowledge of only the moment, only sensation, only mind-numbing ecstasy. If she was not quite sane, so be it. When she was in his arms, hers was a madness without terror, without fear.

"Don't stop," she said and pulled him down to her once again. She did not have to tell him twice.

He joined her in the madness, hands and lips exploring her through the thin garments, the gossamer barrier adding an erotic touch to everything he did. She wanted to explore his body in the same way, to strip all his clothing away, but he would not let her, and soon she realized there was added eroticism in the rough fabric rubbing against her barely covered skin.

Too many decisions had been hers in this tumultuous time of her life; she gave herself more willingly than she would have thought possible to his impulses, his desires. He chose well, waiting until she was wild with impatience before easing his hand between her legs and widening the opening in the drawers.

Her body throbbed with a newfound passion. She wanted to tighten her thighs against his hand and hold it in place, at the same time as she needed to leave herself open to whatever he chose to do. All was feeling, all was rapture. Her world glowed in a rosy hue.

Then came the crash.

It took a moment for the sound to penetrate her clouded mind. Nicholas responded more quickly. He bolted from her and turned toward the parlor, from which the noise had come. Heart pounding, she threw herself from the bed to stand close to his side, the tentacles of sexual pleasure not quite loosened as she wrapped one hand around his arm.

He thrust her behind him. "Wait here," he ordered.

It was the first thing he wanted that he did not get. Holding on to his sleeve, she went with him into the next room.

They stopped in front of the banked fire. The sight awaiting her was one she would never forget. The beloved painting of her mother no longer hung above the mantel. Instead, it lay at an angle on the hearth, face up, the fireside poker piercing through the canvas at the exact place where Jenna Lindsay's heart would have been.

Chapter Eight

He held her through the night.

Of all the impossible things that had happened to Makenna over the past twelve hours, none was more upsetting than that platonic embrace. It was also the least significant—it had to be, she kept telling herself—so why did the memory of him remain?

She sat in the parlor huddled beneath a blanket, alone, still in her nightclothes although the sun was well above the horizon, and stared at the cold embers at the edge of the hearth. Everything about her was in turmoil though she kept herself as still as the dead fire.

Nicholas Saintjohn had held her through the

night. She felt him with her still, though he had been gone almost an hour.

Through the initial shock, the tears that finally came because of the portrait, the humiliating, private admission of how she had forced herself upon him, the gradually returning memory of her manic behavior on the beach—through all of that, he had held her.

No questions, no arousing touches, not even the press of lips against her forehead. He had simply lain beside her in the bed and wrapped his arms around her, and then, at the first light, when she asked that he leave, he had done so.

With an apology. He had come close to taking from her what was hers to give only once. He had not the right, and for that he apologized.

He was wrong, of course, but that mattered little. Far worse, he could not have been more cruel.

What was he trying to do with all that kindness? Make her fall in love with him? What kind of woman was she to feel the deadly combination of tenderness and lust for a man when she was so recently torn apart by another?

And how could he have become her primary consideration when it was entirely possible she was losing hold of her sanity? Of course, that was the answer to everything. In her hallucinatory state, she had no control of her actions, her feelings, her mind.

She admitted another truth. Captain Nicholas

Saintjohn, a man of hot flesh and pulsing urges, was as much the cause of her turmoil as the bloodless ghost.

For the first time in the morning light, she forced herself to look at the beloved painting of Jenna Lindsay, now damaged beyond repair. It sat propped beside the stone fireplace, her mother's face as strong and serene as ever, an obscene hole through her painted breast. There was nothing imaginary about the damage. It was unmercifully real.

She stared at the torn part of the canvas for a long while, then slowly let her eyes trail around the room. Had the spirit of the cove invaded the cottage while she and Nicholas were in the next room? Were there signs other than the portrait of that invasion?

Everything around her looked absurdly normal, from the placement of the furniture to the dust motes in the air. She could detect no mist, no lingering scent, nothing. Except the empty place above the mantel where the portrait had once hung. And of course the portrait itself. When she looked at it once again, she stared not at the damage but at her mother's eyes.

They gave her courage. She was not losing her mind. Ascot Chilton might have broken her heart, or so she had thought at the time, but he had broken neither her sanity nor her spirit. Neither would the ghost. Nor would Nicholas Saintjohn, although in his case she was not so confident.

Throwing off the blanket, she went to get dressed, then pulled out paper and pen from a bedside drawer. At the kitchen table, she hurriedly composed a letter, the words coming as fast as she could form them, then threw on her cloak and bonnet. She took care to secure the cottage. Spiritual intruders might invade, but not real ones, not villains of flesh and blood.

Outside she came upon the dog. He lumbered upright and wagged his tail in greeting.

"Where were you last night, you coward?"

His head lowered.

"The last time I saw you was when I went down to the beach. You refused to come with me. I could have used a little barking down there."

She glanced at the dish she had set out for him yesterday after returning from Windham House. The leftover beef was gone.

"Coward," she repeated. "And glutton."

He whined, his head still low.

Bending down, she rubbed behind his ears. "Come on. The least you can do is escort me into the village."

She could barely get her hand away before he tore from her and ran across the furrows of the about-to-be garden, darting to the back gate and barking impatiently. He was not a large dog, but he managed to disturb much of Mr. Jarman's meticulous work.

She made the journey into East Hartsbridge quickly. On this Saturday morning many villagers were about; she acknowledged their glances with a nod and the best smile she could manage, and posted the letter. The vicar waved at her from a block away and indicated he wanted to talk to her. But she did not want to talk to him, and with another wave she returned to the road back to Elysium, grateful he did not follow.

On this return walk the cottage was not her only goal, not even her primary one. She made an important stop along the way, at the trail leading to the graveyard, the last and only place she had seen Biddy Merton.

The dog jumped around her skirts. "Take me to her," she ordered. "Go on. You did it before. Now do it again."

With a yip of acquiescence, he took off at a run down the sloping trail, and she had to hurry after, through the barrier of trees, to the broken fence that bordered the ancient graveyard. Her heart sank. Biddy Merton was not in sight. Why she should have expected her presence she did not know, but she had.

She stared at the headstones coming out of the hard-packed, overgrown ground like broken monoliths. Cemeteries had never held a fascination for her. But this one did. She felt an urge to walk among the grave sites and read the inscriptions carved into the stones.

Old bones know things.

But do they tell what they know?

A bark from her companion pulled her out of her reverie.

"Okay, dog," she said, more unwilling to give him a name than to feed him, "what do we do now?"

He bounded from her around the fence to the far side of the graveyard, paused to bark again, then took off through the far section of trees. Without another glance at the headstones, she followed. Let the old bones think what they would.

The trail extended through the grove, into an open grassy valley, then over a hill and into another grove, thicker than the one surrounding the cemetery. Nestled within the trees, almost hidden by shadow, was a small structure no bigger than a shed.

Remarkably well kept, its boards painted a soft yellow, the thatched roof thick, the small garden at the side free of weeds, it looked like something out of a tale by the Brothers Grimm. But nothing that might serve as home to a witch, though an incurious black cat was curled up on the stoop. She had enough to deal with concerning the ghost of Carnal Cove without adding another supernatural creature to her list.

"Hello," she called out. "Is anyone home?"

At first she got no response. Then the old woman came from around the corner of the dwelling, looking very much as Makenna remembered her: bent, gray, and wrinkled, a faded shawl wrapped around her thin shoulders. This time her eyes were not tightly narrowed. This time they were surprisingly clear, pale blue, and steady in their gaze.

She appeared not in the least surprised at the sight of her guest.

"I need some information," Makenna said without preamble. "You're the only one I can think of who can help."

"Something's happened," Biddy said. It was not a question, and Makenna did not respond.

The woman tightened her shawl around her shoulders. "Ask your questions. I will tell you what I can. But first you must tell me exactly what it is that has brought you here."

She spoke with an authority belying her feeble appearance.

Makenna breathed a sigh of relief. "I want to. Very much."

Shuffling slowly in a pair of worn shoes, Biddy led her around the dwelling to a wooden bench at the side of a small well. The dog remained close by Makenna's side. The cat stirred herself to join them and curl in her mistress's lap as she lowered her frail body onto the bench. Neither animal paid the other any mind, as if they had been in each other's company often.

Makenna was the stranger here. She was also the only one whose heart was pounding. She took time to think, the words slow in coming, but at last she was able to describe her ghost, the moonlit visits, last night's near tragedy at the pier.

She even mentioned the scent of funeral flowers, though she could not have explained why the detail had stayed so sharply in her memory.

Biddy appeared to be dozing, but when Makenna paused, she was quick with a question.

"The ghost drew you onto the pier?"

"I thought so. But I was not in a rational state, you understand. I could be wrong."

Secretly she did not think so, but she was trying very hard to be sensible in a situation that made no sense.

She made light of her rescue. What had passed between her and Nicholas was nobody's concern but theirs. She did, however, mention his presence in the cottage when the portrait fell. Biddy Merton was no fool. She must know they had been in bed.

Closing her eyes, she was back in that bed, at a moment of great vulnerability when the crash came. The horror of what she saw in the parlor returned. She swallowed a rising hysteria. She and Nicholas had shared a moment of privacy, but they had not been alone.

"The noise frightened you," Biddy Merton said. Her voice had a calming effect, and Makenna's pounding heart slowed, allowing her to continue.

"It terrified me. I thought right away of this . . . this wraith, or whatever she is. She seems to have some kind of connection to me. Or maybe it's to the cottage. Maybe she doesn't want me there. Is that possible?"

And then she got to the question that was at the

heart of her visit, no longer concerned about making sense, needing to learn the truth at any cost.

"I had hung the painting very carefully. It meant a great deal to me. Could she have caused it to fall?"

For her it was a preposterous question, suggesting something too terrible to comprehend. Biddy Merton seemed unperturbed as her gnarled hand stroked the cat's back.

"You said the portrait was of your mother?"

"That's right. I painted it myself a long time ago."

"And your mother died when?"

"Two years ago," Makenna answered, though she could not see how that mattered.

"Leaving you alone."

"Yes." She tried to be patient. "My father died before I was born. Neither he nor my mother had any other surviving family."

"Was there no one at all in your life?"

"I don't understand how that would have any bearing on what has been happening."

"So there was a man."

As much as Makenna valued her privacy, she saw no purpose in guarding it now.

"Yes. We were engaged. Then we weren't."

"And you came to Carnal Cove."

"I found the deed to the cottage among my mother's papers."

"She never mentioned the island?"

"Never. I knew she had once lived close by in

Hampshire. As a matter of fact, a small village there is the place of my birth."

"You've never been to this Hampshire village?"

"There seemed no point. My mother and I were happy enough living in London." She hesitated, but she could not still a growing impatience. "Look, I've already told you more about my past than I've told just about anyone else. But it can have absolutely no bearing on what is happening now."

She was being as firm as she could without accusing the woman of wanting nothing but gossip.

Biddy was not impressed. Continuing to stroke the cat, she said, "Tell me about the captain."

Enough was enough. Abruptly Makenna rose to her feet and began to pace in front of the bench. The dog and cat watched her. Biddy stared into the trees beyond her, as if Nicholas would be making a momentary appearance. With the way things were going, Makenna would not have been surprised.

She stopped her pacing and stared down at the woman. "I'd rather you tell me about him. The first time we met you said he offered trouble. The vicar says the same, but no one will tell me why."

"Look at him. Remember what it is like to be in his presence. His kind of trouble is one any woman should understand."

Biddy made a good point.

But Makenna sensed that more lay behind the warning than sexual attraction.

"Everyone I've met has been on the island no more than a few years. What about you?"

"I was born not far from where you stand."

"So you were here when Windward House was built."

"Is this important for you to know?"

"Very," she said, though she would have difficulty explaining why.

"I worked in the kitchen for a while."

She darted a glance at Makenna, then returned to her study of the trees, as if trying to decide how much to tell her, what next to say.

"The old captain, Gerald Saintjohn, built the house for his wife," she said, and Makenna breathed a sigh of relief. Here at last were the facts she had been seeking.

"That was back in 1825," she added. "He brought her here during the summers, together with his only son Charles and Charles's wife Grace. When Grace Saintjohn gave birth to a son, he was brought as well."

"That would be Nicholas."

"Aye, it would. The lad was an imp, even then, scrambling over the rocks, playing in the water, though he was no more than a few years old. Mrs. Saintjohn, the mother, and the father as well, spent much of the time trying to contain him, but he was like the wind. A free spirit. It was the grandfather that urged him on."

Makenna had difficulty picturing Nicholas as a free spirit. He held far too tight a rein on himself.

Except, of course, when the two of them were together.

"He came to the island often, did he?" she asked.

"Only until he was six. That was, let me think, back in '34. It was the year Joyce Saintjohn, the grandmother, died."

Makenna did a quick calculation. In this year of 1863, Nicholas Saintjohn was thirty-five.

"The holidays on the island ended," she said.

"For the boy and the grandfather. The parents came one summer a few years later, and other family members." She looked sharply at Makenna. "There have been visitors as well, but none who stayed for long. In the past ten years there's been no one but the villagers hired to keep the house from disrepair."

"If it's been abandoned, or practically so, why wasn't it sold?"

"When the old captain died twenty years ago, he willed the house and land to the grandson. Nicholas Saintjohn has not made an effort to find a buyer, or so the people hereabouts believe. One or two made an offer, those that could afford to do so, but never received a reply."

"Were you surprised a few weeks ago when he suddenly appeared?"

The cat suddenly rose from Biddy Merton's lap and darted into the trees as if chasing prey.

"Little surprises me, Makenna Lindsay. Neither his presence, nor yours."

As Makenna stared down at the woman, a new

thought occurred, so unsettling it made her skin crawl.

"You expected to see me on the island, didn't you? Why? You knew of the ghost, though you never saw her. Is she the reason my arrival was not a surprise?"

The woman's eyes flicked up at her, then away, into the woods.

"I sensed you would be here, but why I cannot say. It is one of the mysteries I spoke of earlier."

Her answer was an evasion. Makenna's head pounded with a sense of frustration and anger, her helplessness a weight she could scarcely bear. To pursue the issue would prove futile, to forget it impossible. She groped at the slim hope the letter she had posted this very day would explain the woman's attitude. It was clear she would get no explanation from the woman herself.

"Captain Saintjohn brought his son with him," she said. "Most people don't know that."

Biddy Merton did not respond.

"I'm teaching him to draw and play the piano."

Makenna did not expect a look of surprise. Nor did she get it.

"You saw me go there, didn't you? I felt someone watching. I should have guessed it was you."

Biddy Merton did not bother to deny the accusation.

"If the boy is like his father—"

"He's not," Makenna said. "There is nothing impish about him."

The Ghost of Carnal Cove

She felt guilty talking about Jonathan Saint-john, as if she were betraying a confidence that teacher and pupil shared. But suddenly she wondered whether Nicholas had not brought the boy here because of memories of happier times. If he wanted Jonathan to enjoy the pleasures of the island, he was going about it all wrong.

But that was not her worry, nor the concern of anyone else.

"We've talked a long time," she said, "but you've told me nothing about my ghost. Surely Ni— Captain Saintjohn has nothing to do with what I have seen at the cove."

"It is an assumption easily made."

Her heart quickened, and she pounced upon the woman's answer.

"So he *is* involved."

Biddy Merton shrugged, her expression as enigmatic as the woods into which she stared. "He has not seen her, has he? No more than I, or anyone other than yourself."

Makenna sighed in exasperation. Pinning the woman down to a specific opinion was as difficult as touching the ghost. She rubbed her arms to banish a sudden chill. She felt as if a cold wind were blowing across her soul.

"There really is a connection between me and this . . . this thing I see, isn't there? I know it, though you won't tell me so."

Biddy looked at her without response.

"I didn't tell you everything." Makenna spoke

147

stonily, as if to show emotion would break down the underpinnings of her control. "One evening I sketched her walking at the edge of the beach. The next morning the part of the drawing where she had been was blank."

A frown passed over Biddy Merton's wrinkled face. "This did not make you afraid?"

"It terrified me." Her voice almost broke. "I told myself my pencil must have been faulty, or even that I got up in my sleep and erased the image. Foolish though they were, such explanations put my mind at ease. I am not a fanciful woman. I do not believe in ghosts. At least I didn't before arriving here."

"But you do not leave."

"No."

"Because you are brave."

"Because . . . I don't know why. I guess it's that I don't want to be run off by something I do not understand. By one of the mysteries you have talked about."

There were other reasons she did not pack up and depart, two reasons she could scarcely reveal even to herself. A father and his son, each equally compelling in ways as opposite as they could be.

Slowly Biddy Merton pulled herself to her feet. "I sit too long," she said, stretching.

"I'm sorry," Makenna said by rote, though the apology was a lie. "I have taken up far too much of your time. But after last night you were the only one I could talk to. I wish you had told me more."

"In time, all will be revealed."

When? After I'm completely insane?

The anger and frustration returned. In a worse state than when she had arrived, Makenna started to leave. Biddy Merton's surprisingly stern voice stopped her.

"If you must remain at the cottage, do not see the captain again."

"Surely you can tell me why."

"It is something I feel."

"In your old bones."

"Do you mock me?"

"No more than you do me. You keep giving this same warning but you don't explain why I should listen."

Biddy studied her a moment. "You are a young woman of great stubbornness. I should have known you would be."

"What does that mean?"

Her question was ignored. "I will tell you what I can. The captain has an ugliness in his past. Do not ask me what. I do not know. But when you look into his eyes, look also into his soul."

I have tried, but he keeps his soul a secret.

Without another word, Biddy Merton turned and disappeared into the woods. Makenna stood in silence for a moment. The chill was gone, as was the anger, in their place an emptiness akin to a sense of loss. Making her way back to the main road, the dog guiding her, she tried to remember all the words that had been said, evasive or not.

And despite the emptiness, she tried to determine what she must do about what she had learned.

By Monday morning, after a blessedly uneventful Saturday night and Sunday spent at the piano—except for several passes of the Saintjohn carriage with Gibbs at the reins—she saw her immediate course. Anything beyond the day or the week would have to await consideration. Having investigated her situation as best she could, she must take one day at a time.

Above all else, she understood an immutable fact: staying away from Nicholas was not an option.

Arriving at Windward, she informed Mrs. Loddington she needed to see the captain. Without waiting for escort, she hurried up the stairs, knocked at his door, and hearing a brusque "Enter," did exactly that.

He stood by the hearth, stirring the fire. When he looked at her, he straightened, and a familiar tension raced between them. Her breath caught, and the muscles of her stomach tightened. She could not believe that this strong, dark man with the impossibly penetrating stare was the gentle comforter who had held her through the night.

She stared at the poker in his hand. Hurriedly he set it aside. When she faced him, she did not try to look into his soul. She found difficulty enough in simply meeting his gaze.

"Do you believe I'm insane?" she asked.

Join the Historical Romance Book Club and GET 4 FREE* BOOKS NOW!

A $23.96 Value!

Yes! I want to subscribe to the Historical Romance Book Club.

Please send me my **4 FREE* BOOKS.** I have enclosed $2.00 for shipping/handling. Each month I'll receive the four newest Historical Romance selections to pre-view for 10 days. If I decide to keep them, I will pay the Special Members Only discounted price of just $4.24 each, a total of $16.96, plus $2.00 shipping/handling ($23.55 US in Canada). This is a **SAVINGS OF AT LEAST $5.00** off the bookstore price. There is no min-imum number of books I must buy, and I may cancel the program at any time. In any case, the **4 FREE* BOOKS** are mine to keep.

*In Canada, add $5.00 shipping/handling per order for the first shipment. For all future shipments to Canada, the cost of membership is $23.55 US, which includes shipping and handling. (All payments must be made in US dollars.)

NAME: _____

ADDRESS: _____

CITY: _____ **STATE:** _____

COUNTRY: _____ **ZIP:** _____

TELEPHONE: _____

E-MAIL: _____

SIGNATURE: _____

If under 18, Parent or Guardian must sign. Terms, prices, and conditions subject to change. Subscription subject to acceptance. Dorchester Publishing reserves the right to reject any order or cancel any subscription.

"I doubt it," he said, as calmly as if she asked whether it might rain. "The truly mad are the ones who do not question their sanity."

"Then I will phrase the question differently. Do you consider me a bad influence on Jonathan?"

"In what way?"

She grew impatient. "In any way. I've had him listening to trees, as I'm sure you recall."

"It has not left him speaking gibberish. I doubt it's done him permanent harm."

"I'm serious, Nicholas."

His eyes narrowed at her use of his name. She did not know whether the reaction was a victory or not.

"Then I will be serious, too," he said. "Jonathan has been heard humming one of the tunes you taught him on the piano. I must say he hums better than he plays, but that is hardly the point. Never in his short life have I heard him sing."

Makenna thought back to her own early childhood. Though the memories were vague, she recalled her mother teaching her nonsense songs. Jenna Lindsay had not been a frivolous woman—far from it—but she had encouraged occasional silliness. A father who had been an imp might have done the same with his only child. Or the mother. In all that was happening, the late Mrs. Saintjohn remained an enigma.

But she was not here to judge Nicholas or his dead wife. She was here to help their son.

Or so she had convinced herself as she walked

toward the cliff on this Monday morning.

"I assume, then, the answer is yes, that the instruction will continue."

He nodded. "I never considered anything else."

She prepared to leave.

"Are we not to talk about Saturday night?" he asked.

Her heart stopped. There was nothing about that night she cared to discuss, especially here in an environment entirely under his control, in the bright light of a Monday morning.

And where was Mrs. Loddington's usual interruption when for the first time it was so desperately needed?

She rubbed her palms against her cloak and saw that he noticed.

"You want to talk of Saturday? Then I will. I thought I saw someone by the water, that is all. Someone I had seen before. I tried to follow her onto the pier. You stopped me."

She pushed aside the memory of her hysteria, and prayed that he would do the same.

"I had returned the cloak you left at Windward and saw you from the cottage," he said. "You seemed in distress. I hurried down. Should I have let you go onto the pier? You might have drowned."

"No, of course you should not have let me. I wasn't thinking clearly, something I'm sure you can believe of a woman. I also haven't thanked you for the rescue." She spoke as formally as she could. "I do so now."

"You already thanked me."

Blood drained from her face. She knew exactly what he meant. He insulted her in the most hurtful way a man could insult a woman. She had not considered the possibility that he would, not after the way he had consoled her through the night. But he did. Once a peaceful, reasonable woman, she wanted to hurl herself at him and inflict bodily harm. Instead, she took refuge in dignity, and in directness.

"You mean in bed."

He ran a hand through his hair. "I am a blunt man, Makenna, but even for me that was unforgivable."

She proudly held his gaze. "Yes, it was. If I wasn't thinking clearly on the beach, by the time we got to the cottage I wasn't thinking at all. I won't make that mistake again."

Turning her back to him, she took a step toward the door.

"There's something else you should know about me," he said. "I am not a good man."

She stopped. A twig snapped in the fireplace. Otherwise all was quiet.

"It is obvious you have been considering what passed between us," he said. "Lord knows I have. I apologized for what I almost did, but that's not enough. I could tell you that holding you, kissing you, touching you, brought more pleasure into my

153

life than I have experienced for a very long while. But you would have no reason to believe me."

Was he waiting for her response? Did he expect her to admit that of course she believed him because he had brought the same kind of pleasure to her, except that she had never felt anything like the power of his touch in all her twenty-eight years?

She would burn in hell before such words passed her lips. She took another step to leave.

"I have taunted you every time we have been alone together," he said. "Don't ask why. The reason is far too complicated and I don't understand it myself except that you bring out something in me I had not known existed. But I will not taunt you again. Whatever is happening in your life, whatever has already happened, you deserve better than anything I can offer."

How would he take her silence? she wondered. Whatever response she came up with would seem foolish or wrong or a lie.

"I have blood on my hands, Makenna. I will not put it on yours."

At last she turned to face him, too stunned to say a word. She let her eyes ask the questions her lips and tongue could not speak.

"I can tell you nothing more," he said. "Except to promise that I will not harm you. Ever. In any way."

How wrong he was. Already he had harmed her. He had touched her bruised heart. Despite all her vows, he was forcing her to care again.

It was the one thing she could never forgive.

With the barest of nods, she hurried through the door, sought the music room, and began to pour all that caring into the teaching of his damaged son.

Chapter Nine

The week went very much as the past week had gone, Makenna teaching in the morning, working in the garden, practicing her music, sketching the rest of the day. Throughout it all, she was blessed with intermittent rain and constant clouds.

"Typical spring weather on the island," Mrs. Jarman said. Mr. Jarman grumbled about the difficulty of getting plants in the ground.

Makenna did not complain. There was no moon, and no summons to the cove. She didn't so much as glance at any part of it . . . not the sand or the water, and certainly not the pier.

Like the rain, during the lessons the intermittent sound of hammering returned. On Friday, after the lessons were done and she had pocketed the envelope of money that Nicholas left as her pay, she asked Jonathan about the noise.

"That's Papa," he said matter-of-factly as they shared a plate of biscuits. "He's building a boat."

She tried to picture the darkly dignified Captain Nicholas Saintjohn engaged in hard physical labor, which building a boat surely required. The image kept eluding her.

"I don't believe you," she said. "Show me."

"Mrs. Loddington says I'm not to disturb him."

"Mrs. Loddington is not an artist."

The boy giggled, then clamped a hand over his mouth.

Her heart warmed at the sound. She heard it so rarely. The thought came that she was using the boy to get a view of his father. But not really. A son ought to be able to watch his father at work.

"Remember what I told you artists do?" she asked.

His brow wrinkled in thought. "Artists explore things."

"Right. They also disturb things, remember?"

He took a second biscuit and chewed on it thoughtfully. "I don't think Papa is a thing."

"No, your papa is not a thing." She said it with more fervor than intended, but Jonathan seemed not to notice. "We're not really going to disturb him. We'll simply observe what he's working on, and then we'll leave. He may not even realize we're there, not if he's concentrating very hard on what he's doing."

"What's concentrating?"

"Giving full attention to something. Not thinking of anything else."

"Papa's good at that."

"Yes, he is." Again she spoke with more fervor than she'd intended. "That's why we should go see what's he's doing."

Jonathan's small face took on an expression of mistrust and stubbornness that reminded her very much of Nicholas. Until that moment she had not realized how much they resembled one another.

She liked the expression. It showed spirit. But it also showed a reluctance to test the boundaries of his world. She would not wish for him willful disobedience, certainly not at the age of six, but the lack of a probing mind or a yearning for adventure could be equally bad. Especially when the adventure amounted to no more than seeking out his father at work.

But then she was not his mother. She could be terribly wrong.

"Did the captain tell you not to come outside when he's busy?"

Jonathan shook his head. "He doesn't talk to me very much. Except when he's teaching me to read and write. And geography. He talks a great deal then." He hesitated. "I don't always understand what he says."

No more than he understands you.

Makenna glanced toward the window. Understanding another person could be a complicated business. Nicholas did not understand her any better than he did his son, and she certainly did not understand Nicholas.

I am not a good man, he had said, and then, *I have blood on my hands.*

A shudder ran through her. She shouldn't be thinking of what he said, not now, though the words had scarcely left her mind since she'd heard them. They were terrible ideas to throw at her without explanation. What was she supposed to do, turn him in to Constable Tobias Bent? Had that been his purpose?

No, she was supposed to fear and dislike him. If that was what he truly wanted, he would have to give her more facts.

What a sorry lot they all were, no one knowing what the other thought or how the other felt. Mrs. Loddington must lead a simple life, going by unquestioned rules. And what about Gibbs? He also went by rules, one paramount above all others: protect the captain and obey his commands.

In her own life Makenna had attempted a similar simplicity. Move to the island and keep to herself. She had done the former, although the wisdom of that move now seemed in doubt. Sadly, her attempt at the latter had been laughable. A good day for her was neither seeing nor hearing her ghost.

The same should have been true concerning Nicholas. But it wasn't. At her lowest moment, he had held her through the night. Since that time, not seeing him, not hearing him, brought her no comfort whatsoever.

Thank God he had been there on the beach, else she might have actually run onto that poor excuse for a pier. It could not possibly have held her weight.

A persistent thought occurred, a possibility she had considered when she talked with Biddy Merton but had hastily thrust aside. The times she saw her ghost came before or after an encounter with Nicholas. Were the two connected? Impossible. He was so dark and solid and real, his body formed by hard bone and warm flesh, while the silvery apparition seemed made of mist and moonlight as she eased along the water's edge.

That each had affected her in ways that stirred both heart and soul seemed their only link. And yet the sense of something stronger, something ominous, would not go away.

Jonathan stirred. Makenna started. How long had she been lost in thought? Too long. And the thoughts left her more confused than she already was.

She stood and reached for her cloak, thrusting her bonnet into the pocket.

"The rain stopped yesterday, but it's a little cool this morning," she said. "You'd best put on your coat."

He still looked doubtful. She resorted to the tactic adults frequently applied to children. She used her size and position of authority to intimidate.

Helping him with the coat, bustling about as if she knew what she was doing, she soon had him out the front door, and, with the dog trotting beside them, they followed the driveway down the cove side of the house.

The sounds of hammering had ceased, but it was too late to return to the house. She and her two cohorts were committed to explore.

The cliff top here was much wider than she had supposed from her vantage point of Elysium's portico. Several outbuildings, one of them a stable, lay to the side and behind the house. She also saw the beginning of the winding path Nicholas must take to reach the beach.

For the first time since her near tragedy, she allowed herself to study the cove. Nicholas must have stood close to this same spot when he'd first seen her. She pictured how she must have looked to him, a woman standing on a crescent of white sand, staring out at the water, her cloak blowing wildly in the wind, her long, pale hair whipped into disarray.

She could understand his accusation that she searched for sailors. Sort of. But he had phrased his thoughts far too bluntly. It was, she had discovered, a habit of his. If he was deficit in any area, it was in the art of diplomacy. It must not be a trait important at sea.

When the hammering recommenced, Jonathan halted. They were within a few feet of where the drive curved around the back corner of the house.

"Would you like me to go on ahead?" she asked. The boy nodded, and she glanced sternly at the dog. "Stay," she said, having no idea whether he would obey. But he did, and she proceeded with her quest.

Behind Windward, between two of the outbuildings, an area off the far side of the rocky drive had been cleared for the project. At least it had once been cleared. At the moment it was a clutter of cut wood in a hundred varieties of size and shape, a barrel of nails, saws of various descriptions, as well as a myriad of tools whose purpose she could not begin to fathom. She also saw a large open fire and the biggest kettle of water she had ever seen.

At the edge of the chaos was a spacious, open shed. Nicholas stood under its tin roof, his back to her, concentrating on the upturned frame that was the beginning of a boat. His dark trousers and shirt, pulled tight against his muscular body, were covered in dust, and he had rolled his sleeves halfway up his arms. Catching him at the front of the shed, a breeze played with the fullness of his upper sleeves, and with the thick black hair that lay against his collar. No wind could stir the trousers. They fit him far too well.

She studied the fit, all the way to the ground, where the hammer now lay. At the moment his strong brown hands were stroking a curved portion of the framework with what she could describe only as loving care. A pang of jealousy clawed at her, robbing her of breath. She knew far too well how carefully those hands could stroke. It seemed a lifetime ago that they had touched her.

She also knew how foolish she was being. But the jealousy remained.

The stroking stopped. Though she made no sound, he straightened and turned around. She licked her dried lips. In silence, they looked at one another. He was the first to speak.

"I assume the lesson is done."

Simpleton that she was, she would have preferred a warmer welcome. The lessons were not completed for her, she could have responded. Not with the way she was learning new things about him. But that was not in keeping with his coolness. She found her voice. "We heard the hammering."

"And artists explore things."

"You remember."

"There is nothing about you I have forgotten, Makenna."

The man was nothing if not changeable. There was nothing cool about him now. The driveway shifted under her. She looked at the hollow of his throat. It glistened with sweat.

"You promised not to taunt me," she said.

"So I did. And meant it. But you're going to have to warn me when you approach. And it would help if you grew a wart or two, preferably large and hairy. Like the one in your drawing of me."

How was she supposed to respond to that? She

was having a difficult enough time keeping distance between them. Was she also supposed to engage in repartee? If that's what this was. Somehow what passed between them seemed far more serious. But then, it always did.

The bark of the dog saved her from a response. She vowed to give him an extra serving of meat when they got back to Elysium.

"Jonathan is waiting down the drive. He was afraid of disturbing you."

A look of impatience crossed Nicholas's face. "He won't disturb me."

"Mrs. Loddington says he would," she said, feeling a little guilty at placing blame on the housekeeper.

"I'll speak to her."

"She's doing nothing more than what she feels is following instructions. Welcome him. She'll get the message soon enough." She looked away from him to the upturned frame, then to the pieces of cut wood scattered about the ground. "It's like a giant puzzle. How do you know where all the parts fit?"

He stared at her for a moment. His look could have ignited coal.

"I'm talking about the boat," she managed. "And you know it."

"But you are too deliciously innocent to let such a comment go by without recognition."

If he only knew.

"You're avoiding the question, that's what you're doing."

"Saintjohns have been making parts fit for three generations, Makenna. Ships that can sail the deepest seas. I'll figure everything out."

She was stepping on his pride. "When it's finished, you can take it out in the cove and give Jonathan a ride."

"No, I can't. And don't look as if I'm ignoring my son. The truth is that except as a passenger, I never intend to sail again." He looked away from her and called out, "Jonathan, come on down. I've got something I want to show you."

The summons effectively blocked any questions she might have put to him. Questions like *Why?* and *Whose blood?*

Boy and dog made a hasty appearance. The dog sniffed at the wood and the tools; the boy stared at the boat.

"It's got holes."

"I plan to fill them in. Don't worry. It won't sink."

Makenna watched a minute while he launched into an explanation of where the parts would fit, in the way he probably approached a geography lesson, telling the boy more than he could take in at one time. But Jonathan seemed fascinated. She felt isolated, apart, an onlooker at a private scene. This was no place for her.

As if to prove it, Nicholas placed an awkward arm on his son's shoulders, then dropped it, and

165

she wondered if he was embarrassed at such a show of affection. He spared her a quick glance; she managed a small smile, then backed away and left the two alone.

Halfway down the side of the house she spied the trail to the beach. Despite the cool breeze, the sun was high and sparkling on the water. Spread out before her in such brilliance, the cove looked more beautiful than she had ever seen it—beautiful, innocent, and inviting. Even the broken-down pier looked almost romantic as it fought valiantly to withstand the beat of constant waves. No wonder Nicholas valued the view.

She really did not want to go back to the cottage, not right away. And it had been a long time since she'd walked on the beach. Catching up with her, the dog led the way down the twisting path. Though the grass and shrubs, still damp from yesterday's rain, pulled at her, she had no choice but to follow.

With the sun blazing through the coolness and the breeze turning gentle, she felt no residue of the fear that had haunted her for so many days. For this little while she felt content. For this little while she could believe her specter was no more than the result of a troubled mind.

She stayed a long time on the sand, daring to take off her shoes and stockings and dip her toes into the cold water. With the dog stretched lazily beside her, she sat on the damp beach and attempted to build a castle close to the water's edge.

Her artist's eye pictured something grand and glorious, but her skills at working with wet sand could not realize her vision.

No matter. Slapping at the shapeless mounds gave her a pleasure she could not remember experiencing, as if she were enjoying childhood for the first time. Jonathan should be doing this. Not as part of his lessons, as his father had once suggested, but for the pure pleasure of play.

But how to get him down here?

The same way he had gone to see the boat building. With perhaps a bit more discretion at the beginning of the excursion.

Abandoning the castle project, she returned to her cottage, to the cheerful greetings of the Jarmans, and to a hot meal that was quickly devoured, her own cooking during their absence having proven woefully inadequate.

She continued to feel the contentment of the cove. She had no reason to do so, but she did.

Over the next two days, with the clouds returning, she remained mostly inside. Monday morning she had her approach carefully worked out. After the lesson, in which Jonathan talked about building boats and attempted to draw what he saw in his mind, she excused herself and went up to the library. She passed no one on the way, a fact that made no difference. If Mrs. Loddington had thrown herself across the hallway to stop her, she would have stepped over the woman and continued on.

She was about to knock at the door when she heard the voices of two men coming up the stairs. Nicholas was one of them; the other voice she had never before heard. Her determination evaporated. Feeling as if she were caught in an indiscretion, she stepped into the shadows beyond the door and stared down the hall.

The men walked side by side toward her. To her surprise, Nicholas was dressed in a dark suit, his hair carefully combed, every inch of his tall, lean figure that of a country gentleman, though his walk still bore the loping grace of a man of the sea. His companion was fairer, shorter, and more portly, but he, too, had the air of a gentleman.

"The house and grounds are grander than I anticipated," the stranger was saying.

"My grandfather wanted the best for his wife."

An awkwardness seemed to pass between them, as if neither knew quite what to say next.

They reached the library, and Nicholas bade his guest enter. Makenna shrank deeper into the shadows until the door was firmly closed behind them. If the visitor did not depart soon, she would leave word of her destination and take Jonathan with her down to the cove. She would even ask Mrs. Loddington to prepare a picnic lunch. Whoever wanted to join them could do so if he chose.

She was headed for the stairs when a sharp voice from inside the library stopped her.

"Let's not postpone this any longer, Nicholas. You know why I'm here."

"You are on a fool's mission."

Ah, Nicholas, being blunt as ever. But this time there was a cutting edge to his words she had not heard before.

"Hear me out before you make such a statement."

She should have hurried on—decency and manners required it—but a hurricane could not have moved her from the spot.

"I am not here for myself," the visitor continued. "By your actions you have left two sets of grandparents in misery. I know my sister was far from an angel, but that is no reason to punish our parents."

"You think that is why I brought my son here? To punish Leticia's parents for her adultery?"

"Why else deprive the boy of everything familiar to him?"

"Exactly what? His home? It was a cold place filled with expensive things that had no heart in them. I found no comfort in it, either for him or for me. And his tutor was a fool. He had no companions. His mother kept him close at hand. Unless his presence proved inconvenient, of course. Then he visited my parents or yours."

"They doted on him, and still do. He needs their wholesome influence."

"As opposed to mine, is that it? Don't bother to deny it. I can see I am right. The boy has been abducted by a father who paid to have the mother and her lover burned to death. I knew the arsonist, that much I do not deny. He had once served under me. Too bad he clumsily allowed himself to be consumed by the flames. Otherwise he could have testified as to my guilt."

"No one has accused you of their deaths, though you were drinking heavily at the time and seemed capable of almost anything. Besides, you were at sea when the fire occurred."

"Ah, yes, so I was. But as we all know, though no one was brave enough to point it out, arrangements could have been made on my last visit, when I learned of Leticia's indiscretion."

"I make no excuses for her, but consider the situation. You were gone months out of the year. She was alone."

"She had our son."

"Whom she loved, whether or not you choose to believe it. But he did not fill the loneliness. Surely you understand. She was young."

"Ah, yes, and lovely. And ripe. The pleasures of the flesh called. I understand only too well. I too, have heard the calling. And do still."

The words cut into Makenna like shards of glass. He was thinking of her and, likely, other women as well. There was no joy in his voice. She heard only despair. She ought to cover her ears, to run and try to forget what she had heard. But running would be too late, and forgetfulness would never come.

"Enough, Robert," he said, the despair gone, his voice louder as he walked to the door. He rang the bell. "You cannot take the boy with you. He remains where he belongs, with me."

Makenna stumbled back into the shadows as Mrs. Loddington came down the hallway from the direction of the stairs. Before she could knock, the door opened. The housekeeper stood in the light falling into the hallway and listened to her master.

"Mr. Campbell finds it necessary to end his visit before he planned. Please take him down to the carriage. Tell Gibbs to take him to the village as quickly as possible. If they hurry, he can catch the next ferry to Southampton."

The woman nodded, showing no sign of surprise.

"You're making a mistake, Nicholas," Robert Campbell said as he stepped into the light. "I want what is best for the boy."

"As do I."

"You could visit him whenever you chose. As you have done most of his life." Makenna could hear the anger and sarcasm in the man's voice.

"He is mine," Nicholas said. "I will keep him by my side."

"So you say. But this matter is not over yet. Your parents want him as much as mine do. I am his only uncle. I, too, miss the boy. And don't forget your own sister. She would like him as a companion for her two girls."

171

"Then tell them to visit us on the island. I will not turn any of you away."

"That is not good enough, and you know it."

"I can see it would be much more convenient for you to have him in Liverpool. Too bad I am in your way."

"Do not be too sure, Nicholas. We are not without legal recourse."

Slapping his hat in place, a cloak thrown over his arm, he turned on his heel and followed Mrs. Loddington toward the stairway.

Nicholas held silent and still until Robert Campbell was out of sight.

"You will not have him." He spoke from the lighted doorway, his words too faint for anyone to hear.

Anyone, that is, except a heartsick woman he did not know was near. But, oh, Makenna heard him clearly enough, heard every word. As he left, Campbell had spoken in anger. Not so Nicholas. He spoke with pain, his face torn by an anguish too terrible to look upon.

The door closed, and she was left once again in the dark. When she at last stirred herself, she moved on leaden feet, unable to remember why she had come upstairs. The memory of what she had heard burned all else from her mind.

Makenna went through the rest of the day—the walk home, greeting the Jarmans, listening to their talk—by rote. Her thoughts lay elsewhere.

When she was at last alone, with only the dog as company, she stood on the portico and remembered everything, every moment she had ever spent with Nicholas, everything he had said and done. She thought of what she had learned. And she thought of his pain.

She came to a conclusion that gave her no pride, no satisfaction, no joy. She loved him. Whatever she had felt for Ascot Chilton was nothing compared to the emotion coursing through her now, the pounding heart and fullness inside that threatened to explode, that left her thinking of nothing but him. Wisely or unwisely, unrequited though her feelings undoubtedly were, she loved Captain Nicholas Saintjohn.

He was blunt, he was rude, he could be cold as fiercely as he could be hot. But was he capable of murder? In a rage, perhaps, to protect his son or anyone he cared about. But to arrange a fatal fire with cold deliberation lay beyond not only her comprehension, it would lie beyond his as well. Remembering his suffering, his despair, remembering, too, how he had helped her through a long and terrible night, she knew what she had to do.

He had heard the calling of the pleasures of the flesh, had he? He was not alone.

The decision came hard, defying the last hold she had on reason, but it came from a compulsion stronger even than her need to pursue the specter. Nicholas was made of flesh and blood, and so was she. It was a bond she could not deny.

Changing from the serviceable dress she had worn for the morning lesson, she chose the blue gown she once thought conformed to her body far too well. She did not think so now. Brushing her hair until it shone like polished silver, she let it rest loosely against her shoulders. Without giving more thought to her purpose, she gathered her cloak, decided against the bonnet, and locked the door of Elysium behind her.

As she set out across the heath that led to Windward House, the wind picked up, blowing against her, slowing her step at times almost to a halt. It was as if on this occasion the elements frowned upon what she planned to do. Even the dog growled and ran in circles around her, dashing off the road at one point into the bushes and high grass, then returning to continue his snarling protests.

But she would not be deterred. In the evening dimness she spied the light she had seen on late nights shining from the top floor. If unseen eyes watched her progress from the dark, she was not aware of them. She thought of nothing but what she was about to do.

When she knocked at the front door, Gibbs responded. He looked neither glad nor disturbed to see her. He looked resigned. He stepped aside. "He's all the way up the stairs. Saint Nick, that is. You've not come about the boy."

It wasn't a question. She did not respond. With an order for the dog to remain outside, she hurried

174

past Gibbs, moving up the stairway to the top floor
and, without stopping to consider her course—
she had already done too much thinking—went to
the door from which light spilled onto the hallway
floor. She knocked.

"Go away," Nicholas said from inside. "I told
you I did not want to be disturbed."

*Too bad, Nicholas. That's exactly what I intend
to do.*

She opened the door and stepped inside. He was
sitting in front of a dying fire, a full decanter of
brandy on the table beside him, an empty glass in
his hand. She took a quick look around. The walls
were darkly paneled and hung with maps, the only
other decoration a brass-bound wheel that must
have come from the deck of a ship. Now it rested
above the mantel.

On a shelf she spied a compass and a peculiar
piece of equipment she took to be a sextant. Taking a deep breath, she could almost smell the sea.
Thus had Nicholas laid out his place of refuge, a
captain's quarters as might be found on an ocean-
going vessel. Somehow it looked in place at Windward House. Too, it told her more sharply than
ever that this was not her home. As a woman, she
would not be welcome.

But she held her ground.

"I said—" he began, then stopped when he saw
her.

"I wish I could do as you wish and not disturb
you." Tossing the cloak aside, she shook her head

to let her hair hang free. "But I don't really think you will mind. If you decide you do, you'll have to tell me bluntly to my face."

Closing the door behind her, she took a step toward him, and another. Setting the glass aside, he rose to his feet and watched, his hands loose at his side.

"And you'll have to tell me in such a way that I will know it's true."

She took a steadying breath.

"Do not bother yourself with concern about my virtue. I am not a virgin. There is no reason you should not take what I want to give."

Chapter Ten

He was shorn of the afternoon's coat and tie, his hair unkempt, his face shadowed by bristles. Makenna had never seen him so darkly formidable. In his rigid stance, he seemed as ruggedly unbending as the rock cliff beneath his home.

What he did not look like was a man aroused to erotic fervor because she had come to him.

Her heart pounded so fiercely she wondered if he could hear it halfway across the room. Until this moment she had not considered the possibility that he would tell her to leave. She considered it now. In truth, it became the only thing she could think of. Why was he staring at her? Why didn't he speak?

She fought a rising panic. His day had been far

worse than hers, she told herself. How well she understood his retreat to solitude here in this very special room. And then had come the knock at the door. Her knock. She saw herself as he must see her, brazen, intruding, a woman bringing a gift he had not asked for.

Women were frail—he had told her that often enough—but until this moment she had never agreed with him. Though it would give credence to what he said, she felt the urge to turn and run. Perhaps he would forget the foolish things she had already said or, miraculously, be gentlemanly enough not to mention them.

Then her eye fell on the decanter of brandy and the glass, resting invitingly on the table beside his chair. Nicholas had once drunk heavily, Robert Campbell had said. Since their first encounter on the beach, she had seen no signs that he continued the habit. Until now.

The crystal decanter caught the light from a lamp. The sparkle was enough to keep her in her place. She looked at him while he was looking at her, his gaze forbidding, yet enticing as well, pulling and pushing her until she thought she might scream. Love swelled in her, an emotion of such intensity she had to look away before her eyes revealed too much.

Right or wrong, wise or foolish, she was here. When she left, in a minute or an hour, she would go with the memory of either heaven or hell. Only he could decide which it was to be.

He took a step toward her. Her heart stopped. But he did not come close. Instead, he circled the place where she stood, his eyes never moving from her, like a wolf surrounding its prey. She felt connected to him, a thin wire of tension stretching from his body to hers, and she could do nothing but shift to keep him in sight.

Could this tightly controlled man be capable of murder? She thrust the idea ruthlessly from her mind. It was a question she had already answered. The power pulsing in him must not raise it again.

The silence in the room became unbearable, her final words echoing in the air.

There is no reason you should not take what I want to give.

One reason occurred to her now: He didn't want it. Not tonight. He had too much eating at his mind.

At last he spoke. "You don't know what you're doing." His voice was deep and rich and accusing. As if she had done something wrong.

Her nerves were stretched to the breaking point. She had expected a different kind of greeting, something warmer, something approaching pleasure because she had come to him. Unbridled passion would not have been unwelcome.

Wasn't she bringing him the strongest comfort a woman could give a man? Wasn't she helping him get through the night?

But she did not get a kiss or a touch or the hint of a smile. Instead of passion, she got advice. As always, she would have to deal with what she got.

"Probably not. But I'm still doing it."

He stopped in front of her. "Why? Why tonight of all nights?"

Makenna's mouth went dry. He seemed to know she had listened outside his door. Or guessed she knew his secrets. The man was too clever for his own good. She loved him all the more.

Because I love you. Because I want to share your pain.

It was not a response she cared to put before him. She might never tell him. It was enough for her to know.

But he was not a man to let a shrug answer his question. Since he seemed determined to analyze her presence, rather than pull her down on the rug in front of the fire as she had imagined, she tried to give him a response he would accept.

"Because I am a passionate woman. And you, Nicholas, despite what you claim, are a passionate man. I hate to admit it, but I'm lonely, and so are you."

His eyes narrowed, and she sensed something dark and dangerous building inside him, the wolf ready to spring. Yet he held himself back. She almost hated him for such mastery. Could he not understand how difficult this was for her?

"You speak as if you had a dozen lovers in your past," he said tightly.

"Just one." She kept her voice light, at a cost he

would never understand. "I'm not that passion-ate."

"He's why you're on the island."

"He was. But he's not why I stayed." Anger flared. "Does his existence bother you?"

Nicholas slowly shook his head. She tried to read his thoughts and failed. He stood still, tall and dark and solid, his thoughts, his reactions, buried too deep for her to see. Did he truly seethe inside, or was she only hoping he did? The after-noon had changed him as much as it had changed her. She wanted to understand him even more than she wanted to touch him, though she wanted to touch him more than anything else in the world.

Remembering the anguish on his face as he stood in the library doorway, she walked around him and took up the glass that sat beside the brandy. She moved casually. He must not know how close she was to collapse.

"Looking for Dutch courage?" he asked.

"I don't need a drink, if that's what you're ask-ing. I wanted to know if you did."

"What did you find out?"

"The glass is dry, the decanter full. You've not yet taken a drink."

"Does it matter?"

"I don't particularly like the taste of liquor on a man's breath."

Makenna the hussy speaking. In truth, she had never experienced such a thing. Her only lover had claimed that alcohol of any kind gave him a rash.

She looked around the room, wishing she had courage of any kind, whether or not it came from a bottle. Why was he standing there watching her? Why wasn't he taking her in his arms?

Clearly she was no good at seduction. He was supposed to explode, overcome by his hunger for her.

Humiliation began to build inside her. She grew desperate for a distraction.

"This is like a room on a ship. I thought you planned never to sail again."

"I don't."

"And what about women? Have you forsworn them as well?"

The eyes of a lurking wolf glinted at her. "That's not so easily done."

"You couldn't prove it by me."

Her voice broke. All her insecurities smothered her desire. He was far too absorbed in the day's events to welcome someone as inconsequential as she.

"Look," she said, "this is obviously a mistake. I'll leave you to whatever you were doing before I interrupted you."

Tears threatened. She would rather die than let him see them. Clearly he was not about to pull her down onto the thick carpet and let ecstasy overtake him. Giving him a wide berth, she headed for the door. But he was quick. He blocked her path and, in an instant, he had her in his arms. He slanted his lips across hers.

"Does that prove it?"

Again.

"Or that?"

"No," she said. "You're too much in control."

He trembled. "Ah, Makenna, you cannot know how wrong you are."

He deepened the kiss, covering her mouth with his, letting his tongue probe inside her, thrusting, dancing, until she thought she would swoon.

He broke the kiss. His breath was as ragged as hers.

"You drive me insane," he said, and then, "You should not be here. I told you why. I am not a good man."

The taste of him burned her tongue. All the desire, the longing and purpose that had brought her to his room returned in a rush. She cared little whether or not he was good.

Except as a lover. She knew he would be very good indeed.

"You talk too much," she said.

"I promised not to harm you."

"You're not harming me. Except by going too slow."

"How could I have ever thought women were weak?"

"You had not met me."

She could hardly believe she spoke as she did.

She did not know herself. But, oh, how she wanted to know him.

Cupping her face in his strong, blunt hands, he covered her cheeks with kisses, lingering at the corner of her mouth. She clutched his arms for support.

"Why now, Makenna?" he asked between kisses. "Why tonight?"

The question mattered to him far too much.

Her voice was ragged. "I felt you call to me."

It was not entirely a lie.

"Make love to me," she said.

She did not have to tell him twice. He backed her against the closed door, trapping her body with his, gripping her wrists over her head as he pressed his hard length against her soft flesh.

He worked her lips with his tongue until they were soft and wet and pliant. She sucked him inside her and reveled in the growl that came from his throat. Her tongue danced against his. He did not taste of brandy. He tasted like something far more intoxicating, something forbidden, something rich and thick and erotic.

He tasted like sex.

In desperation she tugged at his hold on her. He freed her wrists. Breaking the kiss, she cupped his face as he had cupped hers and covered his eyes, his lips, his bristled cheeks with kisses. Again came the growl. It burned away the last of her humiliation. Nothing she would do with him tonight, nothing he would do with her seemed outside the realm of possibility.

His hands were not idle. They eased to her waist, then upward to hold her breasts. When his thumbs found the hard tips, she thought she would burst through the confines of her clothes.

"You are a dream," he whispered into her ear, then touched his tongue to the lobe.

She shivered. Everywhere he touched seemed connected to everywhere else. She was feeling his tongue very low in her stomach.

"I'm real," she said.

"No. Let me believe in the dream. It tells me life is not without hope."

"Then I'm a dream. Don't awaken too soon."

"I want you naked."

"Undress me."

"I always do what you say."

She couldn't suppress a laugh.

"That's a beautiful sound," he said. "Almost as beautiful as you."

At the moment he was staring at her breasts, having unfastened the front of her gown in the time it took her to draw a breath.

She wasn't breathing now.

Neither was he. He'd discovered she wasn't wearing anything over her bosom except the blue dress. Wait until he explored beneath her petticoat.

He fondled her nipples as if they were precious jewels.

"I wanted you to know I was sincere," she said, unsure if he could understand her ragged speech.

"I've never seen anything more sincere." He kissed one pointed tip, then the other. "I can't decide which one is more so."

With a few deft movements he finished the disrobing and stepped back to look at what he had revealed. Her own boldness took flight. She wanted to cover herself and begin the lovemaking again, more slowly, without the flicker of lamplight playing on her naked flesh. Her shyness made no sense. She had been the one to urge him on.

But she had not anticipated the lupine light in his eyes. Once again he was the wolf studying his prey.

The study began at her hair. He ran his fingers through the long locks, brushed his thumbs against her lips, then down to the pounding pulse point in her throat. A glint flared in his eyes as they moved on, to her breasts, her waist and hips, to her pubic hair, her long legs, then back to the juncture of her thighs.

Her knees gave way. He caught her before she fell and held her close, bare flesh against the roughness of his shirt and trousers. She hadn't truly collapsed. The pretense was the only way she could think of to hide herself. Two purposes were served. She felt his tall, hard strength along the length of her body. And she felt his hands on her skin.

He kissed the side of her neck, blew on the sensitive nape, let his hands explore her backside, cupping her buttocks and holding her close. Impatient, she worked at the front of his shirt, artist's hands proving their clever worth, and enjoyed her own exploration, letting her fingers search out the contours of his chest, brush against the coarse body hair, play with nipples that were as erect as hers.

"Undress me," he said.

She tried, but her fingers were not clever enough for him. He had to help her. And then they were lying on the carpet in front of the glowing embers. He had taken time to extinguish the lamp. They had only the glow. It was enough. It danced over the two of them. She imagined that a portion of that glow came from within her.

Like the ghost.

The thought was like the stab of a knife. She grew frantic to blot it from her mind. Rubbing him with her hands, she kissed his face, his throat, his chest, her fingers as hot as his body, and he responded in a way that made her think of no one but him. Their hands and lips explored each other until they were tangled together and pressed so tightly they might never be able to part.

Mind and body were one. A storm raged in them both. She pulsed in a new rhythm that seemed to match his. When he eased his hand between her thighs and found the waiting dampness, he growled in pleasure. She had never heard anything so arousing.

Except when she took the bold step of taking his erection in her hand. The growl became a gasp. She did not know which sound she preferred.

Nor did she have the opportunity for contemplation. He eased her to her back, breaking the delicate hold she had on him. They were not separate for long. She parted her legs, he laid his body on top of hers, and they were joined, each progression as natural as the ragged breaths they drew. He paused a moment at her tightness. She had not made love for a long time, and then only twice. When she compared those times to what Nicholas was doing to her, she could scarcely call her experience making love.

Their bodies fit in a way she thought a miracle. His thrusts brought a throbbing she could scarcely contain. A force built within her. She matched his thrusts, their bodies pounding against one another in what might seem a punishment except that it was the most deliriously pleasurable sensation she had ever felt.

When the climax came, she shouted out. He covered her mouth with his and swallowed the sound, holding her tight, letting their matching tremors build, then slowly, almost painfully, fade away, until she was left with that sweetest of sensations, the knowledge of having been truly and thoroughly loved. In body, of course, only in body, but it was all that she had asked of him and far more than she could ever have anticipated.

Wrapped in each other's arms, they clung to one another tightly until at last she could feel the shared wild pulsing ease. The descent into reality came slowly and for her did not completely erase the high, screaming wildness he had aroused. Nor did she wish it to do so.

After what seemed both an hour and an instant, he stirred and lay beside her, his head propped on one hand, the other hand resting possessively on her abdomen. In that moment she became aware of everything: the regard in his eyes, the possessive hand on her stomach, the room so alien to her, the brandy, the dying fire. And of course the way she was stretched out beside him, naked flesh to naked flesh.

She wanted blurred contentment. She got skin-prickling details.

Anxiety took hold. Could he possibly be about to thank her, the way he might thank Mrs. Loddington for bringing him afternoon tea? Not even he could be so insensitive. Why couldn't he simply hold her? After what had passed between them, he was supposed to be lulled into satisfaction, sucking comfort from her the way an infant suckled at its mother's teat.

But Nicholas was not a man to accept comfort, his jagged edges were not so easily smoothed.

"Now is not the time to talk," she said.

"How did you know I was going to say anything?"

She let the question go. How to tell him there was nothing he could say, nothing he could possibly want to say, that she would want to hear.

She curled into him. "Just hold me," she said. "Nothing more."

She could feel the tension in him. Like a coward she kept her head bent, her eyes closed, concentrating on the one thing he had said that brought her joy.

. . . life is not without hope.

He kissed her hair but he did not speak. Contentment came at a leisurely pace, but when it settled over her, it slowed the pulsing of her blood, and another miracle happened. Gradually, resting in his arms, she grew drowsy, and without planning to do so, she drifted into sleep.

Later, how much later she had no idea, she jerked awake to find herself covered by a blanket. Nicholas sat in the chair, fully clothed. Despite the cover, a chill shivered through her. She felt vulnerable and most certainly embarrassed. And abandoned. She should have awakened in his arms.

In a perfect world he would be declaring his undying love for her and listening to her matching declaration. He would have told her that the troubles of the past were nothing to him now, that she had brought a dimension to his life that made it complete.

But the world was far from perfect. He sat in his chair and waited as she stirred to consciousness. And he watched her without expression, as if she were no true and permanent part of his life, but an intruder as much as she had been on the beach.

He might as well have carved out her heart. A sob threatened. For her own sanity, her own pride, she must not reveal any sign of sentiment.

Holding the blanket close to her breast, she sat up and pushed the hair from her eyes. She could feel his gaze on her like an unwelcome weight. She could hear his every breath.

"You could have had the decency to stay naked, too," she said.

He smiled. Under other circumstances, his response would have pleased her. She had rarely seen such an expression on his face.

"Do I amuse you?" she asked.

She sounded sharp. She wanted to cry.

"You surprise me. You always do."

He knelt beside her. Taking her by the shoulders, he held her against him. The blanket fell to her waist. She wished with all her heart it had not done so. She did not want to be aroused.

Nor did she wish to arouse him, though she was glad to lose the sense of being an intruder. She needed time to consider what they had done.

"I'll undress if that's what you want," he said.

She pushed him away and pulled the blanket to

her throat. God help her, she did indeed want him naked again, but not for decency's sake. She had something far different in mind.

"Give me a moment's privacy," she said. "I'd like to get dressed."

His eyes glinted darkly. He took a long, torturous moment to consider her request. At last he stood and turned his back. She pulled on her clothes, giving up on her tangled hair, then reached for the cloak.

"What are you doing?" he asked.

"Leaving. I did not come here to stay the night."

"Don't be absurd."

Dear Nicholas, true to himself no matter the occasion.

"I'm not being absurd. When I got here, I thought at first that perhaps I was. I know I won't be when I leave."

He blocked her path to the door. She felt the wolf in him return and wondered if she ought to feel threatened. It was, she thought with a shudder, a little late for such a consideration.

"I don't understand you," he said.

"You've indicated that before."

"Shouldn't you want me to tell you how I feel about what we did?"

"Is that what women usually want? I know you liked it. I would be a fool to think otherwise."

Oh, how brave she was being, how bold, how like the woman she wanted him to believe she was. But her eyes burned with unshed tears. She had not known how consuming making love to him would be. She felt as if there were nothing left of her that was not touched by him.

He pulled her in his arms and kissed her. It was her undoing. She kissed him back.

"I more than liked it," he whispered against her swollen lips. He kissed her reddened cheeks. "God help us both, Makenna. I cannot help myself."

She knew, as well as if he had spoken his thoughts aloud, that all the details of his past and present, and of the uncertain future, were rushing back. She had not held them at bay for long.

She wanted to kiss the hands he said were stained with blood. Instead, she pushed them away. "It's late. I must return to Elysium."

His expression darkened as he looked down at her. "You know as well as I that we have started something we cannot stop."

She avoided his eyes. What did he mean by *we*? The decision to come to him had been hers and hers alone. She should have realized he would want the aftermath in his control.

She must not let it be so.

"I know no such thing," she said, but of course she did.

She tried to step around him, but a hand on her shoulder stopped her.

"Wait here," he said.

He was gone before she could protest. Surely he was not summoning Gibbs to get the horse and carriage. Everyone in Windward except Jonathan must know she was still in Nicholas's room. Everyone must know what they had done. She could expect nothing less. But she did not want to face them quite so soon.

Without waiting for his return, she hurried down the stairs and let herself out the front door. He was waiting in the carriageway with only the bridled horse. Throwing himself onto the animal's bare back, he pulled her up in front of him and with one arm clasped around her waist began the short ride to the cottage.

Neither spoke. Silent, too, was the dog that ran behind them. Too easily she could hear the steady roll of the ocean, the beat of the waves upon the beach. The sea was eternal, or so the poets said. Did that make all else fleeting? Perhaps. Yet she thought the night would never end.

She had told him loneliness had brought her to him. She had lied. But afterwards, clasped against him so tightly she could feel the beating of his heart, her memory inflamed by what they had done, she had never felt more lonely in her life.

Outside the back gate he eased her to the ground, then dropped beside her. In the moonlight, she could see his probing gaze. It echoed what he had said to her in his private quarters. They had started something they could not stop.

"Good night," she said and hurried from him.

Against her wishes, he followed her into the garden and watched as she opened the back door and went in. He waited for a light to appear and the lock in the door to turn. With her forehead pressed to the door, she listened to the closing of the back gate and the hoofs of the horse on the road as he returned to Windward House.

The tears she had thought to shed did not fall. Instead, she trembled, not only from the memory of what she had done but from a cause he would not begin to understand. His reality had returned, but so had hers. The night was bathed in moonlight. That could mean only one thing.

She should have been given a respite, a time to think about what had passed between her and Nicholas. But such a moment of peace, ragged though it might be, eluded her. Tonight she had told herself she had acted to ease his pain. But she had pain of her own, an anguish that had nothing to do with her past. The comfort had been for herself as much as for him.

One thought destroyed that comfort: The night was bathed in moonlight. With it would come a special kind of terror born not in the demands of the flesh, not in anything of this world, but in something far too shattering for the sane mind to comprehend.

As if she went to her grave, she moved to the front of the house, to the door that opened onto the portico and onto a view of Carnal Cove. The dog followed, a growl deep in his throat. The iciness of past experience returned. Blood that had so recently pumped hot in her veins now flowed cold.

Standing at the outside railing, she watched the apparition of a white-clad woman walk along the water's edge. She gripped the railing to keep from hurrying down the path. What would happen if she gave in to the force urging her to the beach? Would she follow the beckoning vision onto the pier?

Nicholas would not be there to save her. Not tonight.

Evil or good—from which did the specter spring? She truly did not know. And the strange old woman who might be able to tell her had refused to say. Biddy Merton's lone advice had been to stay away from Nicholas. It was the one thing she could not do.

Closing her eyes, she let the memory of the evening overtake her. It gave her strength, as if her lover's arms still enveloped her and held her in place. Gradually the iciness faded and the obsession to hurry to the shore eased.

Trembling, she was about to return to the peace of the cottage when the sobbing returned. It drifted to her on the night wind as if carried by a moonbeam. At last she began to understand its source. Jonathan Saintjohn did not cry out in a small boy's misery from his cliff-top mansion. This sound was deeper, more ripened, filled with far too much despair.

One possibility remained. A fist tightened

around her heart, and the possibility sharpened into realization. The sobbing that had haunted her from the first night at Elysium came from her ghost.

Chapter Eleven

Makenna spent the hours before and after midnight at the piano. She played wildly, passionately, and at times, despite herself, piteously, but the music brought no consolation. It did not erase the echoes of the sobbing. It did not purge the memories of the day.

The sound of her playing surely carried on the wind to the top of the cliff, to Nicholas in his captain's retreat. He would hear the passion in the notes. He would know the wildness that swelled her heart.

But he would not know its source, love and fear mixed so intensely together she could scarcely determine where one emotion ended and the other began.

After such an unsettled night, cruel day arrived too soon. In its brightness she dreaded going to Windward House as much as she had wanted to be there the previous evening. Exhausted from little sleep, and with a violent headache pounding at her temples, she had not the faintest idea what she would say to Nicholas when and if she saw him.

Or what he would say to her.

She would not change last night for a Rembrandt painting, but that did not make the morning after any easier to get through. The one thing that inspired her to make the journey was the thought of remaining at the cottage. It held memories, too, as difficult as those at Windward House.

Makenna felt trapped by circumstances, as surely as a wild animal caught in the iron jaws of a snare. Her life on the island, which was supposed to be one of quiet seclusion, had become a walk on an endless high wire, with Nicholas awaiting her fall on one side, the specter lurking on the other.

Only one thing about the perilous walk seemed certain. One way or another, she would definitely fall.

Treading slowly across the heath, she made it to Windward and to the music room without seeing anyone but Mrs. Loddington. Grateful to be spared an accusatory look from the watchdog Gibbs, she threw herself into introducing the boy to watercolors, then gave equal enthusiasm to a half dozen simple tunes on the piano. If there was a desperation in her teaching, Jonathan did not seem to notice. Instead, he responded as eagerly as any six-year-old could, only occasionally showing restlessness or inattention.

She marveled at his courage. He must know something about the circumstances surrounding his mother's death. If not, he certainly knew she was gone. Looking at his wide brown eyes, solemn one moment and inquisitive the next, at the gentle curves of his young child's face, the delicate hands he rested on the keyboard, she felt a need to protect him that was so strong it was a physical pain.

And she admitted another truth. She loved Jonathan Saintjohn as much as she loved Nicholas, though in an entirely different way. It was an instinctive love that came from something deep inside her which she had thought would never be nurtured.

Wanting to hold him and give him comfort, she resisted. At the moment, taking any Saintjohn into her arms seemed a poor idea.

The boy could never be hers any more than the father.

"I can't practice today," Jonathan said when the time came for her to leave.

He spoke in a serious voice, as if he expected her to chastise him. It was something she had never done, and she wondered for the hundredth time what his life had been like in Liverpool.

"That's all right," she said with a smile.

"Papa said I could watch him build the boat. He's getting close to being done."

"How wonderful," she said, and meant it, for Jonathan's sake but also for a very selfish reason. Nicholas would be busy with his son. He would have no time for her. She smiled at the boy. "When did he tell you?"

"This morning. Before you got here."

"I don't hear any hammering."

"He said he wouldn't be working during the lesson. He had something else to do."

She did not try to guess what that something could be. It probably concerned the visit of Robert Campbell. It could not possibly involve her.

Bidding the boy goodbye, she hurried out the music room door. Mrs. Loddington met her in the hallway.

"The captain would like to see you."

She spoke the words in a voice of doom. In the dimness she looked taller, thinner, her face paler and more drawn than ever. She was all edges. She was the perfect messenger for delivering bad news.

Makenna's heart fell. What could Nicholas want with her? A lecture? Quick sex before his time with his son? Shocking as the idea might have been a day earlier, it was not shocking now. If she was doing him a disservice, it wasn't much of one. The man was capable of most anything.

But not everything. She had to believe that; otherwise her soul would die.

The housekeeper departed, leaving her alone in the dark, cold entry.

Or maybe not so much alone. Her mouth grew dry and her heart quickened. Someone was watching her. She could feel the glance of unfriendly eyes as surely as if someone had loudly spoken hostile words. The feeling made her skin crawl.

"Who's there?" she called out. The words echoed in the grimly dark hall.

No one responded. She hadn't expected anything else.

She glanced at the closed front door. For a moment she considered a dash for freedom, then saw the futility of such an attempt. Imaginary eyes were not the problem. Nicholas Saintjohn was.

If he wanted to see her, he would do so, in his upstairs library, at the cottage, in the bushes at the side of the road.

Makenna blushed. She was as bad as he for thinking such things. How quickly she had forgotten his anguish, as much a reason for her visit last night as her love.

And she must never forget that she was the one who had initiated whatever it was that burned between them.

A thousand thoughts skittered through her mind and settled into one immutable fact, one that had escaped her love-driven contemplations of last night. All at once it seemed as clear as the day. Despite the disparity of Victorian morality, which gave men the freedom to take a lover, while women were denied the same, he could not risk anyone from Liverpool finding out he was having an affair with his son's music and art teacher. His possession of the boy was already far too shaky. If the truth were known he would have no recourse but to dismiss her.

Though the admission left her feeling hollow inside, she knew he would be right. Filled with the realization of her feelings for him and the newly discovered knowledge of his troubles, she had not thought the situation through.

At least he had not lied and told her he loved her. She wasn't sure if that passed for honor, but she thought it might.

We have started something we cannot stop.

Such had been his feelings of last night. But with the sun, reason must have returned. She had not brought him consolation. She had brought him trouble.

With a sigh, she turned her back on the front of the house and hurried up the stairs. Knocking at the library door, she entered without waiting for permission. He had not given it last night, and she did not want it today.

He was seated behind his desk, pen in hand, a sheet of foolscap unfolded in front of him. He was coatless, his shirt open, his eyes sunken as if he, too, had not been able to sleep. Her heart pounded. In his pulsing darkness, he obliterated the harshness of the day. He made shadows look good.

Taking a deep breath, she closed the door behind her. He set the pen aside and stood. They looked at one another without speaking. She had worn her dowdiest, most ill-fitting black dress, had bound her hair ruthlessly into a bun, made herself as unattractive as she could. Still, he looked, his face as solemn as his son's, his expression unreadable. But there was nothing unreadable in the way he came around the desk and moved across the room toward her, every muscle rippling with quiet determination.

She let out a small cry. When he took her in his arms, she could do nothing but lift her lips to his.

The kiss was thorough, a brief return to the passions of last night. Desire, as hot as it was sudden, tore through her. She could think of nothing but what she and Nicholas did, what they might possibly do. He held her tight, and then he let her go and gazed down into her eyes.

Desire was slow to end. She felt small, vulnerable, and far, far too susceptible to his will. She needed to be his equal now more than ever. Somehow she found the strength to meet his gaze.

"I hadn't meant to do that," he said.

A confession of weakness? Impossible.

"I hadn't expected you to," she said.

"I had things to say."

She stared up at him with all the resolution in her heart. "There is no need. I'll leave."

He put some distance between them. "What the devil are you talking about?" His voice was hard, his eyes no longer warm. He could change his moods far more quickly than she. It was one of his more unnerving habits.

She had no immediate response. She wasn't supposed to know about his visitor of yesterday. She wasn't supposed to have listened outside his door.

"Word will spread about what happened between us," she said.

"I don't give a damn what people think they know."

Oh, but he should.

He turned from her.

"Forgive me," he said. "I'm thinking of myself. It's your reputation that's at stake. I have none to worry about."

She almost laughed. She had not thought about herself. And now that she did, was the possibility of a ruined reputation enough to keep her from his arms? It wasn't, and she told him so.

"You don't know how vicious rumors can be, Makenna." He studied her a moment. "Or do you? Were they the reason you came to the island?"

She shook her head in exasperation.

"You won't let up about my past, will you? My story is hardly original. I fell in love and the man betrayed me. If anyone talked about my behavior, I was not aware of it. If I had been, I would not have cared, any more than I do now. When the . . . affair ended, I simply saw the need to get away. I found the deed to Elysium in my mother's papers and came here."

"You have no other family?"

"No. None."

His gaze trailed down to her middle.

"You could be with child now."

He spoke the words without emotion. He had no need. She suffered enough emotion for them both.

She dug her fingernails into her palms. "I doubt it. I rather suspect I'm barren."

She spoke the truth, but it was an admission she had never uttered aloud. He would never know how difficult it was to get the words out now.

"And if you're not? You do not want me as a husband or father of your child, Makenna. They are not roles for which I am suited."

The anguish returned to his voice. It was nothing compared to what she was feeling inside. He could be honest, up to a point. It was a condition denied to her.

"You're the one who said we had started something we could not stop. You're the one who kissed me not two minutes ago."

"I told you I hadn't meant to do it."

"Which makes what you did all right. Except that it might lead to other things. And their consequences." She glanced momentarily at the stormy seascape over the mantel. More than ever she felt its turbulence. "You have no idea how much you have insulted me."

"I keep doing that."

"I would prefer that you stop. My purpose last night was not to trap you into marriage. I have no intention of taking a husband. I have no intention of asking anything at all of you."

He did not speak for a moment. As he regarded her, the lines at the corners of his eyes deepened.

"I thought you were weak," he said. "I was wrong."

Makenna almost laughed. She had thought she was strong. She was the one who'd been wrong.

But she could put up a good pretense. Even though she could not look at him for long. Not only because of what he said or what he might possibly be thinking. Her problem was more complicated and primitive. She wanted him to kiss her again, passionately, and then engage her in more erotic pursuits. The fit of his clothes was already enough to arouse her, the way he walked, the timbre of his voice.

She kept remembering how he had looked naked as he lay beside her. Was he remembering the same thing about her? The heat flaring in his eyes told her he was.

She suddenly did not know what to do with her hands.

"You sent for me. Why?"

"I thought it was to talk about what happened between us. But the truth is, I wanted to see you. Nothing more. I like looking at you, Makenna. I like holding you in my arms."

As long as I don't make demands.

"Since I put myself there last night, I can't see the problem. Except for what I've already tried to tell you."

"You were lonely."

"Ah, you remembered something I said."

"I remember everything you said. And did. Are you lonely now?"

More than you can know.

"That hardly matters," she said. "The truth is, I did not think the matter through. I did not think about today. But I am thinking about it now. Jonathan has come to mean a great deal to me. I would not see him hurt by idle gossip."

"And how is he to hear this gossip? Through Mrs. Loddington? Through Gibbs?"

"He needs to be with other children."

"He needs to be with me."

The words had the harsh clang of an iron door slammed shut.

"And he needs to be with you," he added, to her surprise. "He's suffered through far too many changes in his life. You are a constant that gives him security. Yet you would turn from him because people might talk." He shook his head in disgust. "I am sorry he means no more to you."

Her pain was all the sharper because it was so erroneously inflicted. Nicholas was not so smart, after all, if he thought she could dismiss his son so easily. She started to speak. He raised a hand to stop her.

"I'm being unkind, right? It is my way. But it does not change the way things are. He needs you." A black shadow passed over him. His eyes burned like coals. "So do I. I don't know about tomorrow, Makenna, but I know about tonight." He ran a hand through his hair. "Damn me for being the man that I am."

Before she could present an argument, he swept her into his arms.

"Tell me to stop," he said, his voice thick. "Tell me to let you go."

She parted her lips, but the words would not come.

His second kiss was more thorough than the one before, as if he read her thoughts and gave her what she craved. When he buried his hands in her hair, the bun gave way to his invasion, much as everything else about her gave way. Tangled hair fell about her face and shoulders. He made her feel beautiful, voluptuous, wanton. She hungered for him as she had never hungered for anything in her life. All the thinking and reasoning and practical judgments in the world would not make the hunger go away.

Wrapping her arms around his neck, letting a sense of rightness flow through her, false though the sense might be, she wanted to stay as she was forever, lips against his, their tongues dancing, bodies melded as if the two of them were one. When she was in his arms, she could not think.

But, oh, how she could feel. Every nerve ending in her body was on fire.

And from no more than a kiss.

When he let her go, she swayed a moment, then backed away. The dizzying yearning was slow to pass. His lidded eyes, his ragged breath, told her it was the same for him.

But such rapture could not last. He knew it as well as she. Had he not told her they could never marry? She had expected nothing else. But still, the warning cut like shards of glass.

And so, too, did the kiss hurt, but in a very different way. She had told him she did not want a husband, no matter what happened between them. She had given him carte blanche to do with her what he would.

It was his power that frightened her most of all. Hand pressed against her mouth, she turned from him and ran from the room, ran from Windward House as if the devil himself were on her trail. The dog, her faithful companion except when she needed him most, loped silently at her side.

As she hurried down the hill, she came to a conclusion that had played at the edges of her mind for a long while. Nicholas was right in one thing. She could not leave Jonathan, not right away. But eventually she would have to. Eventually she would have to leave the father as well.

And, of course, Carnal Cove, whether or not she ever understood the otherworldly happenings on the beach.

Nicholas, blunt and realistic as only a man could be, did not know about the apparition, though she had tried to tell him what she saw. But it was never far from her mind, even when he held her in his arms. Only his kisses made her forget, and then only for a little while.

The specter had invaded her home as well as the cove. There was too much proof for her to believe otherwise. At times the walls themselves seemed to sigh.

Even if she could stay off the beach, she could not remain in Elysium. Sometime before long, she would have to go.

She slowed her pace and gave herself over to more careful thought. Perhaps she could seek out the village of her birth. Wickford Close it was called, in the South of Hampshire. Very small, Jenna Lindsay had said, but surely not so small that it could not be found.

Makenna seized on the thought with a desperation that stunned her. Her mind raced, the idea gathering strength until it became a plan. She could find neighbors who had known her parents, locate the house where they had lived.

And her father's business, of course—there would be records of that. It must have been fairly substantial. Its sale had been enough to support his widow and daughter for years, and now the daughter alone. West Indian Importing and Exporting, as best she could recall, operated out of Portsmouth. He had been on a business trip to the

West Indies when he drowned, unaware he left behind a pregnant wife.

She would investigate her mother's family as well as her father's. Jenna Lindsay's maiden name had been Newbury. She could find out about the Newburys as well as the Lindsay clan. No one in either family had survived. Other than herself. But there would be records of births and deaths and marriages, the important passages of life.

She should have investigated those records long ago, but her mother had always discouraged any such backward looks.

What's past is past. We've got to get on with our lives.

Makenna had complied. With a smile, she realized she was sounding like Mrs. Jarman, repeating the advice of her mother.

But her mother was gone. The daughter had to make decisions for herself, and do a better job than she had lately done. With luck, the answer to her post sent weeks ago could help her here.

Perhaps Wickford Close needed a teacher of music and art. Despite all the problems besetting her, she had proven to herself that she could manage such a position.

She had been wrong to think that in her chosen refuge she could be idle. Look what had happened to her here. The problem, of course, was that she had allowed herself to become emotionally involved with a man. She had made that mistake before. She would not make it again.

It was a vow that could easily be kept. She could not give away her heart because she didn't have it. She had given it to Nicholas Saintjohn.

Yes, the Hampshire village called to her—not as loudly as Elysium had once done, but still it called. She would not go there with joy, or with optimism, but she would go.

Only not just yet. A father and his son would keep her on the island for a while longer. In the next week or month or however long it took for the boy to gather his own strength, she would store up memories for the rest of her life.

Providing she did not hear the sobbing too often. Providing she could somehow hold on to her sanity.

She had almost reached the narrow lane that led from the main road to the cottage when she heard the creak of wheels behind her. Stepping to the side of the road, she turned to watch the approach of the high-stepping horse that pulled the Saintjohn carriage. Gibbs, scowling as ever, sat high on his perch, the reins in his gnarled hands.

She thought he would pass. He reined to a halt. She stared at the flaring nostrils of the horse, and at the animal's dark eyes that had not quite lost the wildness of the untamed. Could it have been only last night that she had sat in front of Nicholas on the stallion's bare back, wrapped in her lover's arms, the tingles of passion not quite faded?

She took another step backward, unable to meet

213

Gibbs's squinty eyes. Somewhere back on the heath the dog had managed to disappear in the shrubs alongside the road, chasing rabbits, probably. She could have used him at her side, barking furiously at the horse, sending the carriage on its way.

"I've duties to tend to in town," Gibbs said, "but not so many nor so urgent I can't take time to say what has to be said."

She sighed in resignation and looked up at his leathery, wrinkled face, his narrow lips pulled tight with disapproval. In times past he might have looked in such a manner at a wayward shipboard cabin boy who disobeyed his captain's orders.

"Say what you will and be gone."

He lifted his sailor's cap, wiped a sleeve across his brow, then slapped the cap back in place atop his wiry, gray-streaked hair. The day was hot. He was sweating. So was she.

"There's rooms at Windward closed and locked. Most of them are such. No need to open 'em up. Won't do a single body any good."

Makenna understood his meaning. He wasn't speaking of the house. He spoke of his master's past.

The muscles of her stomach clenched. He was going to tell her something she did not want to know. And he expected her to do nothing but stand by the road and listen.

"Are there secrets behind these doors?" she asked, unwilling to be so passive.

Gibbs frowned, as if irritated by the interruption.

"Trouble's closer to the truth. Matters of the past best left there. Saint Nick's been through more than most men. It's time he had some rest."

"It's time we all did."

He waved at her in disgust. "So why stir the poor man as you're doing?"

"Poor man? You're speaking of the captain?"

"I know right well enough what's going on between the two of you." He gathered fervor the more he spoke. "I know your kind. Seen 'em in all the ports of the world. You're cleaner than most. Gentler, too, I guess—can't think of no other way to put it. But that don't mean you're not a Jezebel, same as the rest."

"A Jezebel?" Of all the things he had thrown at her, this was the most absurd. She stared up at him in disbelief. "How could you say such a thing?"

" 'Cause I got the captain's well-being at heart. You've got him thinking again. He's warned you there's blood on his hands. You should have listened. He's not a man for lying."

"He told you what he said to me?"

"No need."

"You listened outside the door."

He did not respond. He did not have to. Makenna knew far too well how easily conversations in the library could be heard from the hall.

And, too, the sounds of lovemaking coming from inside another room.

Heat burned her cheeks, from anger as much as embarrassment. She and Nicholas had not been quiet. She remembered how he had tried to swallow her cries.

She had assumed that Gibbs, and Mrs. Loddington as well, would figure out what she and Nicholas had done. But not in full detail, and not while they were in the act of doing.

Gibbs was not finished. He spat on the ground near her feet.

"The captain's a good man. Not a mate served under him but wouldn't do so again."

"So why won't he sail again? Surely you cannot blame me for that."

Gibbs ignored the question. "He's got his weaknesses, there's no denying it. He's done things he's ashamed of, things that don't bear thinking on. That's why I'm here. To take care of him, and protect him when I see fit."

Makenna shook her head. "He needs protection from me, is that what you're saying? Or is it I who needs protection from him?"

The old sailor's pale eyes took in her appearance. She was painfully reminded of the wanton looseness of her hair. She touched her lips. They felt swollen from Nicholas's kiss.

Gibbs's precious Saint Nick had been the one to remove the hairpins, she could have said. Because he wanted to do so, he had covered her mouth with his. But he had been given no choice. She was a Jezebel.

Makenna could have laughed at the senselessness of the idea, but Gibbs would not have seen the humor.

And she was not in the mood for anything as light as laughter. The old sailor had done something far worse than accuse her of seduction. He had thrown out words that sent a knife through her heart.

He's warned you there's blood on his hands. You should have listened.

Gibbs had as much as accused his captain of murdering his wife and her lover. It was one of the secrets locked behind one of those doors.

The old sailor took up the reins once again.

"Heed what I say. If you keep coming up to Windward at all hours of the day and night, there's not much telling what might happen to you. Best you be taking the next ferry away from the cove."

He snapped the whip over the rump of the horse, and the carriage took off toward town, leaving her in a swirl of road dust, and in a swirl of emotion as well. If she'd heard right, and she was sure she had, she had just been threatened.

What harm could he bring to her that she had not already brought to herself?

She stared at the departing carriage until it dropped over a hill and disappeared from sight.

"Say what you will, old man, but you can't run

me off. The spirit on the beach frightens me, as much as the power your captain has over me, but you don't. I'll leave, all right, but in my own good time."

She imagined the quiet lanes and carefully tended cottages of a picturesque village known as Wickford Close.

"I thank God I have a place to go."

Chapter Twelve

Ungrateful.

When the dog shoved his way through the back gate an hour after her uncomfortable session with Gibbs, she took one look at his panting face and came up with the name.

Ungrateful. It suited him, from the tip of the lolling tongue to his tawny hair to the nails he used to dig up Mr. Jarman's carefully planted seeds.

"Earn your keep," she ordered, and guided him down to the beach.

She needed to put distance between her and the road. She was weary of thinking over the things Gibbs had said, weary of threats and insinuations. A clear sky and a bright sun and a breeze filled with salt and grit were more to her liking.

The dog now known as Ungrateful followed her guidance to a spot a half dozen feet from the water's edge. He immediately dug a hole down to the moist, cooler sand beneath the hot surface, stretched out, and went to sleep.

He did it all without raising a single hackle. Without the hint of a growl. Carnal Cove was safe for a while.

Rolling her sleeves above the elbows, unfastening her gown at the throat, letting the wind catch in her unbound hair, Makenna spread a blanket beside him and got out a sketch pad and pencils. She had meant to try an experiment, to draw images of the water, the pier, the ghost. She would set the finished work in the garden and see what it looked like in the morning. She would see if her version of the specter was still there.

But the pencil took on a life of its own, and she found herself drawing the solemn face of a young boy. She poured her heart into every line, much as she had done when she painted the portrait of her mother. She had not been able to capture his father, on that long-ago day when Nicholas tore her work in half. But she captured the son.

Unwilling to stop, she shaded the cheeks until she was satisfied they were exactly right, worked a long time at the unsmiling mouth, gave special effort to the huge brown eyes that far too frequently looked much too serious. On a whim, she added a grand piano in the background, thick bristled brushes for his artwork, and, as the final touch, the outline of a sailboat.

When she was done, she stared at the finished work a long time. Her heart caught in her throat, and she smiled.

Not once had she glanced toward the top of the cliff. At times she felt someone watching her, but she had not looked to see who it was. Instead, she let her hair fall around her face like blinders on a horse. And she thought only of the boy.

Pushing the art supplies aside, she stretched out on the blanket near the dog and fell asleep. When she awoke, the sun was close to sinking in the west. She sat up abruptly, for a moment disoriented. Ungrateful did not stir.

A trail of footprints in the sand led from beyond the pier toward her and back again, in the direction of the cliff. Someone from Windward had walked onto Carnal Cove, had watched her sleep, then gone away. She did not wonder who that someone might have been. The wonder was that he had left her alone.

The second wonder was that she had not awakened and thrown herself in his arms.

Feeling terribly exposed, and once again vulnerable, she stood and brushed the sand from her skirt. Under the weakening sun, a heavy mist began to roll in off the water, and with it a cold wind. They came like warnings telling her it was time to depart.

Gathering up the supplies, accompanied by Ungrateful, she hurried up the twisting path through the sand dunes and prepared for another long night in Elysium. The first thing she did was to feed the dog, the second to secure the doors. Eventually the wind died, but to her great relief, the mist remained, surrounding the cottage, pressing in at the windows like curtains, giving her a sense of security no moonlight could ever again bring.

She welcomed the solitude. For a while she looked at the sketch of Jonathan Saintjohn, which she had propped against the back of the parlor sofa. Love lay in every line; even a non-artist would be able to see it. A personal, private love, as maternal in nature as she could allow it to be. When she'd begun the sketch, her first thought had been to present it to Nicholas. Not now. The drawing was hers alone.

With a sigh of regret as much as pleasure, she rolled the paper, bound it with a ribbon, and put it on the high shelf of her wardrobe in the bedroom.

Behind her dresses rested the portrait of her mother. The portrait with the jagged tear through the heart. To look at it was too painful, and she quickly closed the double doors.

The next morning, rested for a change, she greeted the Jarmans with what she hoped was cheerfulness before she journeyed up the hill. The good fortune that had rolled in with the mist held. Jonathan's lesson was concluded without her seeing Nicholas or, equally disturbing, receiving a message from him.

Neither did Gibbs make a scowling appearance. It was as perfect a day as she could have wished for.

Until she returned to the cottage. Mrs. Jarman, preparing to leave with her husband, stood in the open doorway of the kitchen and pulled a folded piece of paper from her coat pocket.

"I forgot to give you this before you left for Windward House," she said with a smile of chagrin. "It's a letter. All the way from London. The vicar asked me to pass it on. Don't know why I let it slip my mind. But as my mother used to say, there's little good that comes by post. You've been looking so drawn lately, maybe I wanted to hold it back as long as I could. Not that I did it on purpose, understand. Still, a moment's peace never did anyone any harm."

Waiting in the garden behind his wife, Mr. Jarman cleared his throat.

"Oh, my," she said with a flutter. "It's time to leave."

But she did not do so. Instead, she stared expectantly at the folded paper. Makenna thrust it behind her back.

"Don't fret, Mrs. Jarman," she said. "There's no harm in the delay. It's nothing of importance, I'm sure. I'll see the two of you day after tomorrow. And I promise to get some rest."

Before stirring from her place, she waited until

she could no longer hear the creak of the departing wagon. Preparing a cup of tea, she sat at the kitchen table and stared at the unopened letter lying in front of her. When she'd sent out her query weeks ago, she had hoped the answering missive would settle questions that plagued her about the cottage, about the circumstances which had brought her here.

She had wanted it to arrive.

And now the letter was here.

She felt an urge to throw it into the embers in the stove. The reaction made no sense. She had been the one to elicit information from her solicitors, about Hampshire as well as Elysium. What they'd learned could very well determine if her plan to seek out the village of her birth was possible. It was time she became realistic about her situation. It was time she thought things through before hurtling into the unknown.

What was the worst they could tell her? That they had been unable to learn anything about the presence of the deed in her mother's papers? They had said the same before, though their first examination had been admittedly cursory.

Now, after the more thorough investigation she had requested, if they told her much the same thing, she would simply have to put the issue from her mind.

The tea grew cold as she stared at the letter. She had never been one for premonitions. One struck her now, a sensation so strong she could scarcely breathe.

How silly she was being. Hastily she picked up the folds of foolscap and was rewarded with a paper cut. Blood pooled on her fingertip. She sucked it away.

The letter was comprised of three pages, the first outlining the processes by which the solicitors had searched for what she wanted to know. Admittedly they had gone beyond her original instructions, but, as she would read, there had seemed no place to stop.

If she objected to what they had done, they would be open to discussion about their stated expenses. They also regretted if their findings caused any distress.

The latter did nothing to soothe her troubled mind.

Much of the report was written in legal terms, and at length, which told her the investigation had indeed been thorough. It should have been, considering the amount of the invoice written in sharply legible numbers at the bottom of the first page.

She had the money. She gave the sum no more than a casual glance.

Not so the next two pages. She read them once, twice, a third time before their contents began to make sense. It was a cruel kind of sense, however, a summary of findings she could scarcely comprehend. Of all the things she had imagined they might find, nothing approached the truth.

She closed her eyes, but the facts would not go away. The solicitors had been right. They caused her distress. And worse, far worse.

Shoving herself away from the table, away from the terrible words, she went into the parlor and paced in front of the cold fireplace, rubbing her arms with trembling hands, biting her lip until she tasted blood.

Some things were simply incomprehensible. The letter was one of those things.

She ran her hands over her face and to the back of her neck. The muscles were as hard as wood. She tried to think. Obviously, terrible mistakes had been made. She would dismiss the firm of solicitors and employ another. She would send them on the same mission. The second report would be as different from the first as light from dark.

No, that made no sense. She had already hired the best solicitors in all of London. Ascot Chilton had told her so, and she had heard the same from other sources. Ascot might have been a scoundrel, but he was far from stupid. The letter was not filled with errors. The letter reported the way things were.

An anguish gripped her that was unlike anything she had ever felt. Her heart pounded painfully against her ribs. The fierceness was all she could feel. There was no ground under her, no air to breathe. She was a hollow woman in a hollow world. She was scarcely aware of the tears on her cheeks.

For a moment she was frozen in place, her very soul stained with the blackest of paint. As if some unseen force directed her steps, she went into the bedroom, opened the wardrobe, and pulled out the portrait of the woman she had known as Jenna Lindsay.

But there was no such woman. Didn't the letter report that was so?

The same force that guided her to the bedroom returned her to the parlor. Placing the portrait in the place where the sketch of Jonathan Saintjohn had rested, she moved her easel close to it and placed a blank canvas on the wooden pegs. Opening the jars of paints, slapping pigments of color onto her much-used palette, she felt cold, separated from her normally treasured supplies, as if she were outside herself watching what she did.

Since the night the portrait fell onto the fireplace poker, she had planned to re-create it. Eventually, when she was stronger emotionally. But the moment never seemed to come.

She could wait no longer. With her world shattering around her, she needed to believe that if she attempted the painting now, if her hands were as skillful as they once had been, her mind's eye as keen, she could bring her mother back to her.

The thoughts came at her like tiny sharpened darts. She did not care whether they made sense. In her new world of secrets and mystery, anything was possible. Wasn't it? Even the fact that her life was all a lie.

"They say in all of Hampshire there is no Wickford Close."

She spoke to the damaged portrait. Her mother's eyes smiled blandly back at her.

"You say try Sussex, Dorset, Surrey? They did. Besides, you always spoke of Hampshire as the place of my birth. When you spoke of anything at all."

She brushed at her cheeks, hard, as if the tears that kept falling stained her skin and she must erase all trace of them. She did not bother with a basic sketch of her mother's face, as she had done the first time. Instead, she splashed color on the obscene whiteness of the canvas, moving quickly, brush flying, as if to stop would be to lose all hope.

"Oh, but there was a West Indian Importing and Exporting. But the founder and owner still lives in Portsmouth. He had never heard of Wickford Close. He could hardly have done so, since it doesn't exist."

More paint, more slashing strokes.

"He knew of no Philip Lindsay. No wife, no child. He has never married. And he plans never to do so, thank you very much."

She hardly looked at her work, at the bands of color left by her brush. Nor could she look at the original portrait. Instead, desperate for a respite, she closed her eyes. There was no respite, no peace. In her mind's eye she saw the letter, each word carefully written in an ink as black as pitch.

"There is no Philip Lindsay anywhere in all of Hampshire. Lindsays enough, but no one who knew of the wealthy Philip with his company in the Caribbean."

She opened her eyes to the portrait.

"Nor of his wife Jenna, born Jenna Newbury. What? Do you say the solicitors were not thorough enough? Oh, but they were. They sent a team of investigators into the villages and towns. They went through church records, through official documents as well. They found no trace of my father, nor of you. No trace of your marriage."

Her voice broke, but she forced herself to go on.

"And no record of my birth. How could they? Wickford Close does not exist."

And neither did she. Not as Makenna Lindsay. The letter had stated as much. She was free, they readily admitted, to question the finding at length. They would send a representative to the island, if that was what she wished, to discuss both their fee and their findings.

She did not know what she wished, except perhaps to die. But that would be far too dramatic for the quiet, sensible woman she had always been.

Inconsequential was the fact that they had been unable to trace the ownership of Elysium backward from her mother. The last transaction had involved a wealthy Hampshire landowner by the name of Pemberton. But he had died long ago. No search of his heirs had been possible. They, too, had apparently died, without issue.

Whoever they were, apparently they had never claimed the cottage. All records of the deed had disappeared until it turned up in the London papers of the woman who called herself Jenna Lindsay. A woman who, at least in official documents, did not exist.

Makenna's eyes burned. Unable to see, she dropped the paintbrush on the floor and collapsed, burying her face in her hands. Sobs tore at her throat. She felt raw, bruised, and more abandoned than she would have thought possible. How cruel the letter had been, coming as it did just as she was planning her future.

Today she had learned the bitter truth: She had no past. She felt as insubstantial as the apparition who walked the beach. Even her sobs sounded like those of the ghost.

She was scarcely aware of the opening and closing of the back door, of approaching footsteps, of a figure kneeling beside her.

"Miss Lindsay, are you all right?"

And then, when she remained silent, "Please, let me help you. Tell me what is wrong."

The speaker had a kind and soothing voice. The sound of it, the gentle touch on her arm, brought her back to the room, to the place on the floor where she sat, to why she was there.

With great effort, she dropped her hands and stared into the handsome, worried face of Reverend Coggshall. She wished he were not there as a witness to her weakness. But he was, and he was kind.

"Vicar," she said and leaned into his arms.

He patted her shoulder. "Mrs. Jarman came to me and said she had delivered your letter. She feared it contained bad news and asked that I come out to Elysium. Naturally I did, as soon as I could get away."

There were questions in his voice as much as comfort. But she could not bring herself to speak. Not until the back door once again opened and closed, not until, after a long silence, she heard a different kind of voice lash words into the room as sharp as the sting of a whip.

"I did not think you took your painting so seriously," Nicholas said from the kitchen doorway. "Has it reduced you to tears?"

Something snapped inside her, cutting through the fog into which she had fallen, her confusion, the weight of her misery. Strangely, she welcomed the harshness. Here was something familiar, something she had dealt with before. Something she could deal with again. It gave her the strength to leave the kindly solace of the vicar and to stand. It made her forget, if only for a minute, the cause of her collapse.

"Captain Saintjohn," she said, well aware of the vicar's careful regard. "Your visit is a surprise."

He stepped into the room. "Obviously."

The man was a devil. He had a devil's eyes, dark

and watchful, the sharply etched lines of a devil's face. Was that concern in his eyes? Was there worry that she might have been harmed?

She must be imagining it. He offered no comfort. Instead, he challenged her. How could she have ever thought she loved him?

But she gave the devil his due. He did one thing the vicar did not do. He returned her pride to her.

She thought of the letter lying open on the kitchen table. Her letter. Her tragedy. She doubted that either man had taken a moment to read it. The vicar would never think of doing such a thing. Not so Nicholas.

Walking around the two of them, taking care not to touch either one, she got the folded papers and thrust them in her pocket. When she returned to the parlor, her gaze fell on the easel, on the canvas, on the jagged lines of color she had painted instead of her mother's face.

It was the painting of a nightmare. She stared, unable to look away, as stunned by what she had done as anything that had passed. She had thought she was painting a beloved face. She had been painting her version of hell.

And both men knew it. So much for privacy. So much for pride.

She felt brittle, about to break, yet she managed a smile for them both.

"Thank you, Captain, for dropping by. I know you want a report on your son's progress, but if you don't mind, I would prefer to give it tomorrow after the lesson. In writing, if that would be all right."

She turned to the vicar. "Thank you, too, for your concern. Mrs. Jarman was right. The letter contained news of an unexpected death. It was, I fear, a shock, but nothing I won't be able to deal with in time."

So many lies, from first to last. She delivered them with ease.

"When I first arrived, I feared your distress could be somehow connected to"—the vicar glanced at Nicholas, then back to her—"to that matter you came to me about. The one we have discussed on occasion."

The ghost. It kept intruding, even now.

"No, not at all," she said. "What I need at the moment is solitude. Please allow me to have it. As you know, women are silly creatures, given to far too much emotion."

Standing behind the vicar, Nicholas shook his head in derision. She ignored him.

"You do not have to subject yourself to my tears." She gave Nicholas her regard. "Neither of you. In truth, I do believe they've gone away. But I do need to be alone. I'm sure you understand."

The vicar frowned. Nicholas simply looked at her, though there was nothing simple in the look, nothing accepting in the narrowing of his eyes, nor in the tightness of his lips. Not for one second did he believe anything she said. But, nodding curtly, he left, alongside the vicar, after the latter had given notice he would be out to visit her again.

The vicar had come by carriage. Nicholas had walked. At the moment, she truly did not care what had brought him here. She wanted him gone.

The men set out in opposite directions. It was Nicholas who returned. He found her in the parlor putting away the paints and brushes, waiting for the sound of his footsteps, for the call of his deep voice.

He did not disappoint.

His long legs brought him quickly to her side. He stared down at the slashes of paint that made up her hellish work.

"What's going on, Makenna? What's wrong?"

Gone was the harshness. He was all warmth, all thoughtfulness. Once again he was the man who had held her through the night after the damage to the portrait. She was terrified he would take her in his arms and offer comfort again. She could take sympathy from the vicar, but not from him, not now, after all that had passed between them. Too closely it would resemble pity. Especially if he found out what had driven her to despair.

Worst of all, she would break down once again. She had to be done with tears if she were to survive.

Wordlessly, stepping around him, she finished putting away her supplies, though for the first time in her life she did not clean the brushes when she was done with them.

He watched everything. He would not go away.

"Nothing's wrong, not really. Nothing that is your concern," she said and meant it.

He stood too close. She concentrated on the painting, little more than swirls of thick, bright color. It was an abomination, the chaotic work of a soul on the edge of madness. She ought to destroy it. Or keep it as a reminder of the destructive power of grief.

For grief was what she felt. It was as if her mother had died all over again.

Taking the still-damp nightmare canvas, she set it on the portico. Against her will, she looked down at the cove. At mid-afternoon, under a bright sun, it was far too early for the ghost to appear, but still she looked. For the first time when considering the apparition, she felt no fear, no apprehension. She thought of the ghost's sobs and remembered how they had sounded very much like her own, as if she and the specter suffered a grief that somehow bound them together.

The thought robbed her of breath, yet at the same time gave her a sense of peace she had not felt since opening the letter. It was as if her life had some form, after all, a past, a present, a hope for something yet to come.

Foolish, foolish thought. Had she altogether lost her mind? Hurrying inside, she bolted the door after her. The remnants of the momentary peace fled when she looked at the damaged portrait of Jenna Lindsay, and Nicholas standing beside it.

The ghost had caused the painting to fall. She had believed it at the time. Nothing had happened to change her mind.

She took the portrait into the bedroom and returned it to its place at the back of the wardrobe. On impulse, she took the letter from her pocket and thrust it behind the portrait. When she closed the doors, she turned to find Nicholas behind her.

She jumped.

"What are you doing in my bedroom?" she demanded.

Her knees trembled. She would have liked to put more force in her words. She did the best she could.

"I've been here before," he said, as always insinuating, provocative.

"Why did you even come to the cottage? You were supposed to be working with your son."

"I don't think this is the best time to tell you."

She laughed bitterly. "Oh, please do. I promise I'm done with tears. Assuming the reason you came here is unpleasant."

He stepped close. He wore a coat, but the shirt beneath it was open at the throat. She stared at the exposed brown skin and knew it would taste salty and warm.

"Do you find my presence unpleasant? Tell me and I will leave."

"I already did that."

"You were speaking to two men. There's just one man with you now."

He might have been a hundred in number, so strong was his effect on her. She tried to look away, but she could not. What broad shoulders he had for such a lean figure. He blocked out the world.

"It could be," he added in that voice that curled around her spine, "that I'm the wrong man. You and the good reverend looked cozy indeed when I walked in."

She stared at him in disbelief. "You're as insane as I am."

"Probably. But what is it that makes us so?"

He gave her a liquid glance. It poured over her like warm honey. It sweetened her anger to something very different. She tried to breathe, but he robbed the room of air. Around him she could scarcely think.

But, of course, she did not want to. Not when thinking brought back recollection of the letter. Not when it led to the insane ideas, the impossible feelings she had just experienced on the portico.

Another insane idea struck, but it was one she could welcome. If Nicholas cooperated. And she rather thought he would.

In his moment of anguish, she had offered him solace in the only way she knew he would accept it.

It was time he did the same for her.

Stepping away, she tilted her chin at him.

"Take off your clothes, Nicholas. I've changed my mind. I do believe you ought to stay awhile."

Chapter Thirteen

"You sound like me."

It was not a romantic response.

She had not expected one. Nicholas was provocative, seductive, compelling. But he was not romantic. That had been Ascot Chilton's forte.

"But I don't look like you," she threw back at him. "That's why I want you to undress."

It felt good to spar with him. And to know what would inevitably happen between them. There was nothing like hostile words and torrid sex to take a woman's mind off her troubles. It was hardly a Victorian gentlewoman's way of thinking, but then Makenna's troubles were hardly typical of any gentlewoman she had ever met.

She had no past; she did not even have a name she could honestly call her own.

What she did have was Nicholas Saintjohn, as far from a typical Victorian gentleman as he could be. For which, at the moment, she was blissfully grateful.

He slipped out of his coat. "Tell me how I'm different."

She took a moment to answer, letting her perusal take as long as possible, resisting the urge to throw herself into his arms.

"You're taller."

"So is a tree."

She warmed to her task.

"Your hands are bigger."

"As are my feet. Would you care to point out differences in between?"

"I'll get to those parts."

As he well knew.

She studied his face, lean and sharply defined. She managed to avoid his eyes.

"You grow whiskers."

"That I do. I'm growing them while we speak."

"And your hair is coarser."

"Some of your hair is coarse, too."

As always, Nicholas did not fight fair.

He unfastened his shirt and pulled it free of his trousers. It hung open, revealing a column of brown, hair-dusted skin, which required more perusal.

She took a trembling breath.

"Your chest is flatter."

"Thank God."

He made her smile, in a trembling kind of way. He also made her breasts swell and the tips grow hard.

"But not totally flat," she managed. "For which I give equal thanks."

He took off the shirt and tossed it aside, then unfastened his trousers. More skin, too brown to be natural. He must have worked on the boat dressed much this way. Unless he had taken off even more of his clothes. If so, he had needed to be very careful when he used his hammer and saw.

"How far are you going to take this, Makenna?"

"I'll let you know."

More quickly than she would have believed possible, he was out of the rest of his clothes. They lay limply on the floor in front of the wardrobe.

She saw nothing limp about the body they had covered. He looked sleek and hard and strongly muscled, and there was nothing about him that did not look wonderful. Nothing, that is, that she allowed herself to study.

He seemed not in the least embarrassed to stand before her in such a state. It was as sharp a difference from the way she had felt as could be.

She lost her nerve. It was one thing to hold him in the night, his naked body next to hers, to kiss him, to touch him, letting her fingers do the exploring. It was a far different matter to look at him in the brilliance of day from halfway across a room.

"Your feet really are big," she said.

"Coward," he said.

She took the word as a challenge. A welcome one. Wasn't she trying to forget everything but him?

"You've got hairy legs. The calves, at least. Not so much the thighs. Until you get to . . ."

She sucked in a hasty breath. Dampness seeped against her underclothes. Though he had not yet touched her.

"You're more complicated than I thought. And yet efficient." She seized on the word as she brought her eyes to his. "Nothing seems wasted."

"Except time."

"If I'm boring you . . ."

"Do I look bored?"

She thought of his erection. Of course she had looked at it. Wantonly she had wanted to stroke its length, to wrap her fingers around its thickness, to rub her palm against the black pubic hair in which it nestled, to cup his genitalia and learn exactly how complicated he was. His sex had brought her to a rapture that went beyond all thought, all fantasy. And, if her desperate wishes came true, would do so again today.

Flames licked at her blood. "You don't look bored." She had become, it was turning out, a master of understatement.

"This is your game, Makenna. I'll keep it up for as long as you wish. As long as I'm able. But I can't guarantee that everything will remain up. And efficient."

He was misjudging her, not for the first time. What she was doing was no game. She was keeping the world at bay. But it was creeping back, like fog under the door. Reality had an acrid air about it. It burned her eyes.

Pain ripped at her chest. A sob escaped her throat. How could she do this? How could she pretend for even a moment that nothing had happened to her on this terrible day?

Oh, but there was one way that she could. A primal urge tore through her, obliterating the pain. She threw herself against Nicholas, wrapping her arms around his neck. As slender as she was, she made him stagger. But only for a moment.

Strong arms enveloped her and held her close. An insistent mouth claimed hers. She rubbed her hands against the tight skin of his back, drove her fingers into his hair, raked his mouth with her tongue. He always tasted salty, and at the same time wet and sweet, like ripe fruit.

She added a new flavor. She tasted desperation, but that must be coming from her tongue.

Make me forget, Nicholas. Help me not to think.

He did exactly what she wanted, without the words being said aloud.

His back muscles rippled beneath her probing fingers. She felt his intensity, his heat, as if something akin to steam was building inside him, something that threatened to explode. Her skirt rustled against his bare legs. His breathing was harsh, and she could hear the pounding of his heart. Imagination? Probably, but it seemed very, very real. His sounds were as intoxicating as his taste.

Roughly he tugged at her gown, bunching the full skirt around her waist. He growled when he felt the slippery petticoat. When she had gone to his room, she had worn nothing beneath her dress. Not so today. She was armored, but it was in silk, a scant barrier to what he wanted to touch.

He tumbled her back onto the bed and made short work of her drawers. He stared down at the triangle of hair in which awaited her own throbbing sex.

"Nicholas," she said, the muscles of her thighs and buttocks taut.

"My turn," he said.

His clever thumb went unerringly to where she throbbed. She whimpered, a weak sound compared to the all-powerful forces that were flooding through her.

When he abandoned the throbs, she swallowed a cry of protest. She should have trusted him. He was gone only as long as it took him to bare her breasts. His teeth scraped against the hardened tips. His hands took over as he ran his tongue down to where her skirt was bunched at her waist. Strangely, with her dress half off, exposing the private parts of her body to his cunning eyes, she felt more erotic than when she had lain beneath him naked.

Now he was the one who was naked, a condition that pushed eroticism to the extreme.

His tongue moved lower. It found the throbbing. A shock went through her, as if she had been struck by lightning. Nicholas had ever been a storm to her; today the turbulence within him raged. Like the wild wind it roared into her.

He was relentless. She tried to thrash against the mounting sensations, but iron hands held her in place beneath his velvet assault. Her blood pulsed so that she thought it might burst through her veins. At the final moment of passion, his mouth covered the unbridled pulsing, as if he would suck the raging shudders into his own sweat-slick body, as if he could share the climax he had brought to her.

She wanted to curl into him and cherish the moment, letting the shudders gradually ease. But he had other plans. With a final stroke of his tongue, he kissed his way back to her breasts. His ebony hair lay damp against his face, thick lashes resting above the sharp contours of his cheeks. The love she should not feel flooded through her. The love had nothing and everything to do with the thrill as he cupped her breasts, as gently as if they were the greatest treasures in the world.

In that moment, he seemed as vulnerable as she, a power of nature and yet a repository of all the worries that could strike the human race.

He moved over her and stretched his body against hers. When she looked into his glinting eyes, she forgot his vulnerability. The wildness had returned. He held her captive, her thoughts, her heart, her soul, as surely as if he had bound her in chains.

"Your turn," she whispered huskily.

"You think I took no pleasure in what just happened?" He brushed his lips against hers. "I am not so unselfish, my passionate one."

He spoke the truth. She was passionate. And she was his. She hoped never to confess her feelings, but he had to know them, as surely as if the words were written on her brow.

While his tongue teased her lips, his erection did the same to the hot private parts between her legs. She had truly thought she was done with rapture. He proved her wrong. When he thrust inside her, she was ready for him, and she found that ecstasy shared was sweeter than any other kind.

With their lips parted and pressed together, they swallowed their mutual cries, and he held her tightly until the tremors had finally eased. He did not move immediately, nor did she want him to do so. Because she found her greatest happiness in his arms. Because, too, her greatest misery would return when she could think clearly once again.

It was as if she could feel only two sensations,

as disparate as feelings within the same human body could be.

When he eased from her and stood, the happiness fled. But then, it had already begun to do so. The worst part of thinking would be the fact that he would know the moment her troubles had returned. And he would be relentless in finding out what they were.

But they were her troubles, not his. And what would he say to her? She could almost hear the awkward phrases of consolation or, worse, the assurance that she surely misunderstood her situation, either her memories of what she had been told all her life or what the solicitors were telling her now.

It was all too much to contemplate while she was lying on the bed in a tangle of clothes and covers, her body not quite done with pulsing, and a very naked Nicholas watching everything she did.

Two nights ago she had been blessed with sleep. But not today. Nor did he seem inclined to get dressed right away.

And when would she learn that sex offered no more than a temporary escape? It did not change the way things were, especially when mutual affection was not involved.

Turning from him, she curled into a fetal ball.

"Please get dressed," she said.

"Now that you've had your way with me?"

Dearest Nicholas, as darkly insinuating as ever.

"I wasn't the only one who had my way."

"I wanted to hold you a while longer. After I took off your gown."

He sounded tender. She did not want tenderness. It weakened her.

"I'm exhausted," she said and meant it.

"If that's a hint that I should leave, think again, Makenna. Something's going on here. You don't have to deal with it alone."

But that was exactly what she needed to do.

"Do you know how to put water on for tea?"

"I might be able to manage it."

"Then, please, prove it."

"After I've dressed."

"That seems a good idea."

She listened as he scooped up his clothes and left, closing the bedroom door behind him. Forcing herself from the bed, she was relieved to find that Mrs. Jarman had left a pitcher of water on the bedside table. Dear Mrs. Jarman. But then she had also sent the vicar to witness her despair.

Bathing as best she could, she put on a clean gray gown, brushed her hair and pinned it into a bun, and went out to deal with the man who was as much a problem as he was the light of her life.

He was seated at the kitchen table, a cup of tea in front of him, a second cup awaiting her in front of the opposite chair.

"I managed not to burn down the house," he said.

She sipped the tea. It scalded her tongue. She

was glad. It gave her something to think about.

"Am I going to have to get the letter or will you tell me what it said?"

She stared into the cup but knew that would not do. He needed to look into her eyes.

Before she could speak, he reached across the table and brushed his thumb over the shadows beneath her eyes.

"You are exhausted," he said.

"It's your fault."

"I don't think so."

She did not try to argue with him.

"I already told you what is troubling me. The letter brought news of a death."

And so it did, in a way, if you could call news of a nonexistence a form of death.

"It would have to be someone who meant a great deal to you. But your parents are gone."

"Oh, yes, they are gone."

Suddenly he shoved his chair away from the table. The tea jostled in the cup and spilled into the saucer. He turned from her, then back again, and his eyes flamed with certainty.

"Of course. Your lover. Who else could cause you such distress?"

He gave her the solution she had been searching for. She could have kissed him. But he would not have understood.

She lowered her lashes. If he believed that Ascot Chilton was dead, she would make no attempt to change his mind. Of course, the solution was not perfect. He would believe she had tried to forget her grief by making love to another man.

The reality of the lie, and the enormity of it, washed over her, and a new kind of pain rushed in. She could imagine the names he might call her. He might not keep them to himself.

Difficult though it was to do so, she stood. She could not bear his looking down at her the way he was.

"I had thought I was over him."

"So you indicated."

"The letter was a shock. That's all."

"A shock."

"A surprise."

"And nothing more. Don't lie to me, Makenna. Don't lie to yourself."

He came around the table and cradled her face in his hands.

"The trouble with being human is that we can't help loving the people we do." He kissed the shadows under her eyes, then brushed his lips across hers. "God help us. We don't seem able to help ourselves."

He turned to leave, then paused and looked at her once again.

"Don't worry about the lesson tomorrow," he said. "I need to make up for disappointing Jonathan today. We'll spend the morning working on the boat."

Without another word, he left. It wasn't until he was out of sight that she remembered he had not told her what had brought him to Elysium this afternoon.

But that was a minor issue.

The trouble with being human is that we can't help loving the people we do.

The words had come from deep inside him. She could not believe he had spoken about loving her. Too much pain had been in his voice, too much darkness in his eyes.

She had heard that pain before, had seen that darkness too many times. He was thinking of his own past, of his own loss. He was thinking about his wife.

An hour later dusk was creeping onto the cove. In a while the moon would be high. In the cloudless expanse of the universe she could already see the North Star. It hung in the darkening blue sky high over Windward House.

She went onto the portico to await the inevitable. She could arouse no sympathetic bond with the ghost, but neither did she feel fear. She was beyond feeling anything at all.

It wasn't the ghost who came to her. The scratching at the back door and the low, insistent whine gave notice that Ungrateful had returned, after abandoning her for the unending afternoon. With a sigh she left the portico rocking chair and went to set out his food.

The back gate was partially ajar. Nicholas must not have closed it securely as he was leaving, but then he had been thinking of other things.

When she first looked down at the dog, she thought he had already provided sustenance for himself. On the ground in front of him lay a bone half the length of her arm. She knelt to exam it. All signs of flesh were gone, and the bone itself, a grayish white, was stained with what appeared to be dirt, as if it had been buried for a very long time.

"What did you do, boy, dig up someone's grave?"

The moment the words were out of her mouth, she regretted them. For that was exactly what could have happened. Her study of art had included a cursory look at anatomy. The bone lying at her back door was too long and thick to belong to any animal likely to be on the Isle of Wight. A horse, perhaps, but nothing else.

But it could very well have belonged to a human.

She looked at the dog. He was panting, and there was pride lighting his eyes, as if he said, "Look, Mama, what I brought you. I'm a good dog."

She scratched behind his ears.

"If only you could tell me where you got this."

He barked, jumped backward, then barked again.

She stood. "I suppose you're answering me. You're smart, but you're not that smart."

He darted toward her, then retreated, and she

could have sworn he motioned with his head for her to come with him.

"It's getting dark, Ungrateful. We can go on an adventure tomorrow."

He stared up at her for a moment, then darted past her to the door, picked up the bone between his teeth, and in an instant was gone through the open gate.

He gave her no choice but to run after him, calling his name, which, it occurred to her, was new and therefore unfamiliar to him. Not that he would have obeyed anyway.

He ran from the lane to the main road and headed in the direction of town. Even as she joined in behind him, she knew where they were headed. When he came to the path leading away from the road, he paused to give her time to catch up with him, and she knew she was right.

They were going to the run-down cemetery in the middle of a dark and eerie woods.

With the sun disappearing, the air took on an uncomfortable chill. She was without a cloak, but to turn back would be impossible. Tall grasses caught at her skirt, and an owl hooted from somewhere in the approaching trees. Breathless, she ran on, barely able to maintain the steady pace of the dog.

She lost him at the edge of the woods. Halting, she became aware of the wind in the trees, the scraping of branches against one another, the shadowy outline of rustling leaves against the darkening sky. As if the night had arms, it held her in its cold embrace. She felt chilled to her marrow. As well, she felt driven to go on, impelled by an unseen supernatural force as strong as the wispy ghost.

Her escort was not to be seen. She stumbled down the trail without him, guided by a pinpoint spark of light that beckoned from ahead. When at last she reached the clearing, she saw its source. Standing on the far side of the fence that enclosed the graves, Biddy Merton waited, a lantern in her hand.

Bent and gnarled, she looked a part of the scene, as if she had sprung from the ground, as slanted and unfeeling and ancient as the gravestones before her. She nodded, showing no surprise to see her visitor, but she did not speak. Instead, she slowly turned her head toward a corner of the cemetery.

Ungrateful sat in the corner, waiting patiently. Makenna opened the creaking gate and made her way slowly past and around the headstones. An animal rustled in the weeds, and once again the owl hooted its mournful song.

Makenna's blood ran cold, but she could not stop until she stood before the shallow grave behind which the dog awaited. Biddy Merton slipped silently beside her and raised the lantern. Light fell on a scattering of bones much like the one Ungrateful had brought to her. They lay in disorder on top of what appeared to be clothing, and beneath that a rotted piece of canvas. It was difficult to tell for certain in the night. The fabric of the clothing, if that was what it was, had long ago decayed, black fungus covering it in streaks, and the light was as erratic as Makenna's heart.

Without doubt the bones were human. But what human? And why had the dog unearthed them and brought her to see what he had done?

And why had Biddy Merton been awaiting her arrival?

The moon chose that moment to rise above the tops of the trees, casting a macabre glow onto the aged graves. As the wind howled through the branches, only one thing seemed certain. This was the perfect ending for the worst day of her life.

Chapter Fourteen

"It looks human to me."

Constable Tobias Bent trudged in a circle through the mud left by an early morning rain and stared into the shallow grave, dimly illuminated by the sunlight filtering through the surrounding trees.

"Yes, I'd say definitely human."

Neither Makenna nor Biddy Merton disagreed. Both stood outside the cemetery fence, giving Bent ample room to do what he needed to. Thus far, a quarter hour into his investigation, he had done little more than walk and stare and scribble in a small notebook he had pulled from inside his uniform coat.

A tall man, uncommonly gaunt, East Hartsbridge's lone police official bore a long, sharp face, thin lips, and dark, narrow eyes whose primary characteristic was the occasional tic that jerked the left side of his face into a strange kind of wink, as if he were making a joke of everything he said.

But he showed no other sign of humor, nor, Makenna feared, of imagination. He was, she decided, a man given to stating the obvious. At first light she had gone into the village to summon him. Unaware of the existence of the long-unused cemetery, he had needed her to guide him to where he now stood, thick-soled shoes made thicker by the mud, his coat hanging loosely on his shoulders, the sleeves striking two inches above the wrists of his simian arms.

Mrs. Bent, the dressmaker who had so efficiently sewn Makenna clothes suitable for the island, should have been able to alter the sleeves, but her husband did not seem the kind of man to notice his appearance.

His roughly shorn brown hair was as thin as the rest of him. He was holding his hat in his long-fingered hand as if to show respect to the dead, anchoring it under his arm when he wanted to write.

Biddy Merton, showing her own kind of respect, had covered the grave with a sheet of canvas, protecting its grim contents from the night dew. It had been Makenna's idea to weight the edges of the canvas down with heavy rocks, in case another animal as enterprising as Ungrateful should try to disturb them.

To do otherwise would have seemed a sacrilege.

The canvas was now tossed aside, along with the rocks. Everything in the grave was as Makenna had first seen it, a disjointed skeleton lying on top of a swath of dark, rotted fiber whose shape and exact color were impossible to determine. As she stared at the ill-cared-for remains of what had been a human being, she felt sadness for a life so unceremoniously disposed of.

Whoever he or she had been, when the end came, no passing bells had peeled or death knell rung to solemnize the occasion. Everyone deserved the tolling of a bell.

"Dr. Beaumont will be along shortly," Bent said. Before leaving the village, he had taken the precaution of sending his wife to the doctor's residence with the news of the discovery. At the moment, circling and studying with an occasional scribble in his book, he seemed reluctant to touch the bones. Makenna sympathized, but then, she was not an officer of the law.

Ungrateful's bark broke the stillness of the graveyard, and in a moment Dr. William Beaumont hurried through the trees into the clearing.

From their brief meeting at the vicar's home, Makenna remembered him as a soft-spoken man with a kindly, avuncular face. This morning there was an excitement in his eyes and a quickness to his step she had not noticed before.

"I haven't thought of this place in years," he said, letting himself through the gate and glancing at the rows of uneven headstones. He nodded to Makenna and Biddy Merton. "Would have passed right by the trail off the main road, but your dog was there to guide me. The animal is well trained."

Both women let the comment go. The doctor might not have heard what they said anyway. Already he was crouching beside the open grave, studying the remains as carefully as he might a living patient, his small valise on the wet ground beside him.

After a moment during which he scarcely moved, he reached carefully into the grave, which was no more than two feet deep at its lowest point, shifted the bones, picking up one, turning it in his hands before returning it to its place and going on to another.

Bent knelt beside him, watched, but said not a word.

"You see what I see, Tobias?"

The constable's face twitched and his left eye winked. "It's definitely the remains of a human," he said.

Beaumont took the pronouncement with equanimity.

"And one who was not treated too kindly," he said.

He stood and stretched his back. Tobias unwound his scrawny body and looked down on the doctor.

"My thoughts exactly, Dr. Beaumont. Throwing the bones into the ground like that without proper words said over them, it's heathen, that's what it is."

"It's more than that," Beaumont said. He looked at Makenna. "I'll need to do more study, of course, back in the village, but it seems clear enough that whoever the man was, he did not die a natural death."

Old bones know things.

The words kept echoing through Makenna's mind as she sat in a private side room of the Crown and Anchor, waiting for Dr. Beaumont to appear. Women, especially those unaccompanied by a man, were not a common sight at the village's only pub. She'd had no trouble convincing the proprietor, a wary-eyed man named Hugh Snell, to place her where she couldn't be seen by everyone who entered.

Old bones know things.

After last night and this morning, she could think of little else. Or perhaps it was that she did not wish to do so. Her own situation was too painful, too perplexing, to contemplate right away. Here was a mystery that, except for Ungrateful's participation, did not involve her. She might experience sadness over the cruel grave. But she did not have to suffer. The corpse had nothing to do with her.

Old bones know things.

When Biddy Merton had uttered the words, had she been thinking of the bones in the shallow grave? Makenna had thought she was speaking of herself, but now she was not so sure. When asked if she knew anything about the discovery—the question being the constable's lone effort into an investigation—the woman had given him the same enigmatic look she frequently gave Makenna and muttered something about mysteries being everywhere.

At last the doctor arrived at the pub in a flurry, his eyes bright, his movements fitful, as if he could scarcely contain his excitement. He barely had time to sit in the chair facing Makenna before the proprietor was setting a pint of ale in front of him, and a cup of tea in front of her.

He took a deep swallow of the ale.

"I shouldn't be talking to you before making my report to Tobias, but he's busy writing reports himself, though what he has to say is a puzzle."

"But you will talk to me," she said.

Beaumont's eyes twinkled. "You just try to leave, Miss Lindsay, and you'll find yourself bound to that chair. I need someone to talk to who might have something intelligent to say in return."

Since she could think of little that was even coherent, she doubted that her comments would satisfy the good doctor. She did not, however, bother to tell him so. For reasons that she herself could not totally understand, she had taken a proprietary interest in the shallow grave. She needed to hear everything Beaumont had to say. In the hours since Ungrateful had shown up at her back door with his surprise gift, her interest had become almost an obsession.

He grew solemn. "I don't mean to make light of the situation. But it's interesting to me. No, more than interesting. It's fascinating. I've done some studying on bones. There's not much else to do to fill in time between patients except to study." He lifted the tankard of ale. "Or drink, and I'm not given to more than a pint or two a day."

"You know bones," Makenna said, doubting that the comment filled the doctor's expectation of an intelligent response. "Old bones," she added, to herself as much as to him.

"These aren't so old, not by the standards of that cemetery. Those grave sites go back a hundred years or more. The bones dug up by your dog belonged to a man no more than middle-aged. I'd put him a decade or two younger, but I have no proof of that."

"You're sure the corpse was a man."

"Yes, I am, though I have to say medical science has a long way to go in understanding the human body. At times the two words don't even go together."

"Medical and science, you mean."

Another swallow of ale. "I knew you were a smart woman. You'll understand what I'm about to say. The bones of a man are longer, thicker, denser than those of a woman, or of a child. After the undertaker brought them in, I weighed and measured them, treating them with respect, you understand. I'm a God-fearing man and know that whoever he was, the deceased was one of His creatures."

He let out a long, slow breath and stared sorrowfully at Makenna. "The person who buried him should have been so thoughtful. Or whoever killed him. I'm thinking they are one and the same, although again I have no proof."

A cold sense of dread trickled through her. "How can you say such things?"

"Because the evidence is there. Our victim had suffered a broken arm when he was a child, but it had knitted so that it wouldn't have given him more than a twinge or two if he used it wrong. But he had a fresh break in his upper spine that must have happened at the time of death. Healing had not begun."

"I'm sorry, Dr. Beaumont, but I don't understand."

"I'll speak bluntly. You seem like a woman who can handle it. Our victim, and I'm wishing here he had a name, died of a broken neck."

"Couldn't he have died in a fall?"

"If so, someone would have alerted the constable. Or called me. I started in practice here some thirty years ago. I don't believe he died longer ago than that. Here I could be wrong, but I don't think so."

He finished the ale, and the proprietor was instantly placing another tankard in front of him.

"Bring Miss Lindsay a brandy, Hugh," Dr. Beaumont said. "She's looking a little pale, and that tea doesn't seem to interest her."

Hugh Snell left, then returned not quite so instantly to place a small snifter on the table. Makenna took a small sip and felt the liquid burn her nose and throat, forcing her to cough. The second sip went down more smoothly, as did a third.

She looked away from the concerned eyes of the doctor. "I don't know why this has upset me so much," she said.

"I can guess. Your bad news already has you distressed. Remember, Miss Lindsay, you got the letter only yesterday."

She looked back at him and spoke sharply. "How do you know about the letter?"

"The Reverend Coggshall. Of course, Mrs. Jarman had already spread the news that you had received a post from London, so the man was hardly betraying a confidence. Besides, he was not the only one with you."

"You mean Captain Saintjohn. I'm his son's tutor," she said, as if that would satisfy the curiosity in the doctor's eyes.

It didn't, but she said no more and the doctor hurried on.

"The vicar said the letter contained news of a distressing death. And then the dog brought you a human bone. After such a day, most women would have taken to their beds with a severe case of the vapors. But you spent much of the night tromping around in an old graveyard covering up a newfound grave."

He said the last admiringly. How little he knew about her, about all she had faced. What would he think if she told him about the ghost? About how she could now think of the specter without the terror that had struck her at first? He would consider her almost inhuman in her strength.

But he would be wrong. She would also have to tell him what a weakling she was around Nicholas. To be completely honest, she would have to describe exactly the ways she was weak.

She wasn't strong. She was heartsick.

"Ah, Dr. Beaumont, there you are."

Constable Tobias Bent strode into the room, giving Makenna not so much as a nod. Hugh Snell was close on his heels.

"Nothing for me, Hugh," Bent said in his most officious tone. "I'm on duty, you understand. I've got to keep my head clear."

He dragged a chair close to Beaumont's and pulled out his notebook. His face twitched and the left eye winked. Instead of asking questions, he silently went over his notes. Respectfully the doctor did not interrupt the reading. Makenna took another sip of brandy. It kept her from screaming for the constable to get on with what he had learned.

For it was clear he had learned something. He was almost bursting with the news.

"At first I thought there wouldn't be much to tell from the clothing. Rotted so that it fell apart in my hands. But when it was new, it was quality. The wife took a close look at it. She's what you might call an expert on such things, being a dressmaker and all. She said it was wool, probably from one of those expensive mills up in Scotland. And the stitching, what was left of it, was done by an expert hand. A London tailor, most likely. Whoever the dead man was, he was not poor."

A double twitch and wink.

"For it was a man. The suit of clothes said so. Unless you've got a woman masquerading as a man, which hardly seems likely, does it?"

He waited for congratulations from the doctor. Beaumont did not disappoint him.

"Good for you, Tobias. That was clever, asking your wife to help. You have confirmed my suspicions about the sex of our victim. Do you have any idea how long ago he might have been buried?"

"That's a mite more complicated. The wife . . . er, that is to say, I don't have any knowledge about how things rot in the grave, animal or otherwise. And the body had been wrapped in canvas, protecting it from the elements. But it's been a while. Yes, it's definitely been a while."

Beaumont nodded. "How about identification? Was there anything in the grave that might give us a name?"

"I was waiting for you to get to that. If he'd had papers on him, they're long since gone. Anything leather was taken, too—belt, shoes, a packet that might have held papers. It seems that whoever stuck him in the ground was careful enough to remove whatever might tell an officer such as myself who the fellow was. But they overlooked one thing." Twitch and wink. "A handkerchief monogrammed with the initials RD. I found it myself by digging around in the grave. In bad condition, it was, but the monogram was clear enough."

He sat back in the chair and came as close to beaming as a man of his gauntness could manage.

"Good man," said Beaumont, quick to respond.

Makenna kept her silence, hiding her disappointment, realizing for the first time how much she had wanted Bent to turn up an identity for the mystery man. It was a foolish reaction over something that meant nothing personal to her.

Didn't she have enough real worries without taking on one such as this?

While Bent was beaming, the doctor described his own findings and suppositions. He ended with the broken neck.

The constable leapt from his chair, sending it over backward with a crash. He proceeded to pace. Hugh Snell peered into the room, shrugged, and went away.

"A murder, right here in East Hartsbridge," he said more than once. "Murder most foul, or so the bard said. Couldn't have put it better myself. I'll need to notify someone in Newport. They'll want to send someone to the village. Or maybe not. It could be the investigation will be left to the local authority. Meaning me."

He was speaking fast, to no one in particular except himself.

"There might be a promotion in all of this. Won't the wife be proud."

It seemed the final pronouncement on the situation. Neither of the constable's listeners offered a word.

As Makenna finished her brandy, she looked from man to man. A strange thought struck—the consideration that it was good to be with people again, even Tobias Bent and Hugh Snell, but especially Dr. Beaumont.

The brandy might be influencing her, or her weariness, or one of a dozen other circumstances. Still, it was clear even to her addled mind that in coming to the Isle of Wight, she had isolated herself far too much.

The somber thinking returned in force as soon as she got back to the cottage, isolated once again.

Life, she discovered, went on in the midst of death, whether the death was real or not. The real one had happened decades ago, Makenna reminded herself, as evidenced by the findings of Dr. Beaumont and Tobias Bent. The more recent, her onetime lover's passing, had been an assumption she had not bothered to correct. As far as she knew, Ascot Chilton was alive and well and happy with his wealthy cousin far away in London.

The true loss was the ending of everything she had known of her past. Throughout the misty, ghostless evening and into the next morning as she trudged to Windward House, contents of the letter kept stabbing at her in memories too painful to contemplate.

She sought refuge in the boy's lessons. If she found excuses to touch Jonathan more than usual, to guide his hands, to congratulate him with a pat on the shoulder, to stroke the dark hair from his eyes so that he might better view the piano keys, he gave no sign he noticed.

But he did not pull away from the touches. At times he seemed to seek them out. But that was probably her imagination providing her with a comfort she needed more than she needed air.

The lessons were just concluding when the door to the music room opened and Nicholas strode inside, a coat thrown over one arm, his hair disheveled, his eyes as dark as night.

"Papa!"

Jonathan stared wide-eyed at his father, but Makenna could detect no sign of distress. No excited outpouring of love, either, but that would have been too much to expect.

Makenna could scarcely manage to look at him. His last words before leaving her two days ago had clearly indicated that he mourned for someone else. So why did she want to throw herself in his arms and cover his face with kisses? Why did she want to cling to him, force him to make love to her whether or not his affections were totally involved?

She knew the answer. She was a fool. And she was without shame.

"Captain Saintjohn," she said, rubbing her palms against her skirt. "What an unexpected pleasure."

Nicholas stared at her hands. "Is it?" He turned to the boy. "Jonathan, Mrs. Loddington is here to take you to an early lunch. We'll talk later. There's still some finishing up on the boat we have to do."

Makenna looked beyond him to the housekeeper, who was standing in the entryway.

Dutiful son that he was, Jonathan slipped into his small jacket and went to her. Nicholas closed the door. The two of them were alone. She tolerated his perusal of her, but just barely. He reminded her of the way Dr. Beaumont had studied the bones, with a dark degree of warmth thrown in, an addition that was his and his alone.

She wondered if he had heard of the events of yesterday. She doubted it; unless Gibbs had gone into town, something that did not happen every day, he would have had no way of hearing the news.

He and, sadly, his son were more isolated than she.

He tossed his coat aside. "You look terrible, Makenna."

She gasped. "That's not a nice thing to say."

But she knew he was right. She had tied back

her hair without bothering to smooth it from her face, thrown on one of the mourning gowns she'd brought from London, and during the drawing lesson had ignored a smudge of black chalk on her cheek.

It was not her finest hour. But neither was it his. She could not fault him for the way he appeared in his open-throated shirt and fitted trousers—as always, he looked wonderful—but for his manner. In his bluntness, Nicholas could be a boor.

He did not let up.

"You're exhausted. Are you painting the circles under your eyes?"

"They're natural enough."

"You need to take better care of yourself."

"That's my concern, isn't it?"

"Not necessarily."

Alarm bells rang in her head. She put up a defensive hand. "Please, don't say any more."

"How do you know what I plan to say?"

"I never know for certain. But I have my fears."

"Fears? That seems a harsh way to put it."

His eyes glinted. The glint was like a warning flare.

"Poor Makenna. Carrying on an affair with me has quite worn you out. You've lost weight. You obviously are not sleeping. And I have yet to see you smile when I walk into a room. It is lowering, my dear, I must tell you."

She closed her eyes until the threatening tears burned away. Only Nicholas could offer his first endearment couched in sarcasm that negated the words.

"I didn't realize you wanted smiles from me. I rather thought you wished my mouth otherwise occupied."

That got close to a smile from him. But it died too soon.

"I want too much," he said.

She could have told him the opposite was true. He did not want even a portion of what she wanted to give.

"I need to go, Nicholas. Mrs. Jarman will be waiting with all the food I could possibly eat. And then I'll get some rest. Does that satisfy you?"

It was the wrong thing to say.

He was across the room in an instant. When he took her into his arms, she made no attempt to pull away.

"With you, Makenna, I am never satisfied."

He thrust his fingers into her hair, and the inadequately pinned bun dissolved in a tangle of long, silvery curls.

"I've never seen hair the color of yours," he said, as if he were seeing it for the first time. He slanted his lips across hers. "I've never tasted anyone so sweet."

Was he being deliberately cruel? She looked into his eyes and saw no dissembling. What she saw was desire, so hot it scorched her.

She covered her ears. "Go away, Nicholas. Leave me a little peace."

271

"Leave you to grieve, that's what you mean." He tugged at her hands and held them in a tight grip. "You will listen to me. You have no choice. I came to the cottage two days ago to tell you I had been wrong. Though I would be a damnably poor husband and father, I would never abandon you. Never. I've lost too much already. I could not lose you or our child."

"There's no—"

He stopped her words with a kiss.

"Nicholas, I am not—"

He was more persistent than she. This time when his mouth covered hers, she did not struggle to end the kiss. Instead, she opened up to him and let his fire enter her body, sucking at the sweetness of his tongue, moving her tongue against his, welcoming the familiar lightning of pleasure that shot through her in an instant storm of passion.

He dropped her hands to caress her breasts. Wrapping her arms around him, she cupped his buttocks and held his hard body as tightly against her as emboldened strength could manage. Her own body prepared itself for him. She could feel the dampness between her legs. She could feel the swell of her breasts.

So lost was she in her need for him, she was only dimly aware of his easing embrace, of his lips pressed to her forehead, of the curse words he muttered under his breath.

At last she heard what he was listening to, the crunch of wheels in front of the house, the neigh of horses, the creak of springs as at least one carriage came to a halt. It sounded to her stunned ears as if an invading army had come to call.

A knock sounded at the music room door.

"We've guests, Captain," Mrs. Loddington said on the other side. "I thought you would want to know."

She had the good sense not to open the door.

Nicholas stepped away but kept his hold on her shoulders.

"Later," was all he said.

No, she wanted to tell him; for them there would be no later. Whoever had arrived would change everything. She knew it in her heart.

Shrugging into his coat, he went into the entryway. Hastily, Makenna gathered the hair pins from the floor and thrust them into her poorly arranged bun. But she did not follow her lover. Instead, she stood in the sanctuary of the room, praying beyond all hope that whoever arrived would pass on by without glancing in.

The double front doors creaked open.

"Nicholas," a woman cried.

"What are you doing here?"

It was a typical Nicholas greeting, gentled by no sign of graciousness.

The visitor did not seem put out.

"And isn't that a fine way to say hello? We haven't seen each other for months. I know I should have waited for Robert's return, but I couldn't. Here, give me a kiss. Well, that will have to do. You never were one to show affection, were you? I see your time on the island has done little to change that."

Makenna heard the swish of silk as the woman entered Windward House.

"You really must do something about that naked carving over the door. I brought the girls, and I'm not sure bare breasts are really the first thing they should see."

"The breasts have no nipples."

"If you think to shock me, you know that's impossible. My, what a gloomy place. You really ought to do something about it."

The light from the music room drew her there, and she stopped in the doorway and stared at Makenna.

"Oh, I didn't know anyone was lurking about."

"Miss Lindsay is not lurking," Nicholas said.

The two women looked one another over. The newcomer was clad in a dress and matching coat of brilliant green, her black hair stylishly arranged beneath a feathered black hat. She was small and young, and dark and lovely with delicate features that made her look like a pixy. But she had deep, watchful eyes that would miss little. It was evident she did not like what she saw. Makenna feared that the woman knew exactly what Nicholas had been up to when she arrived.

Makenna wanted to smooth her hair. Instead, she stiffened her spine.

Nicholas stepped up beside the young woman,

who leaned against him with a smile of possession as she studied her.

"Sarah, may I present Miss Makenna Lindsay. She instructs Jonathan in the arts."

"Miss Lindsay. The arts, is it? You must be very skilled for Nick to allow you near his son." She put a great deal of meaning into *very skilled*.

Nicholas gave no sign he noticed. "Miss Lindsay, this is my sister, Sarah Harwood."

Makenna nodded. "How wonderful for Captain Saintjohn that you're here, Mrs. Harwood. He did not tell me of your arrival. Otherwise I would have canceled the lessons for today."

"Please don't cancel anything because of me. Knowing Nick, I'm certain he has duties he expects of you. My brother likes routine. It comes from years at sea."

So saying, she turned and wound her arm through Nicholas's. "Please, send your servants out to start emptying the carriages. I've brought a shocking number of clothes. Francis tried to shame me, but the dear doesn't understand the importance of appearance. After five years of marriage, you would think he would have learned."

While Sarah Harwood maundered on, Makenna took the opportunity to steal out the front door. Three carriages lined the driveway. People were beginning to emerge, women mostly, none dressed quite so finely as Nicholas's sister.

Makenna did not count them, she didn't give anyone a glance. Instead, she hurried around the carriages, down the drive, and onto the road that led to Elysium. Whether he wanted it or not, Nicholas was about to be surrounded by life in the form of his sister, two nieces, and their entourage.

While she was surrounded by the influence of death.

As she hurried down the hill toward Elysium, the sounds of chatter, of laughter, rang in her ears. She had no idea how Nicholas would take the invasion. But it would be good for Jonathan, and for him alone she would be glad.

For herself, she could not be pleased. Sarah Saintjohn Harwood had known right away the relationship between her brother and his son's teacher. To Makenna, her love made that relationship special. To Sarah Harwood, it must seem commonplace.

Entering the cottage, Makenna tore the pins from her hair and shook it free. She hurried onto the portico and down the path to the beach, letting the wind catch the long, loose strands, breathing in the smell of the sea. Mostly she listened to the pounding of the waves on the shore. Together, wind and sea blocked out all other sound.

She stood a long time at the water's edge, watching the circling of a cormorant against the clear blue sky. She could feel so much, too much, slipping away. But then the loss was of things that had never belonged to her.

Tonight she would almost welcome the return of the ghost. No one else saw the gossamer apparition. No one heard the mournful cries.

For a short while weeks ago, after her consultation with the vicar, she had considered asking for an exorcism. But not now. Not after she had lost so much.

She had not lost the ghost. The sight and the sounds of it were hers and hers alone.

Chapter Fifteen

With the rise of the moon the ghost returned, but this time without sound, without sobbing. Instead, she walked at the water's edge, as always away from Makenna, her long, diaphanous gown trailing in the waves that died against the damp sand of the beach.

Makenna stood on the portico, drawn to her but not compelled to rush down and follow in her wake. At her side on the portico was Ungrateful, hackles raised. She got the idea he was trying to protect her, though she did not feel in danger. She felt mystified and sad, but not afraid. After that one time when the specter had led her onto the pier, no threats had been directed toward her.

Just a sorrow as deep and wide as the ocean and

as endless as the sky. Since the letter, Makenna had suffered that same feeling.

Kneeling by the dog, she scratched behind his ears to ease his distress. He remained stiff and alert, her sentry against the mystical world, and she decided he was misnamed. He never answered to Ungrateful anyway. She would have to come up with something else, something more suitable.

Eventually, as night fell and the ghost faded into the mist, she went inside and sat at the piano. But first, she carried the canvas with the wild streaks of paint to a refuse bin Mr. Jarman had set up by the shed. Next she took the damaged portrait of her mother from the wardrobe and propped it where she could look at it when she needed and wanted to.

She played for a long time, but not wildly, not passionately. The music on this night was in a more pensive mood. It held no elements to stir a man's blood.

When she was done, she returned to the portico for one last whiff of the sea breeze, one last look at the stars. But she spent little time studying the sky. Instead, her gaze went to Windward House, to the highest floor, to the room that served as Nicholas's retreat.

No light shone from the window. It always had, every time she looked at it in the dark. But not tonight. The blackness of the window seemed to her a wound, as if the house itself had somehow been injured.

When she went back inside, she let the dog follow her. He did so as if this were his routine, his right. He slept on the floor at the foot of her bed. If he made a sound, she did not hear it. Exhaustion gave her one of the things she needed. It gave her sleep.

The next morning she heard a carriage on the road and went out to see Gibbs at the reins of the Saintjohn carriage on a journey into town.

She motioned for him to stop.

"Damned foolishness," he growled, waving a piece of paper about. "I'll have to order a wagon to deliver even half the things on this list. And a dozen servants to boot."

"How is Jonathan?"

Gibbs squinted down at her. "Shouldn't you be going to the house to find out for yourself?" he growled.

Makenna sighed. Like his beloved Saint Nick, the old sailor always stayed in character. Nothing she did pleased him.

"I thought that with the company, he would be too busy for lessons."

"Could be. There's not a quiet corner to be found in the place. Doors opening and slamming shut. Orders thrown about like I had six hands and a like number of legs."

"If anyone asks, tell them I'll wait to be summoned." She did not get the words out easily. "It's likely he'll be too busy to miss me, anyway. And as for the servant problem, see if you can leave word for the Jarmans. If they would like to help out at Windward, I can get by without them easily enough. Tomorrow or for however long Mrs. Harwood's visit lasts."

In the latter, she spoke the truth. Mr. Jarman had been working on rebuilding the shed, but he was almost done. And Mrs. Jarman was likely to wear out the floors and furniture of the cottage with all her scrubbing and polishing.

But Makenna would miss the boy, more than anyone could know. Perhaps it was best to begin the inevitable separation, though she had not planned to do it quite so soon.

Her separation from the Saintjohns lasted no more than an hour. She was seated in the parlor repairing the hem on one of her London dresses when a shadow darkened the portico door. Without knocking, Nicholas strode into the room. As always, he filled it. Even the piano seemed small by comparison.

"What are you doing?" he asked.

She spared him only a quick glance before returning to her sewing. "Do you know you never smile when you see me?"

That stopped him for a second. It wasn't nearly long enough for her to overpower the quivering that started in her belly every time she saw him unexpectedly. Especially when he wore his thundercloud face.

"You're supposed to be teaching my son."

"Your son is too young to handle both the lessons and all the confusion that must be taking place at Windward." She paused a moment. "I spoke to Gibbs this morning when he was on his way into town."

"Ah," he said.

He sat in a facing chair. She noticed he was wearing a coat and cravat and his hair was almost neatly arranged. He ran a hand through it, however, loosened the cravat, and with his coat hanging loosely open, leaned back, one leg bent over the other.

So much for neatness. The sand on his shoes gave evidence he had come to Elysium by way of Carnal Cove. She wondered if he had sneaked out of the house.

The quivering turned to tightness. She stuck herself with the needle. With a yelp she put her fingertip in her mouth.

"I could do that," Nicholas said.

"What, sew?"

"No. Suck your blood."

Tossing the gown aside, she gripped her hands together in her lap and tried to look prim, a formidable task when her insides had melted to jelly from wanting to touch him.

"You sound like a vampire," she said.

"I sound like a man who's been too long away from you."

"I was at Windward yesterday morning."

"It seems longer. Besides, we were interrupted."

Makenna's cheeks burned. "Please, Nicholas,

I'm embarrassed enough knowing what your sister must have thought. The terrible thing is, she was right."

"She was also rude."

The statement surprised her. She had not thought he'd noticed.

"I told her so, too," he added.

She looked at him in dismay. Inevitably she would see Sarah Harwood again. She did not want to face her as an enemy.

"Maybe she had a right. You're her only brother."

"How do you know that?"

She could hardly tell him it was from listening outside his door during Robert Campbell's revealing visit.

"She was very protective of you. It seemed a logical assumption."

It wasn't an outright lie. Makenna was getting good at evasion. She was also good at distraction.

"How is Jonathan getting along with his cousins?"

His features softened. "Surprisingly well. But not so well that he doesn't need you."

"Perhaps he could come here for the lessons."

"Turning coward?"

Yes.

"No. I'm trying to be practical."

He stared at her so long without speaking, she wanted to scream. When he did speak, she was thrown into her own silence and could not say a word.

"Why didn't you tell me about the grave?"

"I didn't think it was important," she said at last.

"Your dog brings you a human bone, you go out to the woods and find a shallow grave and have to send for the constable, yet you don't think it is important?"

"It didn't concern you."

"Everything important to you is important to me."

She had a difficult time not seizing on his words, twisting them into more than they meant. The truth was, he was a man who had begun making love to her and he didn't want to stop. She could not let herself believe that his words meant anything more than that.

She gave up sitting and went to the door, where she could look out at the ocean. Once it had seemed a boundary to her new world. At the moment it looked like a way of escape.

"You haven't told me how you found out."

"When Sarah arrived on the ferry, she heard talk."

"Of course. Did she know any details?"

Makenna could feel a pair of dark eyes on her back.

"Only what I told you. Perhaps you could tell me the details."

For reasons she could not begin to understand, she found herself unwilling to mention things like a broken neck and expensive clothes and a possible reason for the shameful burial. Dr. Beaumont's scientific examination and the ambitious interest of Constable Tobias Bent had already invaded the sanctity of the unknown man's final resting place, which had not proven so final after all.

Somehow she could not blame the dog for the discovery. He was only doing what dogs do.

People probed and people judged and people inflicted hurt on one another, whether or not the hurt was purposeful.

She turned to Nicholas. "The grave was years old. Whoever the man was, he died a long time ago. And yes, the remains were those of a man. Dr. Beaumont measured the. . . ."

She broke off and stared at her hands. In an instant Nicholas was standing close.

"You're surrounded by death, aren't you?" he said.

She knew he was thinking of the letter as well as of the shallow grave.

"Surrounded seems an exaggeration."

"In the music room yesterday I spoke too little of my intentions. I meant to say more, but I was . . . distracted."

She remembered how he'd invaded the music room, sent his son away, and begun to make love to her. *Distracted* seemed an inadequate word for the lust that had consumed them both.

She feared it was about to do so again. Her heart raced.

She stared at his loosely tied cravat. "What a terrible creature I am to keep you from doing what you want to do."

She tried to keep her voice light. But she could not help remembering how Gibbs had called her a Jezebel. He was right and wrong at the same time. Nicholas was attracted to her. Why shouldn't he be? She was willing, she was embarrassingly enthusiastic, and she was convenient.

But Jezebels did not give their hearts for life, something she had done, although no one would ever know.

"As I recall, you said you would be a damnably poor husband and father."

"I also said I would never abandon you. I'm not a man for subtlety, as you've found out. I will take care of you in any way you need."

He was back to the possibility of impregnation. As if that were the only issue of importance between them.

The hurt became unbearable. She slapped him, then stepped back, stunned by what she had done.

His eyes glittered down at her. "No one's ever done that before."

She stared in horror at the imprint of her hand on his cheek. It seemed a symbol of all she was not and everything she was becoming. She wanted to kiss the redness. She wanted to kiss him everywhere her lips could reach.

And touch him everywhere her hands had already been.

Instead, she used her strength to lock her gaze with his.

"I'm no more subtle than you, Nicholas. I will not accept your charity."

"There was more than pride in that slap."

He knew she loved him. He had to know. She slipped away from him and moved to the piano, staring down at the keys, willing her mind to pick out melodies.

Her mind would not obey. She thought only of Nicholas, of the thoughtful look that had suddenly chased the angry glint from his eyes.

"How can you accept my care when you've just lost the man you loved?" he asked.

She bit her tongue to keep from crying out. Ascot Chilton was a milksop, and an unethical one at that. And as for Captain Nicholas Saintjohn, he—

Firm hands took her by the shoulders and turned her. Demanding lips came down on hers. Iron arms embraced her and she fell into the most thorough kiss she had ever received. Lips and tongue, heat and moisture, the taste of wildness that was as much a part of Nicholas as the turbulence that stormed beneath the surface of his self-control.

Occasionally the turbulence broke through. It broke through now. She felt it in her own racing blood. She moaned into his open mouth. He moaned into hers. It took a strength beyond all measurement to break the kiss, to push him away, to listen to the blending of their separate ragged breaths without throwing herself at him once again.

"We're like animals," she said without looking up.

"Is that a bad thing?"

"I don't know."

He did not speak right away. The silence that fell between them struck like pinpricks on her skin, a million tiny stabs of regret and longing. Could he not hear her quiet cry of pain? Could he not hear the breaking of her heart?

He stepped away. She expected him to mention an unborn infant, his noble offer, her unreasonable response. But he surprised her.

"We'll expect you at Windward House at the usual time tomorrow. Do this for Jonathan, if not for me."

It was a cruel and undeniable request. He neither expected nor received a protest. After he had let himself out through the portico door, she went outside and watched his long legs take him down the winding path to the beach, his coat flapping, his hair ruffled by the wind. Without looking back, he strode along the hard-packed sand close to the water, all the way across the cove, past the rickety pier, to the harsh cliff and a second path that took him to his home.

Incredibly, she almost smiled. Whatever Nicholas really was—arrogant, demanding, villainous in ways she could scarcely consider—he was no milksop. She admitted an ultimate weakness: She wouldn't change him if she could.

"Jonathan!"

The name rang out in a childish voice outside the music room door. A second voice chimed in, sounding much like the first. The boy's name became a chant.

Jonathan's lips flattened. "Girls," he muttered in disgust.

Makenna thought of the two fair-haired, blue-eyed moppets who had waved to her from a high, open window as she walked up to Windward House. Their giggles had drifted down like sunlight. She returned the waves, but a sharp voice had already ordered them away from the window.

Two hours later they were knocking at the door.

The object of their pursuit scowled, and his hands came down with an uncharacteristic crash onto the keys.

"Darlings," their mother's voice trilled. "Let's not disturb your cousin."

Too late. The lesson was effectively ended; the time had come anyway for Makenna to leave. She had hoped to get away without adult observation. The hope dimmed.

She brushed a lock of hair from Jonathan's brow, then dropped her hand as if she were burned. What was she thinking of?

The boy showed no sign he disapproved of her touch.

"We ought to let them in," she said. "What are their names, by the way?"

"Charity and Grace."

"Sweet names."

"They're pests."

"They like you, otherwise they wouldn't be calling for you. I guess it's because you're older and know more."

"I can do more, too. They don't know how to hold a hammer."

He made it sound like the ultimate disgrace.

The door opened, and two girls in frilly pink skipped into the room, followed by their mother. Behind them in the hallway a middle-aged woman in black stood with hands at her waist. Unlike the others, she remained in the hall.

"It was so quiet in here, we wondered if you had gone," Sarah Harwood said.

This morning she was dressed in a more subdued gown of pale yellow silk. It brought out the brilliance of her eyes. Dark, watchful eyes, far too much like her brother's.

Makenna stood away from the piano bench. "We were just finishing."

She walked to the table holding her bonnet. She was wearing her plainest gray, her hair in its severest bun. She even wore gloves. No one was going to say she did not look respectable in public, no matter what her private behavior might be.

"Please, Miss Lindsay, don't leave so soon." Sarah looked at her nephew. "Why don't you take the girls outside? Your father is working at the back of the house, and I'm certain he would welcome company. Miss Reynolds can go with you." She looked at Makenna and mouthed *the nanny*.

Reluctantly Jonathan got up from the piano bench and walked toward the door. Makenna suspected the reluctance was a little feigned. Here was a chance to show his pesky cousins a few of his carpentry skills.

As to whether his father would welcome the help was another matter. She felt rather sorry for the nanny. Accompanying three active youngsters to the back of the house was not something she would want to do.

The women had been alone for only a minute when Mrs. Loddington came in with a tray.

"I thought we might have tea in here, if that's all right," Sarah said. "I haven't had a chance to air out any of the rooms. Goodness, Nicholas kept this place as closed as a mausoleum. Very little is fit for human habitation. Thank you for sending the Jarmans to us. They're upstairs somewhere opening doors."

She leaned closer and spoke in a lower voice. "She does talk a bit, doesn't she? But she's a frightfully good worker. The husband, too. What a contrast he is. He rarely says a word."

"They've both been very good to me," Makenna said, unwilling to hear any criticism of the couple.

She would rather have driven spikes under her fingernails than share tea with the young woman. She also saw the wisdom in getting the confrontation with Nicholas's sister over and done. Taking a chair, she watched as Sarah took her place beside her and gestured for the housekeeper to set the tray on the table between them.

"Sugar? Milk? I'm afraid there's no lemon in the house. Gibbs swore he could not find a single one in the village."

Makenna even felt like defending Gibbs, something she had thought never to do.

"Plain will be fine."

Sarah poured, added three lumps of sugar to her cup, and settled back.

"Please accept my apology for yesterday."

Makenna almost dropped her cup. "Whatever for?"

"You know what for. I was abominably rude. But I had come to provide my brother with female companionship, only to find he'd already taken care of it for himself. Oh, dear, that came out wrong. Francis says it's a good thing my foot is small, since it finds itself so often in my mouth."

"I am Jonathan's music and art teacher, Mrs. Harwood."

"Call me Sarah. Otherwise you sound like one of the servants, and Nicholas has told me you are far from that."

Makenna took a sip of tea. "Has he?"

"Yes, you're Jonathan's friend. In the little time

I've been around him, I can see your influence. He was a very unhappy little boy when he left Liverpool. I always tried to . . . well, we won't go into my feeble attempts at being an aunt while his mother was still alive. And then came the fire. We certainly won't go into that."

Questions screamed in Makenna's head. The cup rattled in its saucer. She set it aside.

"I care for Jonathan very much." She let herself say that much.

"And his father?"

Makenna stood. "I really must go."

"I'm hopeless. Please sit down. It's just that I love my brother madly. I wish he would get over that nonsense about being responsible for three deaths. I'm certain he wasn't, and even if he was, it's time he forgave himself."

Makenna could hardly believe what she heard. Three people had met a horrible death. Perhaps the arsonist had misunderstood what his former captain had said to him, had assumed a request that was never given. If they'd talked at all. But she couldn't forget who had died. It mattered not that Rebecca Saintjohn had taken a lover. She had been Jonathan's mother. For that alone, she deserved respect and grief.

"This is none of my business," she said. "You really should not be talking to me about it." She did not add that she wasn't even supposed to know about the fire and resultant deaths, or anything else about Nicholas's troubles. In truth, she knew more about his past than she did her own.

"All right," Sarah said with aplomb. "Please do sit and tell me about the bones."

The request came without warning. Makenna surprised herself by doing what was asked, telling Sarah far more than she had told Nicholas. His sister somehow managed to get her way as much as he did, but using a far different technique.

She heard herself telling Sarah pretty much all that she knew, ending with the speculation concerning the cause of death.

"Murder," Sarah whispered, eyes bright and wide.

"Unproven."

"Oh, I'm certain it was murder. Murder makes the story far too delectable to be wrong." She sat back in the chair. "What did you say the initials were? RD?"

"Yes, they were on the handkerchief."

Sarah tapped a polished nail against her teeth. "It couldn't be. But, yes, it could." She shot Makenna a smile of triumph. "We must send Gibbs for the constable. I've got valuable evidence he must hear right away. I won't say another word until he gets here. I know you don't believe that's possible, but you'll find that when I'm properly motivated, I can be as stubborn as my brother any day."

Chapter Sixteen

"Richard Danvers."

Sarah made the announcement as one might herald the name of a new heir to the throne, needing only trumpets to make the scene complete.

She was standing in front of the library fireplace beneath the Turner seascape, addressing an audience that consisted of Dr. Beaumont, Constable Tobias Bent, Makenna, and, of course, her enigmatic brother, who kept looking at Makenna instead of at his very proud sister.

Makenna had wanted to include Biddy Merton in the gathering, but knew she would not agree to come.

"Richard Danvers," Sarah repeated, as if she had not been heard the first time. Everyone but

Nicholas stared blankly back at her. He was busy noting Makenna's reaction.

Sarah frowned. "I guess no one remembers him. But you ought to, Nicholas. Mama told me about him ages ago. She surely told you as well."

"You're the family historian, Sarah."

"I've had to be. You were always at sea. You can't use that as an excuse for everything, you know." She did not pause to see if she gave offense. "I never met the man, of course. He died long before I was born. At least he went missing, and everyone assumed he had met with a terrible end. Which, as it turns out, he had."

She talked fast. Bent gave up on trying to scribble in his notebook.

"What can you tell us about this Richard Danvers?" he said, then sniffed as if he had asked something very important, something no one else had thought of.

Sarah smiled gratefully at him.

"He was not really a part of the family, though his parents and ours have been friends for ages. He was something of a rake, I gathered from what Mama said, and was estranged from just about everyone."

Dr. Beaumont spoke up. "The initials match, true enough. Is there any other reason for thinking our victim is whom you say?"

"A very good reason. He came to Windward House I don't know how many decades ago and"—

her voice lowered dramatically—"was never heard from again."

Bent returned to writing furiously.

"Surely the family investigated the disappearance," Dr. Beaumont said.

"That's the best part. They didn't. He had been involved in some kind of scandal, which wasn't unusual for him. This time, however, apparently a respectable woman was involved. Not his usual sort. He wrote his mother saying he was going to take care of things. That's what Mama said he wrote. Take care of things."

She made the words sound ominous.

"Sarah," Nicholas said, "do you have any idea what you're talking about?"

Dear Nicholas, Makenna thought. It was exactly what she would expect him to say. It also happened to be what she was thinking.

Sarah was not subdued.

"I shall write Mama. And write Mrs. Danvers. She's still alive, and the two of them correspond quite frequently. The supposition at the time was that he took care of things by disappearing. It was so like him to shirk responsibility."

Nicholas did not let up. "For what was he responsible?"

"The ruination of a virgin."

That brought raised eyebrows on the part of the doctor and the constable. Nicholas knew his sister too well to be shocked. Makenna might have been so had she not spent an hour with the young woman in the music room.

Nicholas was merciless. "Since you've identified the victim, as Dr. Beaumont calls him, perhaps you can put a name to the virgin as well."

"Nicholas, you know I can't. Maybe she was already on the island when he arrived. That's why he came here. It had to be. It all makes sense." She looked at Makenna. "She could have stayed at Elysium. Mama always said there was something strange about the place. I was surprised when Nicholas said his son's teacher was living there. I thought it would take someone rather strange to live there. But after I met you, of course, and we had a chance to talk, I knew I was wrong."

Wrong about what, Makenna had no idea. By the end of Sarah's oration, she had already quit listening. She stopped after *She could have stayed at Elysium.*

She thought only of her ghost.

Talk went on around her, but it faded until the words blurred into one another, like watery paint on a canvas, leaving behind no distinct impression, nothing meaningful.

She could have stayed at Elysium.

Makenna looked around at the people in the library, seeing them but not hearing what they said: proud Sarah claiming a solution to the mystery of the bones, Dr. Beaumont with his scientific measurements, Tobias Bent with his ambition. And Nicholas, who had so recently offered a loveless union if she were with child. That was what she had assumed he meant. He was being noble, willing to sacrifice his freedom for her.

But he had his own terrible past to contend with, though his sister had tried to make it sound inconsequential.

Makenna had her sobbing ghost. And now Richard Danvers. And more—the deed that came from nowhere, Biddy Merton's mysteries, Jenna Lindsay's lies. They had to be linked together. But how? The room itself faded as the voices had done. She grew cold. Pinpricks of fright crept across her skin. A dozen questions pounded like hammers in her brain.

Someone was shouting. She blinked and saw Nicholas standing over her. She saw him clearly, the tight lips and sharp cheeks, the thick brows over worried eyes, the shock of hair that never could remain in place.

"Makenna, what's wrong? You're pale as a ghost."

He wasn't shouting, he was talking softly. He knelt in front of her and took her clenched hands in his.

"I told you," he said in a voice only she could hear, "I will take care of you."

It was too much. With a cry she jumped to her feet. Her chair fell over backward with a crash.

"You must listen to me, Nicholas. I am not expecting your child." She made no attempt to keep her voice low, though she looked only at him. "And if I were, it wouldn't make any difference. Can't you understand?"

With a sob, she ran from the room. Behind her she heard Sarah call out, "Leave her be, Nicholas. For God's sake, leave her be."

She flew down the stairs. In the front doorway she met Jonathan and the two girls, behind them the nanny.

The boy's eyes widened as he looked up at her. "Is something wrong?" he asked.

She fought for control, even managing a smile. "Nothing is wrong, I promise. I've just got a bit of a headache. You go on about your play."

She touched his small shoulder as if for the last time, then threw herself down the road that led to Elysium. But she did not stop at the cottage. Instead, she hurried on to the path leading to the ancient cemetery, bypassing the now empty open grave, through the woods and across the field, not stopping until she was in the midst of the second copse, at the center of which lay the house of Biddy Merton.

But the woman was nowhere in sight. She did not respond to Makenna's frantic calls. Only the black cat was present to greet her. The animal blinked from its perch on the bench beside the small cottage but did not otherwise move.

Makenna rubbed her arms. She could feel someone watching from the surrounding trees.

"Biddy!" she called out, but heard only the wind in the leaves.

The trees moved in on her. She blinked but could still feel their encroachment. Her heart pounded in her throat. She must be insane to feel such a thing. And why shouldn't she be? Nothing in her world made sense.

She backed away from the clearing, then turned around, forcing her legs to carry her back to the cemetery and on to the high main road. By the time she was there, she had grown calm and her pace had slowed. She must act with deliberation. She could not let hysteria take control of her again.

The dog came from the direction of Elysium, barking and jumping about as if he wanted her to follow him. He had behaved the same way the night he brought her his prized bone. The night he guided her to the open grave.

She shivered, but she followed him, to the almost finished shed, to the vicar's carriage sitting in her private lane. Why it appeared ominous, she did not know. What she did know was that whatever had brought Reverend Coggshall from town, it was not to deliver good news.

When she went inside the gate, the dog darted past her and stopped at the back door, panting impatiently for her to let him in. With growing dread, she did so, continuing to follow him through the kitchen and into the parlor, stopping at the front door. She opened it to find two men standing with their backs to her, staring down at the cove. They turned, and she stared at them woodenly, unable to feel, unable to speak.

She did not glance at the vicar. It was the second man who claimed her attention. He was dressed as the London gentleman he was, hat and gloves in hand, his fair hair carefully combed, his pale eyes warmer than she had ever seen them, even in moments of what he called passion.

"Makenna, my love," he said in his soft, carefully modulated voice.

"Ascot," she said barely above a whisper. "What are you doing here?"

He opened the door and stepped inside, forcing her to back up. The vicar kept a discreet distance on the portico, his attention returned to the cove.

The ecclesiastical coward.

"I could stay away no longer," Chilton said.

She closed her eyes for a second, disbelieving.

"You should have tried harder," she said.

"I should have come to my senses sooner. My cousin . . . it was a stupid and momentary madness. She is no longer a part of my life."

"She left."

"She saw the futility of continuing a relationship when my affections were engaged elsewhere."

Makenna could translate his words readily enough. The wealthy and beautiful woman had grown tired of financing Ascot's ventures as a purveyor of art and had gone on to more enticing and profitable pursuits.

And more passionate lovers, which, Makenna

now knew, should not be difficult to find.

Chilton ought to have seen the coolness with which she listened to him. But he had never been a sensitive man, though she had once thought him so.

"I have no right to ask your forgiveness, but I do." He walked closer. This time she held her ground. "Let me touch you, my darling Makenna. I have dreamed of kissing you once again."

The slamming of the kitchen door interrupted her response. Elysium had another visitor.

Ascot Chilton stared beyond her and she slowly turned, knowing already the identity of this newest arrival. No one came into a room quite like Nicholas. Without saying a word, or even making a sound, he thundered as he walked.

He chose to speak.

"Put the man out of his misery, Makenna. Can he kiss you or not?"

She opened her mouth but no words came out.

Coming into the parlor from outside, the vicar added his presence to the crowded scene. Perhaps he wished to offer a benediction over what was likely to become a fray.

The dog had the good sense to duck beneath a chair, abandoning his mistress to this latest twist of fate.

"I thought he was dead."

Makenna sat in the parlor doing her best to avoid Nicholas's hard gaze. He stood in front of the hearth, against which she had propped her mother's damaged portrait. He contrasted sharply with Jenna Lindsay's serenity.

"You assumed he had died," Makenna said.

"You let me believe it."

"I have a difficult time changing your mind about anything."

"You should have ordered him off the island."

"By what authority? I told him to stay at the inn in town, that we would talk later. Given the circumstances, and the witnesses, it was the best I could do."

She had thought her composure and quick thinking a miracle. Apparently Nicholas did not agree.

"What do you plan to talk about?"

He went too far. Anger flared.

"None of your business." She flew to her feet. "You leave, too. I do not want you here."

But he stood in place, as unmoving as the rock fireplace behind him.

"What was in the letter? If not his death, what?"

She backed away. "None of your business."

"You haven't been the same since it arrived."

And she would never be the same again. The words caught in her throat. A feeling of desolation swept over her. It was a sensation with which she was becoming far too familiar. It was a condition she had to keep to herself.

"However I am is equally none of your business."

He was not so easily rebuffed.

"And what was that all about in the library? You left me with an hysterical sister on my hands and some very pointed stares."

"You provoked me."

"I'd like to do more than that."

Whatever he was implying, she ignored it.

"I have faith you can handle anything," she said. "My only criticism is that you don't know when to leave."

"You've got more criticisms than that. I'm rude, a terrible father, I keep too much to myself. I'm sure there are other problems. Oh, yes, I don't know what the devil is going on with you."

"You are not a terrible father. I'll give you that. You're just inexperienced."

"Ah, but everything else was right on the money." His eyes glinted. "You haven't mentioned what kind of lover I am. How do Chilton and I compare?"

She shook her head in disgust. "Is that what is really bothering you? I'll have to give it some thought."

He grabbed her by the shoulders and brought his lips harshly down on hers. This time she did not collapse. Instead, she fought him, and he was the one to back away.

"You can be incredibly cruel." To her disgust she began to cry. "I forgot to say that."

He brushed away a tear with his thumb.

"Makenna," he began. She heard regret in his

voice, and tenderness. She could bear neither one.

She hurried from him into the bedroom, threw open the door to the wardrobe, and grabbed the letter off the top shelf. Slamming the door closed, she turned to see him standing behind her.

"Here," she said, thrusting the letter into his hands. "I wrote my solicitors asking them to trace the history of the deed to the cottage. And my own history as well, though that was not stressed as much. They took the matter further than I had intended. They turned up things I did not want to know."

All energy fled. She felt as if she had bared her soul. Sitting heavily on the bed, she stared out the window, unable to watch him as he read. He made quick work of the letter, then moved beside her. She spoke before he could.

"As you can see, I do not know who I am. Everything my mother told me was a lie."

She felt too much a victim, sitting on the bed with him staring down at her. A victim, like the late and unlamented Richard Danvers.

She stood and walked away from him, standing at the window, throwing it open and letting in the fresh breeze.

"You might as well know everything. When your brother-in-law came to see you, I listened outside in the hall. I know how your wife died. I know about the accusations against you. When you stepped into the hallway to watch him leave, I was standing in the shadows. I saw your pain."

A stillness settled over him that was louder than a shout. Emotions trembled inside him, emotions she did not want to name. She had feared receiving his pity. But it was not pity that turned his features to stone.

"You came to me that night," he said. "Do you like men with blood on their hands, Makenna? Is that what brought you there to offer yourself to me? Or were you performing an act of charity, relieving the pain you thought you saw?"

How could he say such terrible things? He was so close to the truth, yet as far away as the moon.

I came because I loved you.

She shuttered her feelings. "You'll have to figure that out for yourself."

As she stared at him, she knew this would be the last time they faced each other like this, each hurting the other, each needing what the other had to give. She saw in that instant that he loved her as she loved him. He could not say the things he did, could not accuse her and hold her and come to her when they both knew he should stay away . . . he could do none of those things without the force of love driving him on.

Love was the only thing that could make sense of it all. The certainty ought to burn away her despair. She should be shouting with joy, wrapping him in her arms and telling him he did not need to fight her, did not need to push her away.

But she also realized something else. He could not admit that love. Whatever had happened in his past made him build a fortress around his heart. Love was a weakness rendering him vulnerable to further pain, or so he would think. That first evening on the beach, when he'd approached her with inexplicable anger, he had seen what might develop between the two of them, long before she saw it.

It sounded impossible, yet she knew it was true. Such a thing could have happened only at Carnal Cove. It was that kind of place, mystical in more ways than just because it had a ghost.

An expression of joy would not do, not now. He couldn't accept it. He was being too hard, too cynical.

But there was something else she could offer. Something he was too lost in his feelings for her to turn down.

She took the letter from him and set it aside.

"You now know the worst about me. I'm hurting, Nicholas, as much as you. Please, make the pain go away."

Chapter Seventeen

"Where are you hurting?"

My heart. My soul.

"You know where, Nicholas."

He touched her breast.

"Here?"

She nodded. He was close to her heart.

He took her hand and pressed it against his chest, where she could feel the manic beating of his own heart. It pounded in time with hers.

Their bodies pulsed together in other ways. She did not want talk. She didn't even want to look at him. She wanted their separate bodies to blend so that for a little while they were one.

She wished it were night and not bright day. She got lost more easily in the dark. In the darkness

Nicholas was at home. It was his element. She needed to be part of whatever was his.

Tugging her hand free, she undressed. He sensed her urgency, for he did the same. This was the last time, and he had to know it, too. His eyes locked with hers, he pulled the pins from her hair and ran his fingers through the long strands. It was a simple act and as sensuous as anything he might have done.

It took great strength to stand before him without collapsing against his chest. He pulled her to him and ran his hand down her side, along the length of her trembling thigh, reached his hand beneath her knee and eased her leg upward. She felt his erection against her abdomen. How easily he could slip inside; he had to lift her only a little and they would mate.

But that would be too soon. She needed to know him every way that she could, on this, their last time together.

Touching would not be enough. She needed to taste him as well, to listen to his breathing, to hear the groans that caught in his throat. All her senses must be involved if she were to carry complete memories of him through the years.

Except the sense of sight. Already she could draw every plane, every curve of muscle on his body, the public places the world could see and the private ones as well, the intimate parts that made him a man.

She kissed the hollows of his cheeks, his eyes,

his lips, pressed her tongue against the pulsing in his throat. The beat was manic still. Because he loved her. Because what they did went beyond a physical act.

She pushed his arms, his hands, away from her body and eased her way down his chest, circling his nipples with her tongue, then lower, her lips sensing the tightening of his stomach, until she was kneeling in front of him.

"Makenna," he whispered, and she thrilled to the husky sound of her name.

She gave him the ultimate demonstration of her love, taking his sex between her lips, licking a drop of moisture off the tip. She could hear his ragged breathing as the pressure of her mouth grew firmer, as she became more confident in what she did.

Harder, deeper, her own breath ragged with the knowledge of what she brought him, her own heart beating in a frenzied rhythm within her breast, she lost herself to space and time, she lost herself to the world and knew only him.

With a gasp, he pulled free and knelt in front of her. Her head reeled from the suddenness of the move. His lips took possession of one breast, and then the other. His tongue was rough against the tender tips. With his usual graceful and purposeful movements, he lifted her to the bed and loved her as she had loved him, lips and tongue and hands involved until they were a tangle of arms and legs and she knew not where their separate bodies began or ended.

When at last he eased inside her, she was surprised at the gentleness of his moves. But not by the fullness of him, or the way he made her feel complete.

The thrusts were slow, as if he would milk every ounce of pleasure from the mating. She felt the heat build in them both, the quickening tremors burning her blood, obliterating all thought, taking her to a place where only the two of them existed, a place where there were no troubles, a paradise free of pain.

She drew pleasure from the thought—when she could manage to think—that she took him to that same paradise.

Afterwards, when the tight spirals of rapture had finally unwound, for him as well as for her, she held him for longer than was wise, but never, never as long as she wished. No such time existed in the world.

Her breathing slowed, as did her heartbeat, and the anguish of reality returned.

She sensed he wanted to talk. She knew him far too well. She would have preferred he take her by surprise. But she knew what he wanted to say, words of sympathy for her lost past, assurances of his care and protection, even—the horror of the idea cut into her heart—an expression of gratitude for what she had done in this ritual of making love.

She pretended to sleep. Whether or not he believed her pretense, he contented himself with stroking her hair. He eased from the bed, and she listened as he dressed. He leaned close, lifted her hair to kiss her cheek, and whispered in her ear.

"Later, Makenna, we will talk. You cannot run from me forever."

The part about talking later was, she thought, close to what she had told Ascot Chilton. She wondered if Nicholas realized it as well.

After he had gone, she heard the dog patter into the room and curl into a ball on the rug next to the bed. As if he would protect her. As if he were an attack dog.

It was his illusion. She envied him. Her own illusions had died.

A storm blew in at sunset, lashing at the cove in unrestrained fury, the wind and solid rain so intense, water seeped in under the portico door and around the front window. She spent the hours keeping the cottage dry and soothing her terrified protector dog.

The next morning dawned bright, the sky scrubbed into a brilliant blue, the sunlight gleaming off the water like a sprinkling of diamonds. Feeling frisky, the dog barked to be let outside. She put him in the backyard, where he promptly rolled in the puddles and mud.

She found herself laughing at him and envying his unrestrained joy.

"Now there's a sound to warm the heart."

Makenna looked from the dog to the back gate, where Mrs. Jarman stood. As kindly and well-intentioned as the woman was, the sight of her stilled the laughter.

"Aren't you going to Windward House?" Makenna asked, spying Mr. Jarman standing behind his wife.

"We are, if you can spare us. There's work enough to do, and you know yourself we're not people to shrug work. But we wanted to know if you made it through the storm all right. There's trees down in the village, and a roof or two gone. We've not had winds like that in a long while."

"I'm fine," Makenna said. "It's the dog you should worry about."

"Now don't you be letting him track that mud into the cottage. I'll be forever getting it clean."

"Don't worry. I'll protect your floors. But there's something you can do for me. If you see the captain or his sister, say I won't be coming up to the house for lessons."

Mrs. Jarman nodded as if she understood what Makenna truly meant. Perhaps she did.

"For how long will you stay away?"

Forever.

"For a while. I'll let the captain know."

"It's the boy who'll be disappointed. I heard him showing the girls—Charity and Grace, that is, a pair of charmers if I ever saw any—he was showing them what you taught him on the piano." She smiled. "And he didn't stop there. Quite lordly he was, trying to get them to hold a drawing pen the way it ought to be held. But gentle, the way you must be with him."

Makenna pictured the scene. "Oh," she said a little breathlessly. "How nice."

She must be a terrible person to let such pleasantness break her heart.

"I almost forgot," Mrs. Jarman said. "What with the laughter and all, the main reason we stopped by slipped my mind, though it's always good to see you, understand." She thrust out a covered dish wrapped in cloth. "You won't be eating proper, with the two of us working for the captain. And that sister of his." She rolled her eyes. "She seems a flighty thing, if you take no offense at my saying so, but she knows what she wants."

"Mrs. Jarman," her husband said with a familiar warning in his voice.

"She's kindly, too. There's no harm in her," Mrs. Jarman said. "Now you take this and see that you eat every bite."

Mr. Jarman took the dish, tromped through the mud, and put it in Makenna's hands. But he did not let go right away. She looked up to see his coarse features softened by the warmth in his eyes.

"You take care, Miss Lindsay. Without children of our own, I'd say you're like a daughter, but that'd be speaking above my station."

He left before she could respond, and she stared

Evelyn Rogers

at the closing gate. Never in her life had she heard more kindly words. She needed them more than he could ever know.

Setting the food inside, she led the dog around the cottage and, stopping on the portico to gather up the drawing supplies she had left there, along with a tarp she had found in the shed, she wound her way through the damp sand of the dunes to the cove. She didn't stop until she neared the rickety pier.

The night's storm had whipped the ocean into a frenzy. She had never seen the waves so high, frothing and foaming as they broke and crashed against the beach. Normally the steps leading to the pier began a half dozen feet in front of the water's edge. Even at high tide she could reach them without getting her shoes wet.

On this day she would have had to slog through two feet of surf to reach the pier.

Spreading the tarp on the sand, she set out her supplies, then took a stick she had found along the way and, with a cry of "Fetch it," tossed it into the water.

To her surprise, the dog did just that; she continued the game, never throwing the stick very far into the surf, until he was free of mud and ready for a rest.

And she was ready to begin her task.

With the dog snuggled into a shallow trench he'd dug in the wet sand nearby, she settled herself onto the tarp and began to draw. She felt eyes on her, but it was a sensation she had experienced before. She did not look around. The pen moved quickly over the sketch paper as she re-created the shore, the pier, the sky, and last of all, the ghost.

Unable to leave the work alone, she added shading and details such as shells on the sand, and a bird flying overhead.

Birds did not frequent the cove, and more than once she had wondered why. But occasionally a brave gull or cormorant ventured close, and it was from the memory of one such time that she added a lone gull flying high in the sky over the water.

Eventually she had to call the drawing done. But one more task awaited her. She removed her shoes and stockings and set them aside at the edge of the tarp. Hiking her skirt to her waist, ignoring the roar of the waves, she walked into the water toward the pier, took a cautious step up the unstable ladder, and then another, stopping when she could place the drawing on the pier itself, weighing it down with rocks she had put among her art supplies.

Then she backed away to safety on the solid beach, the damp bottom half of her skirt trailing in the sand.

"Okay, whoever you are, remove yourself from the drawing if you will. Show me you are still there."

The breeze off the water blew stronger, whipping her loose hair, almost causing her to lose her balance, it came at her so suddenly.

But she held her ground.

"I am not so easily frightened anymore," she said, raising her voice as if the ghost needed to hear her above the wind.

The dog lifted his head, blinked curiously at her, then went back to his dreams.

"Who are you?" she called out. "Why do you show yourself to me?"

She heard only the whistle of the wind and the crash of waves on the shore.

"Who was Richard Danvers to you?"

She hadn't thought to ask the question, but it came from somewhere deep inside her, the same place that saw a link between all the events that had happened since she'd arrived at Carnal Cove.

On a morning begun with quiet determination, desperation and despair had found their way inside her and taken control. Here on this isolated beach, she was stranded in a universe that had no boundaries, yet seemed to squeeze in on her until she could not breathe.

"Was he your lover?" she cried. "Did he ruin you? Did he come here to destroy you? Did you destroy him first?"

She threw the questions into the wind, against the brilliant sun, each one louder, more frantic, than the last. The vastness of the water and of the air swallowed them, muting their shrillness until she knew no one could hear them who was more than a few feet away.

Nicholas could not hear them.

And neither, she feared, could the ghost.

Turning, she looked about her at the cottage huddled at the top of the sand dunes, at the curve of the hill that led to the rocky cliff on the north, at the dark and massive structure that was Windward House. She turned again and again, whirling, listening for answers, searching for something or someone that was not there.

Exhausted, head reeling, she fell to the beach, covered her face with her hands, and wept. She had not meant to lose control this way. She had not known that hysteria lurked within her.

But then, of course, she no longer recognized herself as the practical, reserved woman who had come to the island such a short while ago.

That woman had known her name, her past, and, she had foolishly thought, her future. As she was now, Makenna knew nothing, her life both past and present as blank as an unused page in her sketch pad.

At last the tears ended. From her kneeling position, she looked at the water.

"Can't you give me some kind of sign as to the truth?" She spoke barely above a whisper. "I can take anything except ignorance."

Words caught in her throat. She forced herself to go on.

"It's all right if I'm imagining some kind of connection to you, or a connection between you and the man in the unmarked grave. The thing is, I need to know the way things are. The way they were. And God help me, the way they are going to be."

To her own ears she sounded pitiful, her desperation so intense it ought to have drawn answers from the empty shells on the sand. But she heard nothing except the wind and the water and the cry of a gull that looked curiously like the one she had put in her sketch.

Slowly she stood. The dizziness was gone but the exhaustion remained. Putting on her stockings and shoes, she shook the damp sand from her skirt as best she could. She was wearing the darkest, drabbest of her clothes this week. The blue gown, and others sewn for her by Mrs. Bent, were thrust to the back of the wardrobe, where they would remain for a long while.

Wrapping the supplies in the tarp, she led the dog back to the cottage, where she bathed and dressed in another heavy gray gown, throwing her soiled clothes over the line at the back of the house. Remembering the kindness of the Jarmans, she forced herself to eat. She put the leftovers outside for the dog to finish.

He was suitably grateful. She gave him a hug. On this day alone he had earned a new name.

She spent the afternoon puttering about the cottage, playing the piano, even working on a composition she had begun a few weeks ago. But the notes sounded flat, the melody harsh to the ear, and she realized she was waiting for Nicholas to visit her. She was glad he did not, yet she listened for the slam of the back door that announced him and him alone.

She even wondered if Ascot Chilton might call. Perhaps last night's storm had frightened him away. Or it could be that the vicar, having read her reactions correctly, had convinced him to give her more time before approaching her again.

Whatever the truth, she was glad Ascot was not present. Yet she listened for the slamming of the door.

In the late afternoon she heard the call of her name. But the voice was not that of Nicholas, or anyone else she could identify. It sounded too earthly to be her ghost; besides, her ghost did nothing but cry.

She walked out onto the portico. On the hillside to her left, Biddy Merton stood in the wild grass that grew in the dunes and waved. She had never seen the woman so close to the water. She had never seen her on the cove side of the main road.

Her heart pounded. "What's wrong?" she called out. Something had to be.

Biddy Merton gestured toward the beach. Makenna stared down to where she pointed. A small figure crouched at the water's edge, his head bent. Makenna's eyes were good. She could make out the sketch pad in his hand and, too, the pencil with which he drew.

Jonathan was doing what she had done so many times, sketching the water and the waves that hit against the beach. He was alone. The world was large and he was so very small. A cry caught in her throat.

"Jonathan!" she cried out, but the wind caught her words and tossed them back at her.

The dog appeared beside her, hackles raised. Makenna turned cold. The hour was too early for the ghost. The sun had not dropped completely behind the hills. The moon had yet to rise.

The dog growled the instant Jonathan set the drawing pad aside, as if he saw what was to come. The boy stood. The wind whipped at his coat and trousers and blew his hat from his head. Makenna watched in horror as he took a step toward the water, toward the rickety steps of the pier.

Already the dying waves were lapping at his shoes.

But he did not stop.

With a scream she hurtled down the hill.

Chapter Eighteen

"Jonathan!"

Makenna's scream did not stop the boy. He stepped farther into the water, as if in a trance, as if the pier were the most important thing in the world to him. A cresting wave, far higher than the others, shook the already unstable ladder and swept around him, grasping him about the waist before letting go and tumbling on toward the shore.

Swayed by the force of the water, Jonathan trudged onward and slowly climbed onto the first step. He grabbed the slanted, broken wood to take the second and third.

In horror she watched as he pulled himself onto the pier itself, stopping on bended knee in front of the drawing she had left there hours ago. He picked it up, studied it for a moment, then, with the paper in his small hand, took another step forward.

"Jonathan, no!"

But her cry was lost in the wind.

Losing all sense, she stumbled across the sand, but the dog reached the water's edge first and plunged into the pounding surf.

Too late. At the same instant a powerful wave shook the pier, the wind caught the drawing and whipped it from the boy's hand. Grabbing for it, he fell headlong into the turbulent water. Another wave caught him, and he disappeared beneath a swirl of foam.

Makenna threw herself into the water, past the steps, her gaze pinned to the place where he had fallen. The ocean floor dropped far more suddenly than she had realized. Her heavy gown pulled her down, her heavy shoes slowed her until she could barely move, but on she fought, diving beneath the surface, blinded by the sting of salt water, shocked by the cold.

The seconds stretched to eternity before she felt the boy's coat between her fingers. She grabbed tightly, dimly aware of the dog close beside her. She swallowed brine and knew Jonathan was doing the same.

Her feet found the sandy bottom a fathom beneath the surface of the storm-swollen waters. The weight of her clothing overcame the natural buoyancy that might have lifted her toward the surface, and she struggled toward what she prayed was the shore. But she could not be sure. No light pierced the darkness of the deep.

Think, she told herself. *Stay calm.* She felt herself, the boy, the dog, all of them trapped in an undercurrent, and she lost what little control she had.

Lungs threatening to burst, she flailed against the tide, dimly aware of strong arms enveloping her and the boy, arms that pulled and tugged and dragged them through their swirling prison, into the shallow, dying waves, onto the dark, wet sand of Carnal Cove.

On hands and knees, she coughed the brine from her lungs, too stunned to feel relief, to feel joy.

Beside her, Nicholas worked over his son. The boy lay on his stomach, pale face turned toward her, eyes closed, while his father crouched astride him, his powerful hands pushing against the slender back. She struggled to his side, desperate to help, but there was nothing she could do except pray and cry. Her heart ceased to beat. She could not draw a breath of precious air.

A trickle of water ran from Jonathan's open mouth, and then another. Frantically, Nicholas turned him over on his back and covered his mouth with his own, blowing air into the boy's lungs, breathing for him when he could not breathe for himself.

Time stopped and all sound faded. And then the boy coughed. Nicholas lifted his head and watched as Jonathan spat up more sea water, then after an eternity began to breathe on his own. Cradling the boy against his chest, he bowed his head and wept.

Stirring, Jonathan tugged at his father's shirt. "Don't cry, Papa. Please, don't cry." His voice was low, barely above a whisper. He said more, but he spoke into his father's ear and Makenna could not hear the words.

"Nicholas!"

A woman's cry echoed over the wind. Tearing her eyes from the father and son, Makenna looked over her shoulder to see Sarah running toward them, her shadow long and narrow, skipping along the water's edge in the dying light of day. Behind her, his limp slowing his progress, Gibbs struggled across the storm-dampened sand.

Their approach pulled Nicholas from his state of shock, and he stared, not at his sister or the old sailor, but at Makenna.

"I couldn't lose him this way," he said, his voice hollow as if it came from a long way off. And then to the crashing waves: "This godless ocean could not claim another victim. Not on my watch. Not my son."

The words seemed wrenched from his soul.

Kneeling beside him, Makenna wanted to wrap her arms around them both, to tell him that he and Jonathan were all the world to her, that to lose the boy would be the tragedy of her life. But this was not the time to intrude, to reveal the depth of her love. Not with the boy so recently snatched from the grasp of death.

And not with others bearing down on them. Sarah and Gibbs would not understand. Her declaration, too long postponed, was not meant for them. It caught in her throat, and her hands remained clenched against her sodden gown.

Sarah dropped to the ground beside her brother and nephew, further separating Makenna from them.

"My God," she managed between sobs, "my precious little boy. He's all right, isn't he? Tell me he's all right."

"He will live," Nicholas managed, squeezing Jonathan against his chest until the boy squirmed in discomfort.

Sarah brushed the wet hair from her nephew's face and hugged her brother's arm. It was what Makenna had wanted to do.

"He's shivering from the cold," Sarah said. "And so are you. We've got to get you both to the house."

She did not look at Makenna to offer consolation, to ask that she come with them so that she, too, might receive needed care.

Nicholas stood, still cradling the boy close, and looked down at her. The stark, lost look faded from his eyes, and she knew he was truly seeing her for the first time since he'd dragged his son onto the shore.

"Are you all right? My God, you were out there, too. You went after him. I saw you."

"I . . . I'm all right." She felt foolish still kneeling on the wet sand, but she wasn't sure she had the strength to stand. And Nicholas's arms were already full.

She looked up at the boy. Once again he had closed his eyes. The black lashes lay stark and unmoving against the whiteness of his cheeks. But she could see the shallow, blessedly regular rise and fall of his chest.

"See to him," she added. "Sarah's right. He's shivering." She gestured to Biddy Merton, who stood apart from them all, silently watching, her face in shadow from the sun setting at her back, her gnarled hands holding tight to her shawl as it whipped in the wind. "I'm not alone."

"Get on with you, Captain," Gibbs interjected. "I'll see to her."

If he meant the words as reassurance, Makenna did not hear it. The old sailor had never been her friend.

"Come on, Nicholas," Sarah said. "Hurry."

They were all wrenching him away from her. But he did not move. Instead, he stared down at Makenna, then looked from her out to the water.

"Take care," he said. "Jonathan saw something out on the pier. He said it looked like a cloud. He went to see what it was."

His words pierced her heart. He was remembering her talk of the ghost. He was thinking she

328

had not protected his son as he had once protected her.

"There's evil at the cove," Sarah said. "I've always thought so. Mama, too."

Nicholas seemed not to hear her. But Makenna did. And so did Gibbs.

"Come with us," he said. "I don't want to leave you here."

The offer warmed her heart. It must have been said reluctantly, but she could not hear reluctance in his voice.

She forced herself to stand.

"I promise I'm all right. Maybe Gibbs can bring me up to the house later. After Dr. Beaumont has seen Jonathan. He really ought to be summoned."

Sarah tugged at her brother's sleeve.

"It's getting cold, Nicholas. There's little daylight left."

He took a long while to take his watchful eyes from Makenna. She yearned for the man who had accosted her on the beach all those weeks ago, the arrogant captain, the man of resolution, the tortured soul with whom she had fallen in love.

But the Nicholas who looked at her now had lost the fire within him. Only the torture remained.

"You'll take care of her?" he asked, speaking to Biddy Merton and then to Gibbs.

The two nodded, and at last he followed his sister. Makenna watched until the three of them disappeared on the grassy path that wound up the side of the cliff to Windward.

She watched in despair, knowing she should have told him something else, something of regret, of remorse, of anger even. But there was nothing she could say that would be enough. Her ghost had finally revealed herself to someone else, and with malevolent intent. She had tried to drown the boy, much as she had once tried to drown Makenna.

As before, Nicholas had been there to avert tragedy. Would he always be? The answer had to be no. Not even he could defeat an evil that came from beyond the grave.

"Saint Nick will be leaving before long."

Pulled from reverie, Makenna looked at Gibbs. "What did you say?" But she'd heard him clearly enough. The words had been harshly said and, she knew, triumphantly.

"The captain'll take the boy and go back to Liverpool with Mrs. Harwood."

"He told you this?"

"He didn't have to. After today, it won't be long, neither. He almost lost the boy because of you."

She felt more than saw Biddy Merton take a step toward her. She motioned the woman away and turned on Gibbs.

"What are you talking about?"

Gibbs's squinty gaze stabbed her with scorn.

"The boy was trying to please you. He'd seen you drawing from the top of the hill. Don't be thinking I don't know what I'm talking about. I heard him tell his cousins he wanted you back at Windward.

He wanted to draw something just for you." He snarled out the words. "To show off some of the nonsense he's been learning."

Gibbs's harshness hit her as hard as if he were throwing stones.

"Sneaked down the path, he did, while the rest were getting ready for dinner. The captain nearly went out of his mind looking for him."

And then, of course, Nicholas had gazed down on Carnal Cove and seen the same horror that had chilled Makenna's soul.

She squeezed her eyes closed and for a moment relived the moment of time that had lasted forever, the sight of a small, defenseless figure drawn toward the wild waves. Her heart pounded as it had when she flew to save Jonathan, when she threw herself into the swollen surf, when desperate fingers caught at his coat.

Once again the cold water pressed in on her and the boy. In her mind he slipped from her grasp, his small body no more than an undulating shadow as the current carried him to his doom. Silently she screamed out his name, but the shadow moved on into deeper waters.

With a start, she opened her eyes. She was trembling. Staring at her, Gibbs must have noticed. In his own way he was as disturbingly watchful as his captain. He seemed to read her mind. He knew her guilt.

"And so they're leaving."

She could barely get the words out. She had

thought she would be the one to go away. In this as in so many other areas, she had been wrong.

"Aye. And there's something else that needs saying. You don't know Saint Nick nearly as well as you think you do."

He doesn't love me?

She almost said the words. But she could not see how he could continue to hold her in his affections, not after what Gibbs had told her. In canceling the lessons, she had turned her back on the boy, ending their relationship too abruptly, then misjudged how he would react.

The knowledge of that mistake was an agony she would carry to her grave.

"He had nothing to do with the fire. He hadn't seen the bastard that set it in more'n two years."

She took a moment to really hear what Gibbs was saying, to understand that he was no longer talking about today but of another terrible time. She started to declare she'd never thought Nicholas had caused his wife's death. But Gibbs wouldn't believe her. And she could not swear that when she'd heard Robert Campbell's terrible words, her first reaction had not been to doubt Nicholas's innocence.

She held her silence and let the sailor talk.

"He found out what she was up to, the last time his ship docked at Liverpool. She swore all that was over. She made him a promise. I heard it myself, though no one knew I was about."

Gibbs looked her up and down, reminding her

without speaking what she must look like, her hair matted with sea water, her wet gown clinging to her body.

"Women," he said in disgust. "Saint Nick was ever a fool for 'em."

He put her in a class with a long line of female companions who had dallied with his captain. He made the women seem at fault. She was not inclined to argue with him, not now.

But she could not completely hold her silence.

"Why did he say he had blood on his hands?"

"Because maybe in a way he did. That's the way he sees it. We made port in South Africa on a return run from the Orient. We were loaded with some fine silks, expensive silks worth a fortune. A letter was waiting for him telling what happened. He went a little crazy, blaming himself the way he always did when something went wrong at sea. Which it didn't, not often, not with Saint Nick at the helm."

"A letter is a terrible way to get bad news."

Lost in his narration, Gibbs ignored her.

"He was drinking in those days. We set sail for home right away. He wasn't what you might call sober. A storm came up. He misjudged how bad it was. There's no denying it. Truth is, I never saw weather the likes of that. We were blown onto the rocks. There wasn't anything he could have done."

He wiped at his eyes. She could almost believe he wiped away tears.

"Saintjohns don't lose ships in a storm. But this

one was lost, the cargo and three men. You should have seen the captain diving into the sea, doing his best to save 'em, while the sky itself was coming apart. But there wasn't anything he could do. A wave washed them overboard right as we were going down. I thought we'd lost the captain, too. The men cheered when he staggered onto shore, but he wasn't having anything to do with it. He killed three men, he said. There wasn't anything to cheer about."

Nicholas would see it that way. Love swelled in her breast until it was almost a pain.

"That's why he said he would never again take charge of a ship," she said to herself as much as to Gibbs.

"Aye. He means it, too."

She stared down at the beach, to the place where Nicholas had knelt over his son, had said something about the godless ocean not claiming another victim. Too late, she understood what he meant.

And her heart broke a little more at the thought of his anguish. What hell he must have gone through when he watched Jonathan walk into the surf.

When she looked up at Gibbs, she did not wipe the tears from her eyes.

He did not seem to notice.

"I'd best be getting the carriage and going into town for the doctor. The boy needs me more than

I'm needed here. I have no doubt you can care for yourself."

She watched in silence as he limped away from her, his back stiff with the pride that would carry him through his mission, and whatever future missions his captain had for him. Wherever they chose to settle. She did not look away until he had at last disappeared into the shadows of the oncoming night.

A whimper at her side brought her attention to the dog. Dropping to her knees, she cradled him against her, much as Nicholas had cradled his son. She rubbed a hand through his wet hair.

"You tried to save him, too. You sensed the ghost. I didn't, but you did. And you still went into the water."

It seemed to her a small miracle, one of several that had taken place late on this summer's day at the cove.

Dimly she became aware of Biddy Merton moving to within a half dozen feet of her.

"It's time to leave," Biddy said.

But was it? The woman seemed to know so much but said so little. Standing to face her, Makenna felt a flare of anger.

"Did you see the ghost? Do you know what she tried to do?"

Biddy's wrinkled face was without expression.

"I did not see her. But I know. There is much sadness here, Makenna. Come, we must leave."

But anger had driven Makenna beyond caution,

beyond reason—anger and a desperate need to see beyond the hints, the warnings, the threats both from this world and from the one beyond.

She stumbled backward, away from the woman, away from safety, away from the shrouded life she had been leading, a life that was a kind of death.

"There is no sadness," she cried, looking wildly at the waves crashing against the pier. "Cruelty, yes, and evil. An innocent child almost lost his life today. Because of me. I have to find out why."

The dog stiffened against her, hackles raised, at the same moment as the moon rose over the water, casting its eerie light over the cove.

A mist at the edge of the water shimmered into the familiar shape of her specter.

The dog barked, but only once, and the wind died, as if the ghost had the power to alter nature. And so she might.

If Makenna was beyond reason, she was also beyond fear. All receded around her, all but the vision of the ghost's long white gown trailing in the sand, her moon-white hair flowing around her shoulders and down her slender back.

This time when Makenna hurried toward her, the vision did not glide away. Blood roared in Makenna's ears, but she could not stop. She reached out a shaking hand, almost touching the gown, as if it could actually be held between her fingers. She knew it would be like holding on to a cloud.

Jonathan's cloud. The one that had called him onto the pier.

Makenna opened her mouth to speak. The ghost turned, and the words died in her throat. The moon was bright. She saw the features of her spirit, features she knew, features that terrified. Recognition drove a spike into her heart.

Staring at the ghost was like staring into a mirror. She was looking at herself.

Chapter Nineteen

The face stared at Makenna from beneath a crown of moonlit hair that floated on the air, the familiar features expressionless, composed of vapor, of mist that would blur if she touched it, like a reflection in a pool.

The ground shifted under her. She felt cold, as bloodless as the ghost. A scream died in her throat. She felt frozen in time and space, able to do nothing but stare.

"Who are you?" The whisper rasped from between her shivering lips.

The specter hovered tauntingly close, without substance, yet as real as the fright, the confusion, the terror that shredded Makenna's reason.

Without answer, the specter turned and drifted

toward the pier, as had happened so many times before, this time the long white gown trailing not on the edge of the shore but across the tops of the froth-tipped waves, like an unfurled sail atop a ghostly ship.

Without warning the wind returned in full force, beating at Makenna, coming from everywhere and nowhere, imprisoning her in a vortex as wild as her pounding heart. Ahead of her the specter faded into shadowy moonlight, yet fingers as insistent as the wind clawed at her, dragging her from the iron-strong gusts toward the pounding waves.

It was the ghost, impatient with a mere beckoning hand. In the chaos that was her mind Makenna knew it for the truth.

"No!" she screamed as she felt herself drawn toward the waves.

The word echoed on the wind and circled back on her, metamorphosing into the cry of her name.

"Makenna."

Like the wind, it came from nowhere and everywhere, echoing again and again, the voice inhuman, yet strangled with the pathos of humanity. With a start she realized it came from inside her, as if she had called out for herself, though her lips had not moved. She had not made a sound.

Her skin turned to icy marble as she tried to run, without destination, without understanding. But she could not halt the inexorable pull of invisible hands toward the sea. She was trapped in a world not made of wind or water or sand, but a world that was infinitely more complex, the world of mind and heart, the world of within.

But it was not her mind that cried out to her, nor her heart that pounded in her ears.

"Makenna."

This time her name came from the deep, panicked voice of a man.

"I want her," the man's voice said. "She is mine."

"Never," came the raging voice of the woman, and Makenna understood it was the voice of her ghost.

They were words she had never before heard, yet they came as if from a long-dead memory, each syllable expected even as it struck her with a newly discovered pain.

It was as if the ghost possessed her, compelling her to explore the tortures of a long-gone past. The clawing, unseen fingers no longer tugged at her. She was caught by something far stronger, by a spirit that could invade another's soul.

"I've come to right the wrongs I've done."

So spoke the man, as pained as the woman who heard his words inside her whirling head.

"Too late," the woman said.

The answer reverberated into a dozen repetitions, each one softer and more desperate than the last.

"No, Bronwyn, not the pier!" It was a desperate cry.

"You'll not have the babe, Richard. She is mine."

"We'll talk. I'll not take her. I'll do whatever you say, if only you will come back."

There was madness in the woman's voice, reason in the shouted words of the man.

Until his final "*No,*" a wail ripped from the hell of despair.

In answer came the high-pitched, mournful keen Makenna had heard her first day at Carnal Cove.

And then the sobbing that had so often rent the midnight air. The pitiful sound drew Makenna from the imprisoning trance. The voices faded, releasing her from the possession, but she knew them for what they were. She knew the man and she knew the woman, though she had never met them in her remembered life.

But she could know them in death, the woman who had given birth to her, if not the man who had equally brought her into the world.

The spirit of that woman lay beyond the shore, the lure of her stronger than the tide, offering what Makenna had so painfully lost, providing her with a past.

Without considering what she did, she strode into the water, letting the waves buffet her, pounding as if they would drive her back onto the beach, then drawing her forward to her inevitable end.

"Makenna."

Another man's voice called to her, but it was not the mournful cry of her father. This voice warmed rather than chilled, wrapping around her as she stood in waist-deep water beside the steps leading onto the pier.

In the distance, on the undulating surface at the edge of the inlet, she could make out the moonlit form of the ghost. An arm beckoned. Wrapped in a miasma of yearning and need, Makenna could not heed the earthly voice. The warmth had come too late.

She swayed toward the vision.

"I love you."

The declaration was softly said, yet it came to her above the wind and crash of the waves, powerful enough to still the currents, the force of the moon, the pull of the beckoning ghost.

If Nicholas's arm had snaked around her and tried to drag her to shore, she would have fought him with her dying strength.

But he caught her in a far more subtle bond. He caught her with his love. It tore her apart, one primal instinct seducing her toward the mysteries of what had been, another enticing her to the comfort of what ought to be.

"I love you," he said again, and then, "Come back to me. You are my life. You bring me hope. Let me give the same to you."

Come back. They were the words her father had used to call her mother to safety, words that had failed. He should have spoken of his love.

Impatient with words alone, Nicholas strode into the water after her. Sensing his presence, she stared across the waves at the fading vision of the specter. As if a lamp had been extinguished, the moonlight died and the vision was gone, leaving Makenna with a momentary sense of loss. But she had been called to something that could never be. And she had no fear of the dark. Her mind clear, her purpose deeply felt, she turned in the water and welcomed Nicholas's embrace.

Wrapped in each other's arms, they helped each other to the safety of the shore.

"Her name was Bronwyn Pemberton. She came here heavy with child. And with no husband."

Scrubbed of all vestiges of sea water, dressed in the blue gown, wrapped in Nicholas's arms, Makenna sat in the parlor of Elysium and listened to what Biddy Merton had to say.

The dog, renamed Hero, had chosen a warm spot in front of the hearth for a well-earned rest. Close beside him, the painting of Jenna sat upright against the stone fireplace. To Makenna she would always be her mother, the one who had raised her in love.

But Bronwyn Pemberton would also have a place in her heart, despite what her lingering spirit had tried to do.

The old woman had pulled a chair close to the open door overlooking the cove and waited without speaking until Makenna was ready to hear what she had to say. This time there was no talk of mysteries, no mention of old bones.

"Didn't the villagers see her?" Makenna asked.

"She arrived at night, her swollen belly hidden beneath the folds of a heavy cloak. She told those who saw her that she was ill, that she came here because of the healthy air."

"She came to have her baby." Makenna said the words softly.

"And to escape the wrath of her father."

"Pemberton. The name sounds familiar."

"It was in the letter from your solicitors," Nicholas said. "He once held the deed to Elysium."

"He bought it," Biddy said, "so he could rid himself of disgrace."

"Bronwyn told you this?" Makenna had a difficult time saying the name.

"Her sister. The twin who came to help when her time was due. She didn't send for her. The pair of 'em seemed to know when the other was troubled. It's the way of twins, as I've observed."

"Jenna Lindsay."

"Jenna Pemberton. There never was a Lindsay. She made up the name before she left the island with you."

And raised the infant girl as her own. Makenna grasped Nicholas's hand and held on tight, drawing strength from the press of his flesh against hers. How difficult it must have been to raise another woman's child, even her niece, as her own, to give up any chance she might have had of marriage and other children.

And yet Makenna had never felt anything from her but unconditional love. She'd given the same in return. In the past few months, nothing she learned, nothing she saw, had altered the way she felt.

"She always had money. She always took care of me."

"Your grandfather died, leaving everything he owned to her. She wrote the news after she returned to Southampton. The disgrace struck him down, she said. He was a proud and lonely man. Your grandmother had died many years before, leaving him with only the twin girls. Bronwyn was the wild one, his favorite. Until she betrayed him. That's the way he looked at it."

"My father really was Richard Danvers."

"Aye, that he was. A wild one, too. Like the father, he abandoned her."

"But he came here to the island."

"There's no knowing what changed his heart. But he was too late to win hers. She had already given birth. When he arrived, she sent us away."

"Us? You and Jenna and—"

"Her baby. She'd named you Makenna. An old Celtic name, she said. It was supposed to bring you the good luck she'd never had."

The angry words came back to Makenna—the shouts, the pleas, the denials that had torn through her as she faced the ghost on the beach.

"She chose to drown rather than turn to him."

"She hated men."

"Enough to give up her life. Enough to give up her child."

"What happened had little to do with you except her wanting to keep the man who'd abandoned her from taking you away. And she had Jenna to keep you safe."

"So what happened to him? How did he end up—"

"In an unmarked grave? I put him there. The two of us buried him in the dark of night."

"You and Jenna."

"We didn't kill him, if that's what you're thinking. I watched him dive into the water time and time again trying to find Bronwyn."

"You watched him. The way you've been watching me when I walk on the beach."

Biddy nodded, then stared through the open door into the dark of the night, listening to the crash of waves on the shore.

"But the sea did not give up its dead. He was a man obsessed. Already he had dismissed the staff of Windward House, where he was staying. He went there. He drank. We found him two days later, lying at the bottom of the stairs. His neck was broken, but he was still clutching an empty whiskey bottle."

"And so you buried him."

"There was little else to do. He was beyond help. To bring others into the house would bring disgrace on all who were involved. And who was to say we would be believed?" She hesitated a moment. "There was another thing. Jenna feared your father's family would take you from her. She

346

had promised her sister that would only happen over her own grave."

Makenna shivered from the thought of so much waste, so much pain. Nicholas kissed her forehead. "Are you all right?"

She nodded, not trusting herself to speak right away. And she listened as Biddy continued.

"We burned his belongings, everything but what he wore. I had a cart in those days, and an old mule. We wrapped him in an old canvas sail and took his body as close to the cemetery as we could. There we dug his grave. Proper words were said over him. In case you're wondering."

In her mind Makenna saw the protective circle of trees, the broken headstones, the abandoned graves that held old bones. She heard the wind that moaned through the trees and over the burial ground. It did not sound much different from the wind that came off the ocean, which, for Bronwyn Pemberton, served as a watery tomb.

"No one questioned his disappearance?" she managed to ask.

"I put out word that he and the woman from the cottage ran away together in his private boat. It was how he came. Island people did not question the tale. As for the sister and the baby, I took them to another village and in the dark of night put them on a hired boat."

"Why didn't you tell me all of this when you first saw me?"

"Jenna Pemberton forced a blood oath from me

347

that I would never reveal what happened on that terrible night. She set up a fund to see me through the years, but that's not the reason I kept my oath. She was a good woman, needing to keep a secret. And you were the most beautiful thing I had ever seen. I had helped in the birthing. From the moment you came into the world, I had seen to your care. To tell would bring shame down on your head."

"You knew that someday I would return. You kept the cottage waiting for me."

"Aye. And spread stories about the place, of strange lights and sounds that had no human explanation. I did not know about the ghost. I made one up."

She fell silent. Makenna wanted to go to her and hold her, to tell her of the affection she felt in her heart, the almost desperate need to do whatever she could for her, whatever Biddy would allow her to do.

She contented herself with saying, "It's late. You will stay here. I've spent more than one restless night in the parlor. I can do so again."

To her surprise, Biddy put up little argument. Nicholas was the one to give her trouble. He did so outside the kitchen door, after Biddy was settled for the night. She planned to send him on his way, to assure him that she needed time to absorb all that she had learned.

He did not give her the chance. Instead, he grabbed her and held her tight.

"I almost lost Jonathan today. And I almost lost you."

He kissed her, at first tenderly, but passion, anger, fear seemed to boil within him and the kiss became all-consuming, as if he would devour her and keep her inside him forever.

She answered him with equal fire. They consumed one another. It was a long time before they broke apart.

"You do believe I saw her," Makenna said, as much a statement as a wish. "You do believe her ghost haunted the cove."

"Oh, yes." He traced his thumb around her lips. "She wanted to take you away."

"She didn't want me with you. She hated men. I suppose that's why Biddy warned me away from you." And then softer. "For all her money, and the love she received at home, she did not live a happy life."

"But she's at peace now. You must accept that."

"I will. Eventually. It seems possible that in her final gesture, she was not beckoning me to follow her. Perhaps she was bidding me farewell."

She would have given in to tears, but Nicholas would not let her.

"Her wildness destroyed her, Makenna. Does the same wildness burn in you?"

"I did not believe so. But then an arrogant sea captain accosted me on the beach and ordered me to leave. When I am wild, it is always because of him."

349

She stared up at him, at the heavily bristled cheeks, the sharp lines of bones, the darkly glinting eyes.

"And that is why you have to leave me for a while. I need the wildness to settle," she said.

"And that won't happen if I stay?"

"You'll distract me."

He kissed the side of her neck. "Tell me why. Tell me how you feel."

She smiled. "I love you."

"I loved you first."

For all the gravity of the night, there was a trace of levity in his voice, a hint that all would be well in their world.

"Is this some kind of competition?" she asked.

"Yes. And I win. The first time I saw you at the cove, I recognized you for what you were. Trouble. But of a very special kind."

"I made you angry."

"You called me arrogant. And so I was. You terrified me."

"Liar."

"You made me see possibilities I could not afford to see."

"But you were wrong. What you could not afford was to let me go."

He held her close. "I still cannot."

She enjoyed the moment, even as she knew that the longer she remained in his arms, the more difficult saying good night would be.

"You need to go to your son."

"We need to go to him."

"He might be having bad dreams. And I can't leave here tonight. I owe Biddy too much."

"You do not fight fair, Makenna."

"I can't when you're the opponent."

He ran his hands down her back and held her tight against his erection.

"Does it feel to you as if I'm an opponent?"

She took a minute to respond. "Who's the one who doesn't fight fair?"

"All I want to do is make love to you. Before and after we're married."

She pushed him away. The only reason she could do so was that she caught him by surprise.

"Is that a proposal?"

"No. It's an assumption."

Was that a twisted smile on his dark face? The light from the kitchen was dim, yet she thought it might be. Her heart did several flips.

The smile did not last long. "This is the proposal: Will you marry me?"

"You ask, knowing my past?"

"It's your future that concerns me. I'm not a good risk, as I've already pointed out. But I promise to spend the rest of my life making you feel secure and loved."

"You're also very rich."

"That, too."

She kissed him long and hard. A considerable time went by before she could send him on his way.

*   *   *

Two days passed before they could really be alone, two days spent with Jonathan, replacing ugly memories with dreams of how wonderful life was going to be. He took the news of the intended wedding with a shy smile and a hesitant kiss planted on Makenna's cheek. It was the sweetest kiss she had ever received, a fact she did not hide from Nicholas.

"I'll work on sweetness, if that's what you want," he said.

"Not all the time."

The three of them were together in Jonathan's room. She thought for a moment Nicholas was going to drag her to the library and start working on whatever she wanted. She was small-minded enough to enjoy the look of pain on his face that resulted from his restraint.

Sarah had taken the news of the betrothal almost as well as the boy. She had not behaved well on the beach, she confessed, seeing only Jonathan's suffering and not Makenna's. But she would be the best sister-in-law in the world. To prove it, she would leave for Liverpool right away and begin plans for the wedding.

That was exactly what she did, packing and gathering together her small entourage, leaving in her wake the frazzled Jarmans and Mrs. Loddington.

Gibbs did not prove nearly so sanguine.

"Whatever Saint Nick wants is good enough for

me," he said to Makenna when they were alone. He did not sound particularly sincere.

She did not push him for further commitment. Silently she vowed to win his friendship, and if not that, his respect. She expected to have years for the campaign.

In the calm that followed Sarah's chaotic departure, Makenna and Nicholas discussed the wedding celebration Sarah and his parents were likely to plan. Simultaneously they decided to wed in the chapel at East Hartsbridge, with Reverend Coggshall presiding.

Which was exactly what they did, Makenna in a pale yellow gown hastily but beautifully sewn by the constable's wife. Biddy Merton stood at her side, Gibbs next to his captain. Between them stood a fidgety Jonathan, who was quickly turning into the imp his father had been.

Wedding guests included the Jarmans and Mrs. Loddington, Dr. Beaumont, the Bents, and several of the villagers Makenna had met.

The lone guest who did not seem completely at peace was Constable Bent. After the ceremony, at a small reception arranged by the vicar's housekeeper, he took time to harangue all who would listen about the unsolved mystery of the bones. They had been moved to a proper grave in the village, and their proximity rankled him.

"We know they're the remains of Richard Danvers, though we've only the initials as proof. What put him in the grave? Right now a murderer is scot-free."

"Most likely in his own grave," Dr. Beaumont said. "It's been close to thirty years, Tobias, since Danvers died."

"It'll have to remain a mystery," Biddy Merton said. "Old bones know things, but they do not talk."

After that, no one had much to say about the matter.

Two hours following the ceremony and reception, with Jonathan at the cottage with Biddy and the dog Hero and Gibbs ensconced at the Crown and Anchor in a crowd of garrulous old salts, the bride and groom found themselves in the master bedroom at Windward House.

The draperies were drawn, a single lamp serving as illumination. If the moon had risen outside, neither of them wanted to know.

Earlier they had exchanged wedding gifts. Nicholas's gift to her was the boat he had been building, with the name MAKENNA painted on its stern. Along with the boat came a written promise to teach her how to sail, with him in his place at the helm.

Her gift to him was a painting of Jonathan she had been working on for a long time.

Everything had been perfect. She was determined to make this night perfect as well.

"We haven't made love since before that night," she said, knowing that the near tragedies at the cove would always be referred to as *that night*.

The spark in Nicholas's eye told her she said nothing he did not already know.

Taking a filmy swirl of nightgown and laying it atop the high four-poster bed, she decided to fan the spark. On her wedding night she wanted a full-force conflagration.

"I'll have dozens of people to meet in Liverpool," she said, turning her back on her husband and beginning to unbutton her gown. "You'll have to introduce me. I hope your mother will not be disappointed."

No response, except for a rustling she took as impatience.

She finished the unbuttoning and eased the gown off one shoulder and then the other.

"I have a grandmother, too." Here her voice caught and she forgot the teasing. "And cousins and even an aunt or two, according to Sarah. There's a brother-in-law and some nieces and nephews as well. Please stay with me when I meet them. I want you at my side."

Was that a growl she heard? She was saying nothing that had not been said before. Somehow on this night everything about the Danvers family needed to be said again.

"I don't know how much to tell them about my father. Probably everything. Except the ghost."

She dropped the gown to the floor and stepped out of her petticoats.

"I'm glad the vicar sent Ascot on his way before

I had to see him again. How I ever thought I loved him will forever be my own personal mystery."

She could feel the heat of her husband close behind her as she finished her undressing. She was reaching for the nightgown when she felt a pair of hands steal around her waist and caress her breasts, pulling her back against a very hard, very naked male body.

She could not say a word. But she could move, and so she did, brushing her hips against his erection, thrusting her nipples against the heat of his palms.

Nicholas was not a man to let such provocation go unnoticed.

Turning her in his arms, he laid her back on the bed and took up the transparent gown.

"Shocking," he said, but he did not look shocked. He gave every appearance of a man about to explode from pure lust.

Dropping the gown over her body, he licked at the dark nipples visible through the filminess. She arched her back to feel each rasp of his tongue, waiting, panting for his hands to begin their magic.

But he was not done with teasing her. Lifting the gown, he tickled the tips of her swollen breasts with the hem, trailed the soft material down her abdomen and dropped it between her legs, moving the silkiness against her hot, throbbing center, then cupping it with a firm hand against the wet throbs. He shifted and straddled her thighs. When he rubbed his manhood against the gown, it was the ultimate teasing, his flesh close to hers, but not close enough.

She wanted their bodies joined more than she wanted to breathe.

For the first time since entering the bedroom, he spoke.

"Let's make a child."

She died a little bit.

"I can't."

"You haven't. And perhaps we won't be so blessed. But, my dearest beloved, it won't be because we didn't make every effort."

"How can we bring a child into the world? We don't know where we're going to live."

"We won't be homeless. We'll live wherever feels right."

She heard hints of her captain on the beach. He was telling her what they would do. This time she didn't argue. The only approach to make with Captain Nicholas Saintjohn was to let him think he was having his way. If he wanted to live in Australia, that would be all right with her. And if he wanted to make love to her night and day, she was not going to deny him.

On that particular issue, she was just as eager as he.

"We can't make a baby if you keep that gown between my legs."

"Clever woman." He eased it away, arousing her with more erotic tickling.

When their bodies joined, she knew in her heart that within the year she would bear her husband's child. Her certainty was a mystery she did not try to analyze. Instead, she held him tight and welcomed the true beginning of her life.